PENGUIN CRIME FICTION

MOONSPENDER

Jonathan Gash is the pen name of a distinguished English doctor. His "Lovejoy" series, including *The Sleepers of Erin*, *The Judas Pair*, *Spend Game*, *The Vatican Rip*, *The Gondola Scam*, *Firefly Gadroon*, *Pearlhanger*, and *The Tartan Sell* (all available from Penguin), is among the most original and consistently entertaining currently being written. A television series based on the Lovejoy character recently aired on the Arts and Entertainment channel. The latest Lovejoy novel, *Jade Woman*, is also available from Penguin.

MOONSPENDER
A LOVEJOY NOVEL OF SUSPENSE
JONATHAN GASH

PENGUIN BOOKS

PENGUIN BOOKS
Published by the Penguin Group
Viking Penguin Inc., 40 West 23rd Street, New York, New York 10010, U.S.A.
Penguin Books Ltd, 27 Wrights Lane, London W8 5TZ, England
Penguin Books Australia Ltd, Ringwood, Victoria, Australia
Penguin Books Canada Ltd, 2801 John Street,
Markham, Ontario, Canada L3R 1B4
Penguin Books (N.Z.) Ltd, 182–190 Wairau Road,
Auckland 10, New Zealand

Penguin Books Ltd, Registered Offices:
Harmondsworth, Middlesex, England

First published in the United States of America by
St. Martin's Press 1987
Published in Penguin Books 1988

3 5 7 9 10 8 6 4 2

LIBRARY OF CONGRESS CATALOGING IN PUBLICATION DATA
Gash, Jonathan.
Moonspender: a Lovejoy novel of suspense.
(Penguin crime fiction)
I. Title.
PR6057.A728M62 1987 823'.914   87-19768
ISBN 0 14 01.4339 4

Printed in the United States of America
Set in Goudy Old Style

This story is humbly dedicated to the memory of the ancient Chinese patron saints Liu Chin-tin and Tsui Tsung-yuan, who protect from poverty any scribbler who dedicates a tale in their memory.

Lovejoy

A story for Ian McShane, Richard and Yvonne, Susan. And the Coven for kindness and help.

MOONSPENDER

1

This story begins where I'm making love to an ancient Chinese vase, on gangster's orders, watched by eleven point two million viewers.

But first, how to sell stolen hankies, from poverty, in the rain.

By evening the crowds of shoppers had thinned. The wet snuffed daylight off the Lion Walk spire, leaving me on the glistening square while women battled pushchairs into the rain. Those old Victorian lamps would have imbued the scene with a romantic opalescence. As it was, our town council now brittle us to death with a neon glare that hurts your eyes. Daft, like everything modern. I'm an antique dealer so should know.

"Genuine Irish linen hankies," I warbled. People hurtled past. "Hankies. Genuine Lancashire," I tried. Prams zoomed. Where has compassion gone? I honestly wish people would reform. I'll even reform myself when I can get a minute.

"What's this tramp cost, Mel, dear?"

Just my luck. I groaned aloud. Sandy was there, smiling wickedly with Mel, his morose friend. Sandy carried a rotating silver umbrella. Bells and minilanterns dangled from each spoke, the interior shedding a roseate glow on his magenta eyelashes. He suddenly screamed.

"Ooooh! It's not a tramp! It's Lovejoy!"

"Push off, Sandy," I said. It's only friends who embarrass, never enemies. Ever noticed that?

"How much are your rags, Lovejoy?" Sandy prodded them with a finger. Cerise and ivory gloves, I observed, each digit with an external opal ring.

"Six for a quid, Sandy." I hated the hope in my voice.

"Don't, Sandy," Mel said. "They'll be stolen."

"Seven." I wouldn't grovel, but my voice went, "Eight?"

They moved away, Sandy's high heels clacking. Today's motif was a miniver fur soprano cape. He looked ridiculous. I thought, cop this, and called, "Sandy. Your handbag's horrible." It was a fluorescent yellow diamanté.

He halted, stricken, then burst into tears and ran. Mel yelled, " *There*, Lovejoy! See what you've done!"

"Sorry," I shouted after the weird pair. "Only joking."

Jo was by the bread shop. She looked as jubilant as I felt, but drier. "How's it g-g-g-going, Lovejoy?" she said, shivering as a gust caught her legs.

"Great, Jo. They're genuine silk, see?"

She crossed over. "You've only s-s-sold four. I saw."

"Five," I said indignantly. "Well, nearly five." Milking the public's finer feelings is bottling fog.

"Nearly five's f-f-f-four, Lovejoy. Cuppa char?"

Jo's a good lass. Her stutter's a pity. Probably our town's best prostitute, though opinions vary. No statistician's yet applied himself to the problem. Should be a good Ph.D. in that for some willing student. Jo's been very good to me off and on. And I've nearly been good to her.

"Here, Jo," I said. "How much is cat food?"

She came over, hopefully doing her walk, but our football team had lost three-nil and the passing lads were all unmerry.

"Is that y-y-y-yours, Lovejoy? F-f-f-feed it scraps."

Toffee had adopted me two days ago. I'd kept it between my ankles for shelter since the drizzle started. It's black, with a caramel chin. I'd had hell of a row with the driver on the village bus, who wanted me to pay. For a *cat*. The fascist swine. I ask you.

"Scraps have run out." I felt myself go red.

"C-c-c-come on. I can't s-s-s-stand all this pathos." She led the way. I said a come on to Toffee, and we made Woody's caff without loss of life, though the traffic tried.

Woody's is a nosh bar in our town's Arcade. The grub is famed among East Anglia's few survivors for running contrary to all known dietary wisdoms. Woody's Dining Emporium is the home of cholesterol, the oppidum of saturated fats. The dense fug starts corrosion where acid rain leaves off. Even the furniture looks riddled with additives. Among it all was Woody, coughing fag ash indiscriminately into custard, chips, sizzling bacon.

A cheer of derision rose as we entered. Antique dealers, using the term loosely, gather here.

"Wotcher, Lovejoy. How's business?"

"Fine, Podge." We found a table, Jo settling with a sigh. Podge Howarth is a tiny ginger-haired bloke into Georgian furniture. I like him, though's he's barmy. He actually built his own motor car, one of these tiny hatchbacks that expands into a hostelry by judicious tinkering.

Two other blokes were with Podge, just leaving. I said hello with a nod. Ollie Hennessey's a neat compact individual who runs a supermarket; collects Civil War weaponry. He gives me day jobs at peak times like Christmas and August holidays. Me and schoolchildren restock his supermarket's shelves, all illegal labor, of course. Clipper, who was with him, was a surprise because I didn't know they were friends. Clipper's a big beefy man, as thick as he is tall. He's a phony gypsy, lives in caravans with a team of roughs. They work housing estates doing re-sprays of dubious motor cars. As always, Clipper carried a bag that clinked. We all smiled knowingly. Tell you more about this trio later.

A large woolly man whaling into a Woody's fry-up gave a laugh at my name, mouth open so we could all admire his masticated calories.

"Lovejoy!" he roared, face going puce. "What a name!"

My weak grin encouraged him, because he made another couple of remarks as Jo ordered for us. She told Woody she wanted some milk in a saucer and some fish for Toffee. She's really nice. Embarrassed, I muttered that I'd owe her.

"Don't be silly, Lovejoy," she scolded. "What's the sense of getting soaked when you could be having a warm drink?"

I put my tray of sodden handkerchiefs under my chair. Toffee sat between my feet. I'd never had a cat before and wondered, was this a unique moggie, or your run-of-the-mill standard model?

"Here, Jo," I said, my voice low so Toffee wouldn't hear. "In confidence. This cat. What, er. . . ?"

"F-f-female," she said. "S-s-stray, I should think."

"Stray?" I said indignantly. "It's a thoroughbred."

"It's coming to something!" The woolly geezer was enraged because nobody had laughed with him. They knew better. Lily, a rather sad antique dealer on East Hill given to disastrous love affairs, even tried to shush him with warning glances. She was sitting opposite—with?—him. "A street beggar, a whore, and an animal." He glared at us, a professional glarer if ever there was one.

"Horses are thoroughbreds, Lovejoy. Cats are pedigree."

"It came in when I put the bird grub out," I told Jo. "It won't eat fried bread."

"Is this allowed?" the bloke was going on. "What sort of establishment are you running here. . . ?" Etcetera, etcetera.

Jo had gone pale. We tried to keep up our conversation but the odds proved superwhelming. It finally happened when Erica fetched over our grub. She always ruffles my hair to annoy, but she didn't this time. She put down a plate of chips, egg, and beans for me, and Jo's cake.

"Woody's boned a bit of haddock, Lovejoy."

The bloke spluttered. "That whore's cat gets better treatment—"

Life is odd, sometimes. Even the same bit of life's different when looked at from behind different people's eyes. In theory, you'd think it to be all the same quality of material. Like, I can take abuse months at a time. In fact I do. I've been scathed by experts, so abuse is snow off a duck to me. I'd hardly noticed what he was on about until I saw Jo fumble trying to slip me a note underneath the table.

"Eh?" I said. My mouth was already full. I'd waded into the grub. "What's up, love?"

"I've j-j-j-just r-r-r-remembered s-s-s-something, Lovejoy." She was making to leave. And to give me the money so I could pay for the nosh. Her face was death, suddenly much younger in its despair.

The woolly man was beside himself. "Hey! A stuttery tart! What a find! I'll bet when she—"

Heat filled my face, and I thought, Oh Christ, here we go. Embarrassment's always been a prime mover with me. I sometimes wish I could ascend the evolutionary scale, from glands to cerebral cortex so to speak, but it's happenings like this that keep you down. I reached, tugged Jo to stay her.

"No, love. Wait here."

"Please, L-L-Lovejoy." She meant don't make a scene. Woody's is the one place she's allowed in the shopping precinct.

Toffee rose and walked with me, probably thinking, oh well, easy come. I almost fell over her and said sorry. Woody called a weary, "Now, Lovejoy," but I said without rancor, "Quiet, Woody," and gazed down at the bloke.

Some things in life aren't in doubt. Like, the most beautiful bottom ever painted is Louise O'Murphy's Boucher picture, owned by the undeserving of Cologne; it's magic even for eighteenth-century Frame. And it simply doesn't matter that Louise, daughter of a poor Irish immigrant, used up lovers and husbands faster than church and Parisian society could count. The point is that her bottom wins by a mile. No doubts, see? But other things in life are never anything *but* doubt. Like, why should a peaceful caff become Armageddon.

Looking down at this goon's piggy face, I realized I'm a great believer in faces. Sit me in a market square and I'm content all livelong day just watching faces. Mirrors of the soul. Some soul. I took the cruet, unscrewed the salt cellar. Woody's salt is famed for its deliquescence, always clogs the nozzle.

The nerk watched in outrage as I emptied the salt over his plate. The pepper ran easier, out in a cloud. I dropped the containers into the grub.

"Here, you!" he bawled at Woody. "This hooligan—"

"Eat, lad," I said, tilting his plate onto his lap. Then a runny sauce. A plate of pie off Woody's counter smeared on his front, and goulash from John Parkworth—he's Georgian furniture—one table along. Finally, with an excuse me to the appalled Lily, the table itself, and a kick to his right elbow as the goon lay in the mess, because some of these roving dealers carry paperknives. Police can't touch you for a paperknife. He was even louder now, yelping and trying to scrabble. This disturbance wasn't my fault. I mean, I'd honestly not started anything. I'd just been having my tea quietly, for God's sake, and now this mess.

Toffee tripped me just about then. I went sprawling with my knee in Piggy's belly. A pair of brilliant tan toecaps an inch away caught my eye. Immaculate creases in the check trousers, cavalry twill. I sighed, lugged myself into the upper air.

"Wotcher," I said resignedly. It had to be Sykie's elder son Eric. Only a nerk dresses that bad. He stood there, a yard ahead of his brother. Gold rings flashing, diamond facer watch dazzling, green leather shirt. Both Sykes lads hate me. Happily they're scared of their dad. This keeps them under control, but one day they'll go for me.

"Lovejoy. Come on."

"I'll finish my tea."

Sykie's lad drew breath, stayed silent. I rejoined Jo, Toffee as usual giving me nowhere to put my feet. I was frightened. Jo must have seen my tremulous fingers having two goes to spread margarine. Erica came with one of those sponge mops that squeezes itself out when you lever the handle. They cost a fortune but one day I'll afford one.

Jo whispered, "It's the Sykes b-b-b-brothers. Hadn't you better make a run for it?"

Sykie's an honest-to-God cockney, big on the Belly—Portobello Road, London. In fact I've often heard him say he founded the vast antiques market there. He's got a soft spot for me because I rejected his sons as apprentices, told him the truth instead of what he wanted to hear. Yet this wouldn't exempt me from grievous bodily harm, on a whim.

My neurons upped a gear into panic. What had I done lately? Nothing Sykie could be mad at, surely. I hadn't seen him since Christie's big September sale of Keating fakes. Out of my league. Jo gave a brave smile.

"You d-d-d-don't pat a cat," she said, keeping the conversation going for appearance's sake. "That's dogs."

The Sykes lads were lighting cheroots, would you believe, outside the glass porch. "Er, look, love," I said, mopping the last ergs off the plate. "Look after Toffee, eh?" And I was off, eeling hunchbacked past where the fat bloke sat, messy head in his hands and moaning. I signaled Woody I'd settle up with him later, got a sardonic glance. Why does he never trust me?

The Minories is a museum near the castle. By some oversight

our town councillors haven't flattened the lovely Queen Anne house into a car park. It's left as a lovely quaint place, to rot to dereliction. And it would have, except for Beryl the curator, a plumpish bird with dark eyes. Most days she sits alone, ever hopeful for hordes of visitors. The trouble is, nobody comes, only maybe some old soldier out of the rain or a couple of ancient crones seeking warmth while planning their next bingo campaign. I don't trust museums or curators, though I can forgive those like Beryl. She loves old dresses, embroidery, lace, and endlessly fights the council to keep her museum open. She's always just lost another round.

Her face lit up when I creaked that lovely oaken door ajar. She was dusting the collection of dollhouses in the main parlor.

"Hello, love. Room for one?"

"Hello, Lovejoy." She resumed dusting listlessly. "Help me upstairs with the Hoover."

I carried the damned thing, pausing to look on the mezzanine floor. One side, a nursery complete with cots, baby gear, lovely clothes right back to the 1690s. On the other side was a long gallery, originally the maidservant's room. Beryl had some thirty or forty wax dummies in clever tableaux. Ladies out walking, fireside groups, a musical evening, marriages down the ages, even a witch coven, the lot. She'd got one thing wrong—a Wingfield tennis racket was in a sporty tableau dated 1865, but Major Walter Wingfield didn't patent his lawn tennis until February 1874; people nicknamed it "sticky" at first. I'd given her an early Victorian coromandel-wood games compendium, beautifully boxed, to start one display off. I must have been off my bloody head. I stared resolutely away from The Homecoming Sailor scenario—a matelot arriving to the big welcome. I'd faked his scrimshaw chest out of an old wardrobe, painted ship pictures and all. The brass handles I'd aged in a local farm's muck-spreading tank, the best way if you've time.

"It's still here, Lovejoy," she smiled. "Think I'd sold it?"

"Eh?" I said, all innocent.

"The fan. The one you let me have."

My fan—my fan—was also there, in a wedding group, Display Sixteen. A wax maid of honor was behind the wax bride, my 1880 original fan in her undeserving wax hand. It was watercolored, on gilt and mother-of-pearl sticks. I moaned.

"Now, Lovejoy. You *gave* it, remember?"

Smiling, she passed me. I followed, not quite gnashing my teeth but definitely not rolling in the aisles from merriment. Beryl and I had been, well, close once. What women call generosity I call exploitation. Afterward.

"Here, Beryl!" I said brightly as she started vacuuming. "I've a couple of wedding knives for sale." Well, I'd come on the scrounge. First things first.

"Wedding knives?"

"They're always a pair, in one sheath. Brides got them, as a symbol of marital status. . . ."

Beryl stopped, shaking her head. "It's no good, Lovejoy. Just look at this place. Listen." We listened. "Empty. Not a soul. You know how many visitors I've had, for thirty-two lovely rooms crammed with antique householdery? Seven. All week." She looked so tearful I'd have given her the wretched wedding knives, if I'd had any. "And I've finished Queen Victoria's copy wedding dress." I'd noticed it, a lovely work with those double-puff sleeves, the famous eight-paneled bodice, the Honiton lace that sprang back into fame in 1840 and saved whole villages. Beautiful. Beryl's three sisters are seamstresses.

"That bad?"

She stood there, sniffing. "The council's given me a final warning: Improve attendances or we'll be closed." She blotted her face and switched the suction back on. "I've done everything. My cousin Teddie lent a van to tour the villages. Last week my dad dressed as the town crier and stood outside the pubs. Not a flicker of response." Tears started rolling quite unchecked. "What *is* it, Lovejoy?"

"It's people." I held her. "They've forgotten how to recognize love. Don't worry. It'll change."

Well, all in all a hopeless visit. No money. No advance on antiques I'd not quite got. And Beryl wouldn't let me borrow back my fan, even though I swore blind I honestly only wanted to show it to a friend. Typical. I left thinking nothing of it, a mere failed few minutes in a humdrum day.

But it came of importance, in time. After a death. Or two. Or, some said, three.

Hoping the Sykes lads had hoofed it by now, I collared up and left the Minories through the walled garden. The town was quieting in the evening rain, buses draining shoppers from the streets. Luckily it's only a hundred sprinted yards to the north car park. My luck was in, or so I thought. The Ryan household's Bentley was there. I'd only to wait a few minutes, crouching embarrassed among the cars, before the lady herself showed.

The rain had slackened. The town hall lights gave her a sparkling halo as she approached. She looked—is—wondrous. I kept low down while she parted from the bloke she was with. A gay Gaelic laugh. The famous Councillor Ryan himself, dressed in that guineas-and-goblets casualness that costs the earth and silences opposition. He's our town's main building contractor. This means the brains of an amoeba and all its survival skills. You've really got to watch his sort. Certain she was finally alone, I rose.

"Excuse me, Mrs. Ryan," I said humbly. "If I knuckle my forehead, ma'am, can your ladyship give me a lift? Only, the bailiffs be arter me—"

She undid the door her side, carefully doing that nonsmile of the woman who knows everything before you do. "Don't be a fool, Lovejoy. Get in."

"Thank you, Mrs. Ryan." Something black blurred in.

"What's what?" Mrs. Ryan gave a little yelp. "You've got a *cat*, Lovejoy?"

"Well, one of us owns the other. I'm not sure which way round." Politely I asked after Councillor Ryan's well-being and present location, in reverse order.

"James? He's back at the council chamber."

"Pleased to hear it." Three's a crowd. James Ryan had started life as Jimmy O'Ryan. His name had escalated since he'd got pomp, posh, and plenty.

Mrs. Ryan said quite casually, "I'll use the Harwich road, Lovejoy." That would take us past very few houses, clever lady. Women are a shrewd lot. She spoke on even more casually. "Lovejoy. Are you still interested in my pendant?"

"Er, yes." Cunning Lovejoy, not too eager. The pendant was an exquisite Roman brooch, its mount a refashioned foliate gold luna. I'd noticed her wearing it at the village flower show. I cleared my throat, oh-so-casual. There were serious implications here. We hit the bypass and ran out of street lights. The Bentley hummed. Toffee snored between my feet. Nobody spoke. It seemed my cue. "Any chance of another look, Mrs. Ryan?"

"Possibly," she said instantly, but still offhand. "James will be late home. I'll drop you at the chapel, then return later."

"Sure that'll be all right?"

"Perfectly," she said. "Incidentally, did I see you fighting? I happened to be passing a café—"

"Me, fight?" I gave a convincing chuckle. "No, love. I leave that to the professionals."

"It was somebody with a common-looking, ah . . ."

Women always run out of definitive terms, don't they? It happens a lot when their personal values are at stake. I have this theory that women's talk is a dot picture; join the blobs and complete the geranium.

". . . common-looking lady?" I said, linking the dots.

"Mmmmh." She glanced down. "I've told you before, Lovejoy; never while I'm driving."

My hand had accidentally alighted on her knee. "Know what I learned today? You stroke cats but pat dogs, not the other way round."

She laughed. Her face is lightweight, medieval tempera paint on parchment. She's the sort who can don ultramarine earrings and turn smiling from the dressing table mirror to show them transmuted into a blanched eau-de-nile. Honest. I've seen her do it.

"You're off your head," she told me, still laughing. "Before you go, Lovejoy, did you think about it?"

"Eh?" Then, oh dear, I remembered she'd offered me her estate manager's job, would you believe, all guns and yokels. "Can we talk about it later?" is useful; postponement is my big skill.

She dropped me off, saying to expect her. I walked the lane from the chapel, thinking about Mrs. Ryan's persistence. She narked me, keeping on about her rotten job. If only women would stop being so demanding, they could achieve great things. Sometimes a woman is a character in search of an analogy. I stopped thinking complicated thoughts then because I could see my porch bulb shining. Odd, that. Sure enough there were two great dark cars blocking the drive.

Indoors, Sykie was swigging tea. "Wotcher, Lovejoy. You've been quick."

Four goons lolled around, one of them with my mug. He was spooning the last of my sugar, the robber. I shut the door and sat down. "Wotcher, Sykie. Your lads'll be a little while."

He closed his eyes wearily. "Slipped them, did yer? Gawd, them pair." He looked about, indicating the cottage. "Here, Lovejoy. This the best you can do? It's a right bleedin' mess."

That narked me. Admittedly the cottage was a little untidy, but I hadn't been expecting visitors. "Well, things have gone a bit off lately, Sykie."

"They've improved. You've got a job, Lovejoy. On telly."

"Eh?" Television?

He's a heavy man, forever starting up in mid-sentence as if hearing an unexpected visitor outside. "Know that antiques game, where they guess things?"

"That's impossible, Sykie." I cast about anxiously. "I can't look natty even if I try. For television you need glamour."

He was grinning. Sykie does a lot of grinning. "Next show, one of the panel will unexpectedly drop out. They'll pick a member of the audience." He grinned wider, winked. "Guess who."

My voice was a croak. "But what if the expert shows up, Sykie?"

"He won't, Lovejoy. Will he, Dave?"

The sugar stealer gave a cadaverous smile. "No, Sykie. He gets flu tomorrer."

"Sykie, please." I felt like a kid in school.

"You join the panel, Lovejoy. And guess all the antiques right." Sykie looked at his cup and rose. "And for Gawd's sake get a few tins of beer in." He moved out, oafs holding the door. His shoulders heaved, him laughing. Serfs laughed along, always a wise policy. "Just do it, Lovejoy. And you'll preserve all this." He indicated my cottage with a nod. Here it came. "Lovejoy Towers."

They were still booming with laughter as the big saloons crunched down my gravel off into the night. I went back in, narked, Toffee the bloody nuisance between my feet. If Sykie had been a fat geezer trapped at table on his own I'd have sloshed him one. Or not. Lovejoy the hard man, I thought bitterly, black belt in origame.

Ten minutes later the Sykes lads tore up in a Jaguar, asking had I seen their dad. I said he'd dropped in for tea.

One o'clock in the morning and all hell seemed let loose. Blearily I went to the door with a towel modestly round my middle. The eldest Sykes son was there, tough and nasty. He gave me a bundle of money.

"Me dad sez get some decent shmutter, Lovejoy. A proper suit." He paused. "Here, Lovejoy, that your horse?"

"Horse?" I was only half awake.

"There's a nag out here." He was thinking how to pull a racing scam. I can read these nerks like a book.

"Not mine," I said. "Night." And shut the door.

I've no carpet, only a couple of tatty rugs that I leap to like stepping-stones because the stone flags are perishing. I dived in to her warmth with a glad cry.

"Lovejoy." Mrs. Ryan was aghast and whispering. "Who was it?"

"A message." Cunningly I wriggled for more of her warmth while she was distracted. "I've to go on television."

Mrs. Ryan relaxed in relief. "You live the oddest life, Lovejoy." My hand found her breast. I can't go back to sleep properly without one, some infancy hangover, I expect. "You're *freezing*. Did you say on television?"

"Shut up," I mumbled. Women never stop rabbiting. Then I thought a bit. "Here, Mrs. Ryan. Did you leave a horse in my hedge?"

"Of course. I couldn't come in a car at this hour. People would hear." Women are sly. I've often noticed that.

2

Mrs. Ryan left while it was still pitch black outside. The wind had fallen, the rain ceased. She blamed me in a steady whimper of recrimination for (a) the cold weather, (b) having the best of this arrangement, and (c) not even getting up to make her some tea. She looked lovely. I watched her dress. I like morning women. They're all floury and plump. It's only later that they collect those toxins of antagonism that make danger. She wears a proper woman's riding habit. (I think I mean a woman's proper riding habit, but you know, not those jodhpurs that spread.)

"I've no tea left." I spoke from her warm patch with bitterness. "Some gangsters nicked it last night."

She came back and sat on the bed. It's really only a foldaway divan, and tilts you riskily toward whoever sits on its edge. It has mixed benefits. I rolled against her.

"Lovejoy."

"Shouldn't you be going? Councillor Ryan will be—"

"This can't go on, can it?" I gave a theatrical snore. "Don't hide." She pulled the sheets off my face.

"Look, Mrs. Ryan. I've a big day on . . ." But it was no use. Women always have everything their own way.

Before she took off on her animal she said to kit myself out at Kirkham's tailor's in town, on her personal account. I said ta, and promised most sincerely to remember whatever it was she'd been on about.

The day of my television debut dawned into one of those mornings where you have plenty of time but suddenly it evaporates. I don't suppose it happens to other people much, everybody else being so organized. But it gets on my nerves when unexpectedly I'm having to hurtle everywhere out of breath. Worse, the train for London was punctual, an all-time first. Big Frank from Suffolk was alighting. He visits our antiques Arcade on the rare days he isn't being sued for alimony. I like him. He's a real dedicated silver dealer, anything before 1900. He's also a megamarrier, bigamist, and multiple divorcé.

"Hello, Lovejoy. Jeez, you're done up like a dog's dinner."

"Wotcher." I felt embarrassed in my new suit. "Here, Frank. Tell Tinker I've left him an envelope at the Three Cups." Tinker's my scruffy old barker—that's antiquese for a bent Machiavellian scrounger. I pay him in booze. "Help us up."

He bumped the basket into the compartment for me, gaping. "It's a frigging *cat*!" I'd bought the big shopping basket this morning with my newfound wealth. Toffee watched dispassionately while she was hauled aboard, monarch of all she surveyed. I wasn't sure what cats lie on, so I'd bought her a blanket thing. The pet shop girl had tried telling me that cats traveled in a lidded basket. I'd told her to stuff her portable dungeon. "What's the game, Lovejoy?"

"Going on telly." The whistle blew.

"Straight up?" He slammed the door. I put the window

down. "Here, Lovejoy. Got anything like a silver fertility pendant?"

These are mostly oriental, or Regency, except for those of the ancient world, which are semiprecious stone or bronze. "Gawd, Frank. You're not asking much."

He looked so crestfallen—a massive slump for such a big bloke—that I felt sorry. "Okay, Frank. I'll have a try. Still on that collection, eh?" He'd been trying to compile erotic antiques for some local lady.

"Mmmmh. Oh, Lovejoy." The train began to move. "Will you be best man?"

"Me?" I don't usually get asked this, being a scruff. Must be this frigging suit, which served me right. "If you want. How many's this?"

"Eighth. That's why it'll have to be at that redundant church."

Well, I could see why a going parish couldn't risk doing weddings as job lots. Religion's never any help to the living, is it.

Big Frank ran out of platform. We ended up bawling at each other over the wheel clatter, him yelling eleven o'clock at St. Mary the Virgin's church on Saturday week, me bawling a polite ta-for-asking. I sagged in my seat, nearly crushing Toffee in her basket. What with Mrs. Ryan, the tailor's, Toffee, and Big Frank I was knackered before the journey'd even started. So this new wife would be the eighth. Did bigamies count two?

"Morning, Lovejoy." Dorothy was smiling at me from the opposite seat. I hadn't noticed her. "My, aren't we smart!"

"Traveling by train?" I gave back, though I like her because she's bonny and plays the harpsichord for Les Moran's music shop in the High Street. "The broomstick in for service?" Her husband Les is a jealous burke.

She smiled, letting Toffee sniff her fingers. "Now stop that, Lovejoy."

Three months previously she'd been interviewed on local

television talking about witchcraft, midsummer frolics, and all that. "Seriously, Dot. Still a fully paid-up witch, are we?"

"I still . . . commune with nature, if that's what you mean."

"I'm going on telly, too," I said proudly. We chatted of that until she got off at Kelvedon. After that some old dear with cherries on her hat started telling me what she fed her own rotten moggie.

"Cats are superior," she explained, in a terrible sentence I later wished I'd listened to more carefully. "Lone walkers, they. Dogs want friends, especially in the night hours. Old softies."

Daft owd bat, I thought, and nodded off.

The TV building amazed me. If you've never seen these places, don't. They're grottie, a real letdown. I emerged from the station to find this hunchback, gaunt-windowed brick building looking like a Salvosh soup kitchen between a post office and a derelict cinema. I even walked round the place to make sure, until Sykie's lads came out and wearily hauled me in past the unshaven doorman.

"I could do wiv yer, Lovejoy," Sykie's eldest told me, "but you're frigging weird. Bleedin' nag one minute, moggie the next."

The audience numbered about a hundred, mostly the blue-rinse brigade. We sat obediently in rows facing an alcoholic comedian who tried to make his transparent anxiety less contagious by telling a succession of corny Christmas cracker jokes. Finally he surrendered from exhaustion, and left us with a blunt instruction to applaud when he wagged a rolled newspaper.

This particular telly game's moronic, like all the others. God knows why people watch. I used to, before sadists among the authorities played hell about license money and nicked my black-and-whiter. The idea is that somebody comes onto the stage with some alleged antique. "Is it real or fake?" the compère bleats through her lacquered grin. Bloody stupid, because everything's one thing or the other, including people. She continues, "Is it . . . *old or gold?*" The studio audience jubilantly chants this catchphrase, applauding themselves and laughing. (Thrilling stuff, no?) A panel of three tries to guess each antique's value while an antiques "expert" sits there, sneering. His job's to reveal the truth. He says. Former civilizations created brilliant musical liturgies and literature reaching the highest spheres of art. We add stupendous technology to this particular cake mix—and produce gunge.

There's only one dicey bit: You've got to believe the expert. The reason the whole absurd carry-on's so fascinating is of course antiques themselves. They're exactly what life is: exalting, beautiful, and an exhilarating risk. Or fake.

Toffee's feline brain sussed out the scene's potential and wisely switched off. I was just settling next to a nice Birmingham bird who insisted on telling me all about other telly shows she'd been to, when Sykie's action started. A thin terrified woman carrying a clipboard tore on, twisting with anguish.

Would you believe, she announced, but a panelist had—gasp!—flu and a volunteer was needed from the audience. She ran about, demented. People frantically rose to volunteer as one. I sat, bored out of my mind, until a Sykie-prompted knee nudged my seat's back and I obediently raised my hand. I can take a hint. The corkscrewing lady rotated down the aisle and picked me. I gave a glowering Sykes lad Toffee to hold, and followed the lady into a kind of barber's where a lank bird in jeans tried to put powder on my face. I wasn't having that, and saw her off. I made the panel unsullied. The show was Going Out Live, they told us breathlessly, as if we'd all be moribund otherwise.

So we panelists sat there on these neffie tubular steel chairs that hurt your spine. I eyed the others mistrustfully. Two youngsters were penning our names on cards. "Lovejoy," I told my particular youth when he asked. For some reason the duckegg was crawling on the floor. I shrugged. Whatever turns you on.

"And here's Veronica Gold!" a deity boomed. Applause and swivelling lights. This fetching bird marched on amid pandemonium. She's attractive, in a rather threatening manner. Worship me, her smile commands, or I'll liquidate you. We'd been instructed to call her Goldie. The suicidal comic flagged the applause to a mere tumult, and we were off.

"Our panelists this week," Goldie trilled, "are Famous Television Personality . . ." I listened with half an ear.

This FTP was quite a pleasant scholarly bloke who looked in from the country, Peter Something. I vaguely recalled him reading the news years ago. Then an intense lass of savage plainness called Beth, a Famous Feminist Author and Equal-Right Journalist, as if there is such a thing. And me.

"And," Goldie beamed, "tonight's Volunteer Celebrity Panelist, selected for one hundred consecutive viewings of this program—Lovejoy."

"Er, sorry, love," I interrupted. "Never watch it, I'm afraid." Her eyes glazed. "What?"

"Bit of a run-in over the TV license."

The comic wafted the feeble applause into a riot, and blew it out with a horizontal swipe of his newspaper.

"No significance in Lovejoy's name, folks!" cried Goldie desperately.

The comic leaps into action. A gale of laughter, then silence. It was getting on my nerves, but it was their business. If this ludicrous pantomime made me immune from Sykie's righteous anger, I'd play along. I'd been happier flogging hankies.

"And now it's time to play . . ." Goldie chirped gaily.

"Old or gold!" the audience thundered. And on came the first item.

It was a small piece of niello jewelry on a velvet card, brought in by a brown-coated serf. The ex-newsreader guessed it Russian, worth a fortune. Beth the journalist talked until she was signaled by yet another creeping kulak—God, they seemed everywhere, crawling about. Like being in a bloody dogs' home. One kept jabbing a finger at me and then at Goldie, telling me to keep staring at our elegant compère. Obligingly I tried, but kept getting distracted by somebody dangling past in the semigloom beyond the lights.

Somebody had asked me something. "Eh?"

Goldie looked narked. "Beth says stylized French, two centuries old, and five thousand pounds. Your guess, Lovejoy?"

My turn. "Oh, thank you," I said politely. "Crappy modern junk, love. Not worth a light."

A split second of silence, then Goldie smoothly moved on. "So three distinct views. But is it. . . ?"

"Old or gold!" everybody yelled.

Our expert, a museum curator, emerged to a drumroll and pulled a lever. A massive screen above us showed carousel numbers clicking past. They stopped at twenty-six. I fell about laughing. The clapping faltered, stopped.

"Yes, three points to Lovejoy," Goldie announced brightly. "He is in good humor at his success!"

"Not that, love," I said. "You'd never get twenty-six quid for that rubbish. It's penny a ton. Thailand stuff, mass-produced. There's no variation in the niello, see? Ancient niello makers stuck to the old Cellini one-two-three step formula, silver is to copper is to lead. So do the Thais, incidentally, but their absolute mix is—"

"Thank you," screamed Goldie, smiling a terrible smile at a camera. There were lots of these. A red light kept shining, first on one, then another. Pretty clever, really. "And the next item is . . ."

A lady walked on wearing an amber necklace. She was a good middle-aged handful for some fortunate yokel. Her beads were bonny, simply carved, a light orange.

"Amberoid," I said in disgust without rising to examine the necklace and thinking, no wonder we're all morons these days if this is your average telly. Why show dross when you needn't? The lady exhibiting them looked lost. "Not your fault, love," I told her kindly. "Wiser heads than yours have fallen for it. Amber fragments heated together. You can tell by the longitudinal striations. Maybe a couple of quid on a bad day."

In the mutterings that followed, Beth actually won that round because the expert said a hundred quid and she'd guessed nearest.

But when the next serf brought out this vase I really did burst out in a guffaw. I just couldn't help it. It was on the far side so I couldn't see it clearly at first. Its shape told me enough—well, almost. Only as tall as your ordinary neffie modern ornament, it was a pale apple green, bulbous at the base and slender-necked. I laughed because everybody gets scores of these Hong Kong replicas every week. They're less than a quid each, delivered.

"It's another blinking fake," I said, falling about to Goldie's obvious fury. I couldn't help it.

Then something happened. I stopped.

Distantly, yet deep within me, a faint peal of bells sounded. Their chimes intensified, increased, until I was deafened by the resonance. Appalled, I felt myself shake. Their clamor actually set me quivering. Not real bells, you understand, but total.

The serf came nearer, placed the vase on a stand. The pedestal rotated. I thought, Oh God, no. The world was suddenly glowing. Dimly I heard Goldie say, all acid, "Lovejoy's especially amused . . ." but by then I was up and at the vase, apologizing heartbroken.

There it stood, its luscious ancient soul radiating while I chimed like a Sunday church. Sometimes I'm just thick. I could hardly speak from grief at what I'd just said to it. Alone, among this cretinoidal gathering, it was magic.

"Look, love," I told it brokenly, "I'm sorry. Honest. I honestly didn't think. It's just this silly bloody game."

Some people were laughing. Goldie was beaming confidingly at the audience, working their amusement, but I could tell heads would roll for letting me on the panel. That made me feel even worse. "We've never had a panelist make love to a pot before," she simpered. The panic-stricken comic fanned the laughter, uncertain applause.

I wasn't having this vase spoken to like that. "*Pot*? You need a bloody good hiding, you stuck-up ignorant bitch." I apologized to the dazzling ornament. The audience quieted. "Do you mind, chuckie?" I asked it politely, and reached out to touch it, thrilling. And I swear it almost did move, a swift gracious response of understanding emanated . . . I realized there was almost total quiet. Cameramen, the gecko crawlers, even Goldie, were stunned into silence.

"Well," I said defensively. "She's worth the lot of you pillocks. She hasn't come down through all these centuries from ancient China just for you to have a frigging giggle, you stupid burkes."

"Break time now, viewers," Goldie caroled. "Don't go away now!"

Everybody froze an instant, then all hell was let loose. They hoofed me off. Not a chance to say good-bye to that luscious green glass queen. A burly bloke actually hauled me down corridors, smashing through swing doors at a breathless run while I tried to explain in gasps. I had a glimpse of the drunken comic giving me a hilarious grin and a thumbs-up, then I was lobbed out into the rain. The door slammed and I was alone under an archway near the car park. Disgruntled, I went round the corner to a nosh bar and counted time, worrying about Sykes.

Scared? Of course I was scared. How was I to know the show was for epsilon-minus stupes?

Twenty minutes later the crowd emerged, talking and amused. The show had obviously taken a turn for the better. Sykie finally appeared. Mercifully, he was smiling. He gave me a nod, walked by without a word. His Rolls came and wafted him away in grand style, his nerks following in a saloon. One gave me Toffee's basket. She was asleep. Some people nudged each other when they saw me, as if it was all my fault. It was that Goldie. Women always find a bloke to blame, don't they. I was at a loss, hanging about the pavement wondering if Sykie'd send word, but at half-past gave up and caught the tube to Liverpool Street Station.

Thinking about it, sharing a pasty with Toffee as the train rattled into East Anglia, I was quite pleased. It was over and done with, and I'd done as I was told, right? It wasn't my fault I'd mucked up their neffie program. Three little girls got on at Romford and played with Toffee while I nodded off.

An hour later I entered the Railway Tavern. He was there, as instructed: rheumy-eyed, in his tatty army greatcoat, resonantly coughing up phlegm from subterranean depths. Tinker Dill, Esq., my barker. The best antiques sniffer in East Anglia.

"Wotcher, Tinker. Get the notes?"

"Aye, Lovejoy." He slurped his ale to drought, my cue to buy another pint. "'Ere. We in trouble?" It's all he ever says to me, but for once I didn't snap his head off.

"Trouble? Nar, mate. Just wriggled out from under."

Wrong, Lovejoy, wrong.

3

Too drunk, Tinker doesn't function. Sober, he's hopeless. But middling sloshed he's a gem. Now he was coughing really well and tipsily crumpled, all good signs.

"I seed yer on the telly, Lovejoy," he wheezed. "That Goldie tart's got lovely bristols, eh?"

"Good legs, too. What about the auction?"

"Everybody bought everyfing, Lovejoy." Translation: He'd guessed right about all the notable items in the sale I'd sent him to. With the stimulus of a fresh pint, he embellished. "Maggie paid a bleedin' fortune for that set of mugs. Lennie made a balls-up, bidding too fast for that little mahogany Canterbury. Liz Sandwell got the Pembroke table . . ."

This is lifeblood. I listened hungrily. Sounds daft, I know, but every syllable might be worth a mint. It took him six pints to run down the list.

". . . and Jessica got them old shoes cheap, folk said. That's it, Lovejoy."

"Them old shoes" were about 1895, very pointed patent

leather pumps with big flat bows of grosgrain ribbon. I groaned. They were mint collectors' items. I hate these delectables going to the undeserving, which means anybody else.

"Another pint, love," I told Megan at the bar—she was fawning on Toffee—and asked Tinker, "Jessica bidding separate from Lennie?"

"Aye."

Interesting news, this. Jessica is Lennie's mother-in-law, and possesses glamour, wealth, and, rumor hath, Lennie as well. She furthers his interests with all the effort of which she's capable, which is a great deal. Sadly, Lennie is a numskull. You never see Lennie's wife. Scandal gets vigorous local help, one way and another.

". . . you'd be there at ten, Lovejoy."

"Eh?" Tinker had been talking. "Me where at ten?"

"Dogpits Farm. Some tart." He coughed, a long crescendo that shook soot down the bar chimney. I paused with the respect due a world champ.

"What for?" As far as I was concerned Dogpits was a place famous for being where they'd found a little Roman amphitheater years ago, and nowt else.

"How the bleedin' hell should I know?" he graveled out, peeved. His glass was empty. I paid for more lubrication. "And Sykie sent his lads over. Sez be home tomorrer."

"Two places at once?" It wasn't Tinker's fault. A barker's job to collect messages, sniff out hearsay about illicit antique goings-on. I'm the brains of the outfit, God help us. Meanwhile he was eyeing Toffee speculatively.

"Stuffed moggies is good money, Lovejoy."

"Only before 1910, though." Toffee looked at me, but the thought honestly hadn't crossed my mind.

"You can age them. Didn't you show Brad some trick with formalin tablets?"

"You mean stuffed fish and hydrogen peroxide." It had made me queasy for days. Never again. "That it, then?"

"Yih." He nearly shook himself apart with another world-beater cough. "'Cept for George Prentiss."

"George? He still owes me for three Boer War soldiers, Afrikaans, painted lead; and a book." That's the trouble with me, too trusting.

"Not now, Lovejoy. Frigging great farm bull killt him." He spat into the fire. "A rubbish animal, big as a barn."

"Dead? Dear God. When?"

"Last night. Boothie found him, Pittsbury Wood way."

Tom Booth is a famed poacher. Seemed an odd business to me. I said so, and a well-loved voice agreed with me from the taproom doorway. I sighed wearily. It was one of those days. Maybe I ought to have accepted Mrs. Ryan's job and be safely baling straw in some orchard or whatever.

"Pint, Megan." Ledger leaned on the bar beside me. "Evening, Dill."

"Mumble, mumble." Tinker edged away, leaving me all alone. Friends, I thought bitterly, though Ledger's not really poisonous, as peelers go. That is to say he has standards, which have even veered towards righteousness when all else has failed.

"Don't tell me, Ledger," I said. "You watched telly and have popped in for a friendly gloat."

"What are you on about, Lovejoy?" He sounded quite affable, a bad omen. "No. I've come to demand an explanation. In," he twinkled with repellent merriment, "the name of the law."

"Should you be drinking on duty?"

"No. Cheers." He sucked on the rim. The most obnoxious sight in the world, a copper enjoying an illicit pint, whooping it up on our taxes. Fuming, I looked away. Megan's mobile mammae were more gorgeous any day of the week. "George, as you said, is a very odd business."

"Tinker just told me. What was he doing having a run-in with a bull in candle hours?"

He gave me a warning finger. "Shut it, Lovejoy. I ask. You

answer. Follow?" He nodded to Megan for a refill, my only benefit being an upsurge in Megan's nubility as she manipulated the lever. The symbolism was wearing me out. If it hadn't been for this pest I'd offer to give her Toffee for a—"How come, Lovejoy, that George had in his possession a book belonging to you?"

"Me?" I went all innocent.

"Don't irritate me, lad. I've checked."

The book was practically new, a 1962 thing called *Erotic Love*. I'd faked the pseudonymous author's autograph, Sardi, on the flyleaf, a common dealer's trick. If he/she can secretly be anybody, the signature can be in anybody's handwriting. It should have kept me in grub a whole week. George had seen me in the Ship pub on East Hill trying to sell it to Lily. I'd come by the Sardi book almost legitimately by nicking it in a church jumble sale, a temporary loan from the Almighty—one way of improving His poor record of assisting the disadvantaged.

"Ah, *that* book!" I said with theatrical remembrance. "Yes. Original author's inscription, I believe. Not quite my kind of subject, you understand . . ." I'd strangle Lily for bubbling me with the Old Bill.

He frowned. "What I want to know is why George Prentiss should be carrying your book across a field, committing night trespass, and getting gored to death."

"Beats me."

"What I mean is, did George fall, or was he pushed?"

"Ask the frigging bull." And these goons get paid. I ask you.

He sat silent for a few seconds, watching me. Some darts players over by the fire cheered a victory. They practice days at a time, but I've never seen a darts match end by anything but a fluke. "What's the book, Lovejoy?"

I spoke frankly because Ledger's tone had gone normal. "Truth is, I got it at a church jumble. It was big erotic stuff for the sixties. Now, it's old hat."

"Was Prentiss a known collector?"

"George? Hardly. He just helps various dealers with early electrical gadgets. Nice bloke. Sometimes bought a few models—soldiery, model cars, dinkies we call them all in the trade." I told him about the Boer War riflemen. "That was a month back. Real collectors are maniacs. Sell their missus for a beer label if it'd make a set."

He left then, to the Railway Tavern's wholesale relief. Not a word of thanks, note, for the invaluable assistance I'd rendered to the forces of law and order. Tinker shuffled over.

After I'd got him ale-oiled, I asked, "Here, Tinker. What rank is Ledger now?"

"Him? A boss summert. Why?"

"Odd." I kept my voice down. Megan's form undulated nearby as she did her thrilling best with the beer handle. "A boss growser, asking around pubs about a farm accident? He should be watching football on telly with his missus brewing cocoa."

"Workin' a free pint," Tinker said with venom.

"That's it," I agreed, smiling. "Another?" But my mind was going: Pittsbury Wood abuts on Dogpits Farm. I decided then to keep the appointment with Tinker's "some tart" at ten o'clock. You see, I knew something about George Prentiss that nobody even suspected and it's this: George wouldn't be found dead in the countryside. No, sorry, I didn't mean that. What I mean is, George hated the dark. And he hated truly rural countryside almost as much as I do, which is considerably.

Let me explain.

One of my worst disappointments was discovering that life needs management. Like, sometimes a week will start so badly that you simply want to stop it and start again. When an especially bad week happens along, I simply halt it and go about pretending it's last Sunday. I call them my Sunday weeks. I loll, feed the robin, read, go to a nonexistent evensong and hum my way through maybe a Tantum Ergo, all alone in a surprised but empty church. The next morning, lo and behold! It's last Monday again, but second time around, as it were. It confers a kind of spirit-world lebensraum. And guess what? That week suddenly changes. It becomes easy, friendly, and trouble-free. Try it.

I'd learned about George's particular weakness three months before. I was merrily drunk on homemade wine and telling a bored robin how I'd stupidly missed a Benin bronze in a Suffolk auction by stopping for a quick, er, chat with the delectable Liz Sandwell in Dragonsdale. That escapade cost money. Not many people can manage penury, shame, and degradation all at one go, like me. Instantly recognizing I'd fallen unsuspectingly into a Sunday week, I zoomed home to pretend it was the previous sabbath. By evening I was happy, and warbling a Thomas Tallis madrigal to an indifferent universe from the confines of my workshop—no thriving mill; it's a crumbling ex-garage set among brambles.

It was then that George stopped by for a drink. I sang him a difficult second stanza and gave him a jam jar full of my best elderberry. George is, was, a quietly calm bloke. Anyone not knowing him'd call him reserved.

But anyone with half an eye could suss George out as a harmless, tinkering bloke good as gold. We chatted. I sang. He stayed, and stayed. I was frying us both some tomatoes and bread when I suddenly realized two things: It was eleven o'clock, and George was terrified. I goaded my irate neurons into action. They decided something else was odd. George hadn't explained why he'd come.

"Here, George," I said. "Anything I can do for you?"

"No, Lovejoy. Thanks." He gave a ghastly grin. "Only, I was mending Sandy's electrics and forgot the time. That's why I dropped in."

Sandy and Mel I've already mentioned. They live in our village, and are rich, aggressive dealers. Nowt as queer as folk, my old gran used to say.

"To wait for the bus, eh?" Mel and Sandy are also famous for not giving people lifts in their fantastic battleship of a car. "Sorry, George.. My crate's off the road at present." The ancient Ruby, corrosive sublimate of motor, was dwindling into oxides among the foliage—a disagreement with the authorities.

"I saw."

Odd. Only then did I concentrate and actually examine George's features. In my drunken state I'd not noticed, but now I saw the symptomatology: the sweat, tremors, the quick glances. Even as he spoke he leapt out of his skin because of a snuffling at the door.

"For Christ's sake, George. It's only the hedgehog."

Crispin stood there blinking while I went to make its pobs, bread in milk. It has its own saucer. Soon he'd start screaming at night along my autumn hedge, a horrible scary cry to show that he's packing up for the year. George stared fearfully into the dark night, while Crispin slurped his nocturnal calories and gave me reproachful glances. He isn't used to slow service caused by trembling visitors. Narked, I bent down and showed it my fist. "I want no criticism from you, chiseler," I threatened. Mother Nature really irks me. All she does is breed scroungers, then sends them round to me for alms. It's basically bad organization. One of these days I'll send the whole frigging lot packing. "If it isn't you it's the bloody birds hammering on the window," I grumbled. Crispin slurped the last and left, pink feet high-stepping aloofly into the night. No wonder I'm bitter. Dignity comes easy, on other people's graft.

"It's the dark, George, eh?"

"Yes." He unwound slightly as the door closed, and gave me a feeble grin. "I was always terrified, right from a kiddie."

That night he slept on my floor, a blanket and cushion job. And went off right as rain in the morning, noshing fried tomatoes and marching out for the first bus. I watched him go from my porch, gave him a wave. Nothing wrong with having a phobia, as long as you keep quiet about it.

That's what I meant about George not being a lover of night-walking. Maybe he'd had some premonition? A daft thought, really, because I'm determined not to believe in hunches and all that. Real life's trouble enough.

So, the morning after my epic television drama, aiming to keep that ten o'clock appointment, I was plodding between the mathematical white fences of Dogpits Farm while horses raised heads and belligerently stared me down. The house grew love-lier with every plod, a resplendent black and white Tudor voyager among modernity. I wondered hopefully how the lady in residence would take a proposal of marriage from a scruff like me.

Then this bloke came galloping at me on a horse the size of an elephant, intending to whip me, while a bonny mounted girl nearby laughed admiringly. Served me right for daydreaming.

4

Well, I wasn't having that. The first I realized of the assault was a thudding of hooves, and this giant horse was charging directly at me with a mounted idiot whooping like a maniac. In panic I fled and crawled under the nearest fence—faster than most people leap—and started sprinting across a field. The maniac leapt the obstruction—I'd forgotten that horses were natural jumpers—and came thundering after me. Instinctively as the bloody nag hoofed closer I made my dash curve, ever tighter, so the mad cavalry floundered to regain direction. Then I was off, straightlining to a distant hedge. Of course it wasn't all athletics. I was also screaming explanations about being invited to call for a job, and begging in terror, anything, but it was no use. The frigging lunatic kept coming, and the acreage grew wider and me more knackered with pain in my chest and side from exercise. And a bit of fear.

A cheering noise sounded, but it might have been my ears roaring. Maybe the blond girl had friends. Third rush I glanced, terrified, to check her distance, but she was only circling at a genteel trot and calling, "Go on, Christopher," and this goon shouting tally-hos and similar intellectual expletives.

I ducked and weaved, then snatched up a great tuft of grass as the creature crashed past the fourth time. My neck got a lash from the nutter, but it was cheap at the price. As he hauled on the animal's gears I wheezed after them, my legs trembling. The beast turned to find me crouched there. I leapt skyward with a howl and hurled my tuft, shedding black soil, into the bloody thing's face. It reared and the bloke went over. I'd actually started a last desperate sprint before I realized it wasn't coming any more. It trotted off, looking quite jovial, tail up and snorting. Our hero lay there, winded. My ribs burned. A hand fell on my shoulder.

"You're under arrest, Lovejoy."

"Me?" Even that word took three labored inspirations. It was Geoffrey, vigilant constable of our parish, in his size twenty-one boots and posh uniform. "Whafor?"

"Assault," he said proudly.

"Don't-be-bloody-silly, Geoffrey," I panted.

That cheering noise had changed. It was now a chorus of booing, of all sounds my least favorite. Astonished, I looked round. A crowd—honest, a real mob—of people thronged the road beyond the hedge. They carried placards and banners full of exhortation. I didn't bother to look any more; I've never read an intelligible banner yet. To my surprise I spotted a familiar face among the mob. Podge Howarth? Out here?

"Hang on, Geoffrey," I said.

This hulking great huntsman was hauling himself to his feet as I stepped up and booted him in the crotch. He doubled with a whoomph that nearly blew Geoffrey's helmet off. The distant boos turned to thunderous applause.

"Here, Lovejoy. Stop that," Geoffrey commanded. I eyed the horse with hate. Jauntily it eyed me back. I decided to abandon ball-kicking while I was ahead.

"He tried to kill me, Geoffrey," I explained. "I want him

arrested." I decided to snap the goon's whip in a grandiloquent gesture for encore, but the whip wouldn't break. All it did was bend. I felt a duckegg and hoped nobody noticed.

"Come quietly, Lovejoy. Don't give me all this aggro." Geoffrey led me off while this bird on her white nag pounded up and demanded why I wasn't being hanged from the nearest tree.

"I've arrested him, miss," Geoffrey said respectfully. "This felon is now in custody."

Felon? Whacked and bewildered as I was, I couldn't help using up my few remaining kilojoules in an amazed stare. I'll bet anybody a quid that Geoffrey doesn't even know what a felon is.

"He kicked Major Bentham," pronounced this mounted Valkyrie.

The crowd's cheers became jeers. A chant of "No, no, no!" began. My day suddenly brightened.

"I assaulted nobody, did I?" I yelled.

"No, no, *no!*"

No wonder there are goons everywhere these days. The feeling's really great. You can say anything, even gibberish, and still emerge president with the World Bank hanging on every belch.

Fist aloft, I bawled, "Nidginovgorod yeah!" and unbelievably got a "Yeah! Yeah! Yeah!" ripping the clouds over the brook where Tacitus himself had sat and bathed his feet. I thought, I don't believe this world any more. Maybe I'm a throwback, or a sport. At least I would have thought that, except nowadays you've to say heterozygous recessive mutant or some such. . . . Oh, Christ. A large black saloon car was pulling in by the hedge.

A somber man emerged, lighting his pipe. Between flashes and puffs he glanced over to our weird scenario, and beckoned. I plodded over, Geoffrey coming with that head-lowering pose of the superseded bobby.

"Wotcher, Ledger."

He wafted his match out, chin raised like a stag sniffing fire. "Lovejoy. What're you doing booting the local gentry?"

"I'm here by invitation. Tinker gave me a message for ten o'clock, the lady of the house."

"Nothing to do with fox-hunting?"

"Eh?" I turned to inspect the immediate universe. The chanting mob was now walking along the road, placards everywhere. A hairy bloke was pouring stuff on the ground. Athletic-looking men stripped for marathon running were scuffing their shoes in the mess. The penny dropped. They were preparing good old aniseed porridge, which harriers would stamp all over the countryside to mislead hounds. "Not today, Ledger. I've read all the quotations." Nobody was going to call me unspeakable in pursuit of the uneatable.

He actually nearly virtually smiled. Almost. "The major must've thought you were a protester."

"He should have asked." I eyed him with curiosity. "Here, Ledger. You're around a lot these days, aren't you? For a corporal, I mean."

Amazingly he was amused. "Now, lad," he said benignly.

"No, seriously. Fox hunts on your beat, are they?"

"Ledger!" the hooliganess screamed, deprived of her arena massacre. "I demand—"

"Says he's here by invitation, lady." To his credit Ledger didn't give ground as she kicked her horse closer. Calmly he struck a match on his coat, to my unbounded admiration, and the beast nervously edged off. The bird lashed the poor thing, furious. It skittered, eyes whitening in worry. I really felt sorry for it. We losers share empathy. "Miss Candice, meet Lovejoy. He's unscrupulous, a consort of thieves, and in my view certifiably insane."

Civilization waited. Then, "Lovejoy?" she said.

"How do," I said, still trying to be friends.

Ledger swiveled to point at the big house. He'd made up his

mind. "Up that footpath, Lovejoy, you'll see signs To The Restaurant. The lady'll be there."

"You sure, Ledger?" I asked. "Only, that silly sod—"

Ledger didn't even glance at the major, who was hunching his slow way along the fenced drive, a paradigm for us all. "The constable will accompany you to ensure your safe arrival, Lovejoy."

"Am I still under arrest, Ledger?"

"You misunderstood the constable's phraseology," Ledger said, getting in his car. The police have this knack of losing responsibilities. "Call in sometime. I'd like a chat. 'Morning." He was tipping his hat as the police driver left us a cloud of pollutant. The slur was unmistakable. Miss Candice glared at me. I shrugged, carefully keeping Geoffrey's stolid mass between the bird and me, and went over to Podge Howarth, who obviously felt sheepish being spotted among this lot.

"Wotcher, Podge," I said blithely. "Ta for helping me when the Cossacks came." A number of protesters grinned and slapped my shoulders admiringly. A gray-eyed girl in camp-follower attire—shredded jeans, dirty pullover knitted from wholemeal, bark sandals—kissed me and awarded me some poor flower she'd dragged from its bed in the interests of conversation. A button-badge begged Call Me Enid!

"Wotcher, Lovejoy. Didn't know it was you or I'd have—"

"Oh, aye." I kept pace with his trudging circle. Finding him among a mob of peace-loving proearth antihunt protesters is like a frog in fruit—something with no immediate explanation. I mean, I don't care for hunting either, because I always feel like the fox, never the hunter. But that doesn't set me off rioting, usually because I'm being hunted elsewhere. Now, Podge is a laugh. He makes Roman bronze door keys, always has scores buried in his little garden aging. With the soft bronze he uses—his cousin's a Birmingham car dealer—a lovely antique-looking patina takes about a year to develop in a good (meaning bad) summer. A dry hot midyear like we'd just had is murder to a bronze forger. "Look, Podge," I said. "What's going on? The whole Eastern Hundreds're going frigging barmy."

He became even shiftier. "Dunno, Lovejoy."

Puzzled, I halted to inspect the demonstration. You can tell when a bloke's following a bird, can't you. Nodding and beaming as they trogged, I watched them once round to make sure there was no married lady whose eyes wavered in guilt. Was Podge Howarth littering our countryside for sordid sex, or something nearer to his avaricious heart? Yes, he was grinning fatuously at the gray-eyed flower-giver Enid, and her with a wedding ring. Tut-tut. Satisfied, I turned to my police escort.

"Right, Geoffrey," I said resignedly. "Fancy a walk?"

Me and Geoffrey went up the path chatting about my fellow villager Raymond, currently on remand for trying to pull the old fiddle trick with a piece of early Wedgwood.

"Unbelievable, these days," Geoffrey was saying as I helped him over a stile. He has these feet. "Stupid sod."

"Raymond's daft. Won't be told," I agreed. "Want a rest?"

"No, ta," he panted, hobbling and leaning on me, though I was the one who'd been cavalried. "He'll get six months, Lovejoy. Mark my words."

"Stroll on," I mourned. Three of us—me, Big Frank and Margaret Dainty—had clubbed together to finance good old Raymond's escapade. If he got clinked, we'd be responsible for his antique shop until they released him. Unwritten and tiresome rules of our hopeless game. I'd known Raymond hadn't the brains to pull it off, but he's Margaret's cousin and you know women.

Geoffrey halted, mopped the interior of his cavernous helmet. "We're here, Lovejoy. In you go."

Surprised, I stared at the great glass edifice projecting from the lovely old mansion house's side. It was almost an exact shoebox shape, an aluminum-framed slab erected by Neanderthals. It was labeled Modern Farm Centre Restaurant in simulated microdot typeface, red on gold. "Hell fire, Geoffrey. Do I have to?"

"Good morning, Lovejoy," said this lady, smiling from the french windows, so I went in and left Geoffrey to the mercy of his feet. "So you're the unspeakable lout who assaulted Christopher?" Unspeakable after all, note.

"Look, missus," I said uneasily. "I can come back. I don't mind leaving it—"

"Do stay. I need you. Like our new place?"

She led me through a forest of tubular steel tables, red plastic, and unuseable slump chairs designed to immobilize the unwary. Flowers looked ashamed in intense blue slit glass vases, Czechoslovakia's idea of art. Dangling wicker baskets marauded on the ceiling, drooping orange blossoms trying to escape. The whole place had an air of a travelers' Gothic, dreadful. I just made the office without retching. I'd give twice a lot for ten minutes of her, but nowt for her horrible restaurant. Instantly I knew what was wrong: She'd hired an expert.

"Candice told me all about it," she said, lighting a cigarette. She didn't need me. She needed Sandy and Mel, because they could make this ghastly clinical restaurant look really homely, except Sandy'd scream and Mel'd get one of his famous heads.

"Oh, aye." My tone must have told her I'd been the victim of many such impartial reports. Unexpectedly she gave a broad infectious smile, and suddenly I liked her.

She had a kind of tooled elegance some women call grace. Not Mrs. Ryan's vibrant showiness, but a precision-made look that announced: I'm still trendier than anybody. I'm not much up on the subject of women's garb, yet all the signs of wealth were there: the strap-round yeoman boots in pricey leather, the russet worsted skirt, bishop-sleeve silk blouse. Pearls genuine; surprisingly, no rings. Even so, you wouldn't get much change here from a quid.

"I'm Suzanne York," this elegance said. "Thank you for

broaching the defenses. Christopher assumes the estate's already his."

Hello, I thought, heart sinking. The dreaded inheritance bit. When property, by some miracle, is being kept out of the taxman's hands, it's never anything but trouble. Women always find my expression a giveaway. She quickly added, "Well, Lovejoy. My husband's passed on. Raising my niece is a problem, a very costly one."

"The hounds expensive?" I asked. "Your butler poor?"

"Don't start that." She sighed and crossed her legs, picking a tobacco flake off her tongue. "Major Bentham says the hounds will generate interest among the county set, who'll flock to my new restaurant." She eyed me. "You like it?"

"Horrible, love."

She took it on the chin. "Yes, well. Just as well you're not likely to frequent the place, isn't it?"

Touché. "Lady. The, er, reason—"

"And in any case," she said, temper rising, "the best restaurant designers in London—"

"It's great," I cut in hastily. "That's what I meant." After all, anyone who builds a glass and tin shoebox with scarlet tables might be daft enough to hire me.

"You needn't crawl, Lovejoy." She was still mad at me for hating her grottie caff. "It's just that this place is intended for the upper bracket." *And you're not in that class*, she carefully didn't add, but the words rattled about the office just the same.

"Which raises the question of me." I smiled my groveler's smile.

"Your performance on television, Lovejoy." She swung her chair. It was one of those that businessmen use, so they can turn their backs on visitors without having to move. She didn't go quite that far. "Was it genuine, or rehearsed?"

"It wasn't a performance." Her skepticism narked me. "They slung me out." I was indignant.

"I noticed you'd been replaced for the second half." Her interest was showing so I melted a bit. "Do you want a job?"

Suddenly I saw it all. This Suzanne was the person Sykie wanted hooked! I grinned jubilantly. I'd fallen on my feet, actually done what Sykie wanted. "Yes. What is it?"

"I want you to find a genuine antique, for the restaurant." I tried not to wince, imagining a Sheraton chair or an inlaid Ince and Mayhew table among this load of crud. "For a raffle."

"Eh?"

"You see, Lovejoy, a restaurant needs a gimmick. They've all been done a thousand times, the Saxon Axe Bar, King Alfred's Kake Kitchen, Ancient Brit, Quaker's Retreat, all the local history tinseled up."

"And you think an antique. . . ?"

Her eyes were glowing, lovely behind the curved lashes. "Each table is numbered. A fanfare, a drumroll, and presto! The lucky table wins an antique!" She was so thrilled she almost applauded herself. "Isn't it a wonderful opening?"

Which meant the place hadn't opened yet, that only the workmen had so far glimpsed the monstrosity. Thank God for that.

"When's the off?"

"Saturday. What do you have in stock, Lovejoy?" She was out of her depth. "I could call at your showrooms—"

Showrooms? "Er, yes," I said. "But it's more usual for the purchaser to simply say what's in her mind. Then I'd know what items to arrange in the, er, warehouse." I waxed eloquent. "You see, stock is continually changing."

"Business," this dear innocent agreed with a grave frown, "is business. Yes, I do understand, Lovejoy." The contractors must have rooked her rotten over that garish hangar of a restaurant. "Though Major Bentham advises us on the financial side of things."

Just as this particularly nasty penny dropped—the galloping

major her friendly treasurer—I heard a real frightener. It was a long gravelly sound, with strangled barks, then rising to a bubbly gasp. Mrs. York went pale. "Heavens!" she whispered. "What was that?"

I knew, and opened the door. Tinker was at the far end of the restaurant between Geoffrey and the major.

"'Ere, Lovejoy," he wheezed, recovering from his cough. "They just nicked me."

"It's all right, Tinker," I called, and said to Mrs. York, "Thank you. I'll select a number of pieces and have my assistants display them in the, ah, display rooms."

"This lout's another one, Suzanne," called the gallant officer. He could have made ten of Tinker, and held him by the scruff of his neck. Enough to make anybody cough.

"Who on earth. . . ?" Mrs. York was peering anxiously at the trio.

"It's all right, love," I said smoothly. "One of my messengers. We use all sorts of disguises. Mr. Tinker is a Sotheby's undercover man. Not a word, mind."

"Of course." She sounded doubtful so I made a swift goodbye.

By the time I reached them Tinker was puce and could only point to his throat where the huntsman's big hand gripped. Geoffrey was standing stolidly by, embarrassed.

"Half a sec, Tinker." I looked around, pulled a chair close, stepped up, and swung a foot in an arc and up, kicking the major in the belly. His chin came forward and caught the chair back. I actually heard his teeth rattle. Blood spouted from his mouth as he slumped, going, "Ergh! Ergh!" as he fell. I heard somebody scream—probably dear old Candice; it seemed her role in life—and got down, pulling Tinker along and down the steps. The quicker we were out of this place the better, now I'd got the job.

Geoffrey hobbled after us saying wait for me and that. Wearily we helped him down the path. When Tinker had got his breath I asked him what he'd followed me for.

"Nothing urgent?" I asked, hoping.

"Sykie's after you, Lovejoy. He's bleedin' mad."

My blood chilled. "At me? What for? I've done all the right things." I'd proved it to myself over and over. Hadn't I?

"Says he told you to stop home," Tinker said. "Here, Lovejoy. Reckon they've got draught beer?"

I was just drawing breath to say I'd suggest it to Suzanne for opening night when I decided to save the oxygen. A pair of long thick saloon cars were waiting in the roadway. Sykie's two lads stood by wearing happy smiles.

If you don't mind I won't go into details over the next bit. Eric and his brother did me physical damage. That's enough description. It was more or less as painful as what I'd done to the galloping major. It only seemed to last forty times as long.

Doc Lancaster told me I was a bloody fool to keep getting into scraps that I never won, but wasn't it lucky I had good friends like Mr. Sykes who had come to give me a lift home. I said a bitter yes, wasn't it.

"I've been good to you, Lovejoy," Sykie announced as I got painfully into his car. "Haven't I?"

"Yes, Sykie."

"Your face isn't even marked," he added, gratified and forgiving. "You understand the implications, Lovejoy?"

"Aye, Sykie."

"No more naughty from you, eh?"

"No, Sykie."

"Legs all right, are they?"

"A few stitches."

"Good, good." He sounded honestly quite glad. "Always go to the doctor's in good time, Lovejoy. My old mother used to say that."

Sykie swung his motor onto the A604 and put us between

the farms in quick succession, driving patiently, reminiscing about the good old days spent duffing up law-abiding citizens and bribing the Plod in London's East End. He thoughtfully included a number of his dear old mum's homilies for my edification. I said how very wise his mum had been.

"Yes, Lovejoy," he sniffed. "An angel. She raised us to show respect. Visited our Joe in Wormwood Scrubs every chance she got. They don't make them like her any more. Do they, lads?"

"No, dad," his psychopathic offspring said in unison. They were beaming proudly on the rear seats. Four more hooligans followed in the second motor.

They left me at the cottage door. The elder lad chucked a flintstone through my window, grinning at the crash. They really love life. Sykie put his head out.

"What's that implication, Lovejoy?"

"No more naughty from me, Sykie."

"Good. See how easy life is?" He gave a forgiving smile. "Stay home until somebody calls with a job for you because he's seen you on the telly. Right?"

Hell, I thought I'd just done that, but obediently I repeated the instruction. We cowards don't mince matters. "Why not tell me who it is, Sykie?"

"And have you chisel him with one of your crooked deals?" said this paragon of virtue indignantly. He eyed me, grinning. "You needn't wave us off, Lovejoy." The joke being that my ribs were strapped up.

They were all laughing as they drove out of the gateway. It took me an age to reach the keys in my back pocket and open the door. I brewed up, had a pint pot of tea, pulled out my divan, and slept for a million years.

Six o'clock I fried my breakfast, seven thick slices of bread, tomatoes, and sliced apple sizzled in margarine. Noshing and wincing, I did the post. Today there were a good dozen letters. I was sore as hell, but pleased. And determined. I'd survive in this maniacal antique business if I died doing it. These letters proved I was getting there by degrees—as lawyers go to heaven, my old gran used to say.

About these letters. Leaving aside my lies to Suzanne York about warehouses bulging with tsarine splendors, there are only three ways of surviving when times are bad. The first is to go "on the knocker"—literally banging on doors and doing a con on whoever opens the door. It has its moments, but there's always aggro on knocker jobs, what with people wanting ornaments back when realizing their value. So you need gelt and transport for that particular road to riches. The second is to wait in your costly well-stocked antiques shop for customers; must be nice. The third is to bread.

Now, every antique dealer on earth has done a bit of breading in his time. Even if Christie's or Spinks say they're above all that undignified conning, take it with a pinch of salt. They've done their share. My technique's to use the local free paper, the *Advertiser*. Usually I pretend I'm different people. Last week I'd been Bereaved Lady of Polstead, American Buyer Visiting Bures, and Distinguished London Collector. I tell Lize that I act as a free agent for these enthusiastic advertisers. She runs the *Advertiser* single-handed, and wants to believe my lies about being hooked on Good Social Works, so I don't disillusion her. It'd be cruel. Besides, I was using her rotten old cheapo give-away newspaper, so it's really me doing her a kindness, right?

Filling with fried bread and humanitarianisms, I sorted the responses to my adverts. The two dealers replying to the nonexistent Polstead lady were Ellston—a Clacton porcelain dealer—and Mannie, a Vitamin Earth lentil eater who deals in antique clocks. Both piously offered to save the poor widow heartbreak, and do it for nothing. And nick half the stuff while doing it, too, which they didn't mention.

"The swine," I said aloud, with heartfelt indignation. Lucky there was no such widow. I burned the replies. The imaginary Polstead lady's advert had offered *Late relative's collection of ar-*

cheological items for sale to interested buyer. No dealers, I'd written. Tinker hates these jobs with nothing really to go on, but it was time the drunken old devil earned his keep. Times were hard at Lovejoy Antiques, Inc.

My American Buyer advert called for real celebration: *Cash money offered for old pottery figures.* Five replies, only one worthwhile answer. A slow printed hand wrote of a "Pottery piece, a woman carrying two eshets", and said I could call any time on Mrs. Rowena Ray at 2, Sebastopol Cottages, Dedham. It sounded honest and frank—maybe the most really underhand trick of all. It was the sort of thing I'd write, so naturally I was suspicious. However, the use of the old farm word for bucket suggested some grannie flogging off her heirlooms. You never know.

As the "London Collector" I'd enticed *Genuine Householders Only: quality furniture needed for Kensington sale. Highest prices paid.* Nothing about antiques, note. The six responses to this advert were today's best, of course; they represented families. Even if you're only invited in to see a wobbly 1945 bed, it still gives you the opportunity of sussing what else is in the house. . . .

Somebody was knocking. Probably Tinker. Thinking I must have absently shot the bolt I got up instead of shouting, but no, the door wasn't barred. A polite bloke stood there, smiling expectantly. The breeze chilled my knees.

Warily I eyed him for concealed warhorses, whips, the odd phalanx of hoodlums, police insignia, and warrants for my arrest. So far it hadn't been a good day.

"Ah, Lovejoy?" he said anxiously.

"Yes." I was reassured. He got good points for anxiety, because huntsmen, gangsters, and police are famous for its absence.

"I called earlier. Unfortunately you were out."

Could this be Sykie's mark? I usually turn errors into habit, so gave him my best bent eye. Stolid. Polite. Moderately well attired. Smooth hands, and a tie without emblems, so maybe common sense lurked within. The silence was now painful. He shuffled anxiously, earning another point. Aggro doesn't shuffle. He saw my gaze on the plastic bag he held.

"I, er, had to call for some vegetables. Off Billiam Cutting, that writer at Ramparts Corner." He smiled self-consciously. "Cheaper than shops."

"Come in," I said, casting the door and leaving him to shut it. "Want a cup of tea? I've no sugar."

"Do us both good, then."

He took a few minutes to settle. He was Ben Cox, director of a Suffolk archeology trust. "I'm supposed to write first, according to our rules," he said disarmingly. "But . . ."

Yes, I thought, as I washed him my spare mug and tried to find a clean bit on the pot towel to dry it, this sounds definitely more like a Sykes ploy than the landed gentry's posh new manorial caff.

"Difficult." I said understandingly. "Want some fried bread?"

"No, thanks," he said, pleased. "My missus."

"Mmmmh," I sympathized. Women go berserk if you've had anything to eat before coming to their table, God knows why. You'd think it'd be easier for them if people arrived half full.

I got on with my grub. The tomatoes were congealing nicely on the cold plate. If you play your cards right, you can scoop up a whole slurp on one rent of bread. It makes a lovely mouthful. I hesitated to try, having company, but decided to give it a go and failed. It was an omen, but I didn't know that then. He grinned.

"I do that," he said. "Hard, isn't it? Easier on a deeper plate."

"Really?" I was impressed. Education must be spreading. I'd never met a really sensible academic bloke before. "East Anglians call us Silly Suffolk," he added, laughing. "They probably mean me. My wife won't have me doing it. You're lucky, eh?"

"Now," I said. Women don't last where I'm concerned. It's not entirely their fault. They simply lack staying power. My one wife had left quickly, claiming I was zero potential. To this day I've never had a penny in gratitude for all the love and devotion I lavished on her. Well, nearly lavished. She'd even demanded alimony. "Eh?" I asked. Cox had said something important while I'd been romancing.

"I saw your broadcast." He was smiling apologetically. "Very impressive. The second half wasn't half as good. I'm pursuing ancient bronzes. I came to enlist your aid."

Pursuit, like in hunt? Here was a chance to change roles. I nearly asked about Sykie, but remembered in the nick of time I wasn't to mention him. Cool Lovejoy. "Pursue? To where?"

"Ah. I'm afraid we don't know that."

"What antique bronzes, exactly?"

"I'm afraid we don't know that either, Lovejoy."

"Then who nicked them?"

"Well, we don't really know."

A definite pause, but I'm not impoverished for nothing. "Where were they nicked from?"

"Ah, well. I'm afraid . . ."

"Then," I said, a headache coming on, "where were they found?" Pause. "For Chrissakes," I yelled, forsaking my nosh to walk about in anguish, "if you don't know what they are, who's nicked them, where they've gone, where they came from, why the hell do you want me to chase the frigging things?"

He rotated his hat miserably. "That's half the problem, Lovejoy. They're not even discovered yet."

My head throbbed briskly. "Half the problem?" I seethed, sitting and glaring at the table. "Never tell me the other half, mate. You're a nutter."

"Please don't be angry, Lovejoy. Only we're in such a mess."

"I'm not angry!" I bawled, furious. I could have strangled him. I thought, I'll kill Sykie one of these days. It's always me who finishes up in plaster, poverty, and prison, never these barmy sods.

For a whole minute I sat seethed, shoving tomato pips round my plate with a fork. I got twelve in a row. Toffee smarmed her way onto Cox's lap unnoticed, I was surprised to see. He stroked her.

My neurons synapsed with audible clangs. Another Lovejoy winner. Sykie's opinion of academic archeology was likely to impose few demands on East Anglia, or on me. His goons, however, were a feral mob of barbarians, so I'd better get it right this time. Cox might not be Sykie's mark at all.

"Look, Mr. Cox. Was it simply chance that brought you here?"

"Yes, chance, really." He was utterly dejected. Toffee sensed his distress and stared reproachfully at me. "I take it this means you, ah, can't assist us?"

Not Sykie's man after all. "Well, I've got a lot on," I said. "Otherwise I'd come like a shot. I'll try to call on you, say, tomorrow." I meant no. What with Raymond getting nicked over his Wedgwood fiddle, my promise to help Suzanne York's restaurant, Sykie, Ledger the Bodger, I was committed.

"I understand." He was quite gracious about it, which made me feel even worse, and rose, pouring Toffee to the floor. "I do realize it's a commercial world."

He bade a quiet farewell. He waved from the gateway, smiling, and went off carrying his bag of cheap vegetables. I felt mad because I felt bad as I slammed back inside. Toffee was reclining on my rug, exuding scorn. I wasn't taking that from a frigging feline.

"You vagabond moggie," I gritted. "Who gets beaten black and blue? Me! Who starves to frigging death while you don't raise a frigging finger? Me! And who's got to keep this antiques firm going? Me. So less of your frigging lip. Hear?"

She walked away, soulful and censorious, and sat watching the garden birds. Just then the blue tits came tapping on the window for their nuts, the robin started screeching outside for his grub, and Harry my blackbird arrived to glare impatiently from the sill. Must be half-six.

"Why me?" I yelled at them all, apoplectic. "Frigging chiselers, out for an easy touch!"

Mother Nature continued to tap, screech, glare, beg. I was grumbling my old refrain, how had they managed before I arrived, when something odd happened, really fantastic. The telephone rang. Now, because my phone had been cut off for two months. Everybody in the Eastern Hundreds knew it. I was so astonished I sat staring at the thing. It's the ancient black daffodil type because I can't stand those absurd instruments you have to act hunchback to keep on your shoulder.

It rang and rang, then stopped. I was glad, and in relief started to clear my pots away.

It rang again. I pretended it was routine, picked it up and said, "Hello?"

Bad, bad mistake. I should have used wire cutters on the flex. This time it was Sykie's mark for certain.

Hereon life goes downhill.

6

Toffee was getting fed up being carried about in her basket so at nine next morning I presented her to a neighbor's house. Eleanor rushed to the door. I've never known a woman like her for hurtling. She's never still, always late, forever breathless.

"A cat?" she squealed, distraught. "But I haven't time, Lovejoy! I'm so behind!"

When women are in a mad dash you have to take a firm line or you get nowhere. "Toffee's come to play with Henry," I announced in a parliamentary voice. "I've to call on an important client. She can share Henry's grub, no bother." More likely Henry'd eat hers, I thought but did not say.

"Very well," she said, screamed, "The oven!" and zoomed inside.

Humping Toffee, I wandered after and found Henry in his playpen. He's lately learned to maraud unaided, thus gets strapped behind bars so Eleanor can sprint about the county being late for everything. When sitting up he wobbles a bit, but can crawl and bawl with gusto. Seeing me, he gave a great grin and a prolonged yell of greeting. A yard of grot dangled from his chin. You have to keep wiping it off or he's soon swimming in spit.

"Listen, Henry," I said, giving him a mechanical wipe and lifting Toffee out. "This creature is not edible. Comprenny?"

He ogled in astonishment as I deposited Toffee in his pen. They stalked round each other, Toffee with detachment, Henry panting and chugging his one exclamation, a sort of brief oooh. He's no linguist.

"There's a rule, troops," I added. "Neither of you's to eat or deform the other till I get back." I then went to say so long to Eleanor. She'd got into a terrible shambles in the kitchen.

"Quick, Lovejoy, quick!" she squealed, dithering about with a steaming skillet while pans bubbled and the oven blinked signals in red-eyed urgency.

"Right," I said calmly. "Be with you in a sec, love," and left her to get on with it. Honestly, why ask me for help? Bloody cheek. Pans are her job, not mine. Anyway, she's experienced in handling messes—she used to go out with me once upon a time. There's honestly nothing between us now, though. No, really honestly. I do a bit of Henry-sitting now and again when I'm absolutely broke, that's all.

The bus was canceled or late. It never matters which. Jacko, our village opportunist, got his rickety old lorry out and clattered me into town. He sang "La Golandrina" wrong all the way, and dropped me off at the war memorial. From there I walked to the office of Castor Chemical Industries on the bypass, and found the snooty secretary who had phoned me the previous night. I'd asked if it was to do with antiques, and was told yes. Sir John had seen me on television. Sykie's mark? Had to be.

Well, an antique collector is a collector. They're great. I really admire them, even though they're the weirdest mob on earth. Nutters, maniacs, scholars, lovers, the whole lunatic herd. And why? Because they're greed-crazed for love, which is a beautiful, wonderful state to be in. It's the attribute of God. In fact I'll go so far as to say that as long as love-lust is alive and well, God is still in with a chance.

"Take a seat," the secretary said, giving me the woman's totaling look—feet, trousers, jacket, hands, face. Miss Minter had the terrible barren beauty of an air hostess, believing herself stunningly glamorous and at the peak of her calling. A laugh. Every woman I've ever known could leave her standing, even if she did measure right, poor thing.

"No, ta." The office was brilliantly designed in repellent plastics. You'd struggle a month to get up from the fawn suede couch, and never make it. What *is* wrong with everybody these days?

"Sir John will be twenty minutes." She made it sound a promulgation. The world evidently had to go along. Well, not me. I'd done what Sykes ordered, correctly this time. If Carnforth wouldn't see me, he and Sykie could fight it out.

"Tell him I called on time, love. Tara."

And I was down the corridor before she came hastening after me and said Sir John was ready. She looked stricken, so I retraced, thinking this Carnforth must be an ogre. The inner sanctum's door lintel was carved in Greek key designs, a pathetic waste of good wood. Some tree had given its whole life so this Carnforth maniac could carve it wrong. What a world.

"Your typist changed her mind," I said to the curtain that hung immediately beyond. Typists hate being called typists. You're to call them personal secretarial administrative specialists nowadays instead.

The curtain was a heavy modern Thai silk in lime. Somebody dragged it aside and I stepped into the most extraordinary room, so weird I heard myself gasp. Normally I only do that when thumped.

As long as broad, the place had three vast convex mirrors, floor to ceiling. A quiveringly beautiful antique study desk confronted me, Ince and Mayhew, late Regency. I moaned with unrequited lust. The walls staggered me so I literally recoiled. Can you imagine? Me, desperate dealer of Lovejoy Antiques, Inc., practically fainting under the impact of that enormous room's furniture and ornaments. Two Joshua Reynolds pencil sketches dazzled on the right-hand wall. An alpine watercolor by Turner, greatest of them all, shimmered its yellows and whites in a paneled alcove. A luscious Charles Cressent commode stood arrogantly by—this Frenchman originated the commode as we know it, changing it at one fell swoop from a mere humble chestlike lump to a slender-legged Regency triumph complete with crossbow bottom rails. It bestrode an Aubusson carpet, an 1820ish Empire pattern on a lettuce green field that made you wish you could float from respect. Over to the left was an early English face shielder, a pole screen with the most delectable tapestry work. Embroidresses nowadays go too much for collage—not clever ladies who needleworked their feminine loveliness and stitched their signatures in the whole history of man. I stepped forward to see if they'd used undercouching stitch, and saw the fake.

Ivory cracks, especially those hard East Africa ivories, so if you've got any, keep them humid. This was a finely decorated German tankard, silver gilt and ivory—desperately pretending to be seventeenth century. I gazed aslant—sure enough the ivory had fractured and been mended. This is okay, because ivory breaks with geometrical precision, and ordinary glues mend it easily enough. But, forever trying to warp, ivory needs pegging, with metal or ivory dowels, exactly as somebody had done here between two cherubs below the rim. Vinyl adhesives never stain true ivory, so why was discoloration diffusing from that faint seam? Because it wasn't ivory, that's why. I'd have whitened it with hydrogen peroxide, 120 volumes, and—

"Give him the bill, Winstanley," somebody said.

My vision cranked reluctantly back. I hadn't noticed the little wart perched behind that lovely desk. Nor had I seen Winstanley, the nervous accountant now treading—not, note, walking or striding, but treading as acolytes fetch ritual unguents—toward me bearing a paper. Baffled, I stood there feeling a right daffodil. It was a telephone receipt, solving the mystery. So this was the nerk who'd paid my bill.

"It cost me that to contact you, Lovejoy," the voice said.

His head was just about visible. Lacquered black hair ironed down on his pate. Specs, a thin face, and a one-piece tie. I hated that one-piece tie. If you're going to wear a tie, then wear the proper bloody thing, not a cardboard monstrosity a machine makes for you. Much worse, or better, was the mindbending fact that virtually every antique in sight was thrillingly genuine. Except one. Here was the man. Power, wealth, authority exuded from his expression; a bloke at war with anybody and everything.

"I'm waiting, Lovejoy."

Like I say, faces fascinate me, maybe because that's where stares come from. Oblong stares, elliptical stares, stares so straight and rectangular they hit you like the end of a plank. Women mostly have curved slow-worming stares, quite warm for the most part. Children have soft magnolia-colored stares that swarm all over your front and push you about. Henry's is like that; takes your breath away. This gaffer's stare slammed me like a piece of four-by-two.

"Waiting? What for?"

"My money." His fingers drummed, like a noisy arthropod creeping from his sleeve.

"Money? I've not got any of yours." Nor, I nearly added, of my own either.

"Explain, Winstanley."

The serf read from a note pad like a courtroom clerk giving the charge before merciless magistrates. "Nine attempts to phone you, two visits to your cottage, petrol, capital depreciation on the Rolls, chauffeur's wages, time, the motorphone."

Winstanley's voice was shaking. He knew what was going to

happen. I had the benefit of his wobbly aspen-leaf stare, and he had the full benefit of mine. I nudged him aside.

"I'm impressed," I said. I really was. This behavior proved that idiocy flourishes everywhere. "Comrade, your chances of getting that gelt are nil. Stuff the bloody telephone."

"Read on, Winstanley."

Winstanley flapped his notes. "You owe council rates, water rates, electricity, the Bungalow Stores in your village. You owe Mrs. Margaret Dainty four loans and a Lowestoft porcelain jug. You owe Elizabeth Sandwell of Dragonsdale for a personal loan made after you and she went to Birmingham—"

"Here," I said indignantly. "That's private."

"And the police, Lovejoy," said Sir John. "You've been arrested nineteen times. The murder charges we needn't detail, since you were never convicted."

We all thought a bit, but Ledger had admitted I was momentarily in the clear. My confidence resurged. "Stuff the police."

"I will deduct the amount, with compound interest at two percent over the bank rate, from you salary."

Salary? I cheered up. Sykie's mark, definitely. "It's a deal," I said. "And in return I won't tell you which of your antiques here is phony. What's the job?" I maneuvered past Winstanley in as few strides as possible. That lovely carpet. And now this exquisite farthingale chair, taking the wind out of my sails. Find a simple chair with boxlike struts and a slightly raked back, chamfered square legs, and tapestry of blinding sweetness, and you've made your first fortune. They did lovely oak work in 1620. Of course, chairs were only for gentry. . . .

"Eh?" I said, touching the tapestry reverently to feel that chime thrill through my middle. I looked up to find Sir John in a towering rage.

"Did you say phony?" He whispered the word through ashen lips.

"Dud. Forged. Faked. Reproduction. Naughty."

"Impossible, sir," Winstanley added.

"Look," I said. "This job."

"Sit down, Lovejoy." Both Sir John's hands were fibrillating now, tap-dancing spiders. "Out, Winstanley."

A waft and the serf was gone. My new boss's gaze was a rapier, flicking around me before inflicting the wound. He'd got what he wanted, hired a defenseless adversary, an armless sparring partner.

"All right, Sir John," I said. "So we hate each other. I'm poor. You're not. You've gone to a lot of trouble to find me. So you need what I can do. What is it?"

He nodded, that curt head-jerk of the boxer at the opening bell. Part of the wall behind him slid away, would you believe the slice with a Gainsborough landscape, black and white chalk and a gray wash. I already hated him. Moving wall indeed. The revealed space glowed.

A map of Suffolk appeared on the screen. A click, a whine, and it enlarged. I recognized the ordnance survey, saw the rim of Dogpits Farm, Manor Farm adjoining, and Roman Brook, St. Botolph's little river line, the woods, the Blackwater estuary, the red A134 road running to St. Edmundsbury. Naturally, my eyes were drawn to where my cottage stood.

"Recognize anything, Lovejoy?" Carnforth asked quietly.

There was a small red dot in one space, the sort galleries put on paintings that have been sold. It should have been a cross, because it was where George Prentiss had died. For the first time it all came together. I knew what Sykie was playing at, and whose side I was on.

"No," I said innocently. "Should I?"

7

Later I was sitting on a less august piece of furniture—a plank bench in the spit-and-sawdust Ship Tavern on East Hill. It's not bad as pubs go. Like, there are worse sinbins, but not many. On auction days you'll find most of the town's antique dealers in for their lunch hour, which extends from 11:20 A.M. to chuck-out time at three. Tinker was on his fifth pint. The gelt I'd received from Sykie stretched to render Tinker semi-comatose on Greene King ale, his staple diet.

"Gawd, I'm glad ter see yer, Lovejoy," he croaked, climbing back on the bench and mopping his streaming old eyes. He'd just had a beautiful racking cough that had shaken him off the form. Just in time I held up a warning finger. He spat phlegm politely into a finished tankard, froth. I looked away, queasy. He gave a rugose grin. "Thought Sykes had done for you, mate."

"Oh, that. His lads did me over a bit."

"We got a few jobs on, Lovejoy?"

"One in particular."

"For Sykes?" Tinker swigged his ale, eyes trundling in nervous nystagmus through the glass. He's scared of big rollers like Sykes. Irritably I shoved him a bigger note.

"Tell her to keep them coming."

He obeyed, shoving his way through the fug and mob. Absently I watched his shabby form. He had a lot to do, now I'd taken Sir John's metaphorical shilling (he'd given me nowt). A barker's main asset is that he is a lowlife—and nobody lower than Tinker, who kips in church porches, dosshouses. He can go where even impoverished antique dealers—me—fear to tread.

"Lovejoy." Big Frank from Suffolk arrived, soulful and lorn. It's all an act with him. You're supposed to feel a wave of sympathy and give him antique silver to cheer him up. Margaret Dainty was with him: plump, honest, loving. She loves me, but with a kind of cunning mistrust that does our relationship no harm at all.

"A delegation, eh?"

"About Raymond," Big Frank said.

"Who? Oh, aye." Our hopeless hero of the dud con trick. "Leave it to me," I said calmly, smiling. "It's all in hand."

"You sure, Lovejoy?" Margaret sounds mellifluous.

"I'll have Raymond sorted out by eleven tomorrow." Nothing reassures people like a number uttered with conviction. Statisticians live on that deception. "You can take over Raymond's aftercare," I offered, which caused them to vanish back into the swirling carcinogenic fug. I shelved the problem of Raymond, silly burke, and started to think.

Swiftly I ran over Sir John's account. What would be safe to tell Tinker? Allies are all right until the question of trust arises. From there you're on your own. This job needed caution. Poor George Prentiss had learned that. Of course he'd been killed, but the word "kill" says very little. Manslaughter by a bull? Execution? Accidental death?

Which raises the question of Roman bronze.

"No," I'd said innocently at Sir John's map. "Should I?"

"You fail to recognize where you live, Lovejoy?"

"All right." I was offhand, the superdeceiver. "So it's a map of the Eastern Hundreds. Modern," I added nastily. "A quid from the Hythe paper shop. Next problem?"

"Next problem? Rumors, Lovejoy." He put his hands together in a child's pat-a-cake. "Of ancient bronze figures."

"Oh, aye." Remembering Ben Cox, I didn't know whether to laugh or yawn. "Any in particular?"

His chair swiveled with that grating noise made by all electronics from videos to dishwashers. An arrow light pointed on the glowing map. "Site?" he said.

"Colchester Castle."

The arrow flew, alighted on a luminescent estuary. "Site?"

"Sutton Hoo, the Viking burial ship."

The arrow tipped that ominous red dot. "Site?"

"Nowhere?"

He touched secret controls. The screen departed as the Gainsborough slid back like a benevolence. I couldn't help wondering what this bloke had been like as a child. He looked like he'd terrified his way to the top.

"You are a crook, Lovejoy. Probably a killer. There isn't an antique dealer in the Eastern Hundreds who doesn't know of you. You sponge off women. You're filthy—"

"Watch your tongue. I'm a bit shop-soiled, that's all." I bath every dawn, and at least a bum-balls-armpits wash if I'm on the hoof somewhere. I'm always spotless underneath, even if the heating's off and I have to scrub in the chill.

"My conclusion, Lovejoy, is this: Your particular position means you can find out why, even when others can't, anywhere in the eastlands."

"Find out why what where?" Don't say this bloke was another Ben Cox. When I was little we nigged in to the pictures through the lavatory. We considered it the bounden duty of our contemporaries already in the audience to update us on the film's story thus far. I now felt like nobody would even tell me the story's beginning. Poor George knew it, too late.

"Why rumors have reached me of an important find in the Eastern Hundreds. Some say Roman, others ancient British, Anglo-Saxon, early English, the Great Civil War."

"Quite a spread," I said drily.

"No impertinence." He spoke without rancor. "The point is that all the rumors say bronze." He reached for a file. "You will trace the rumors and discover their substance."

"Why me?"

"Because you're a divvie. There is no other in East Anglia." His face contorted a little about the mouth. Fascinated, I realized his facial muscles were trying to indicate mirth. Had they ever known how? "I investigated six false claimants, Lovejoy. Your television display finally convinced me."

"What if I don't take the job?"

"You will." His face did its inward crumple, a horrible sight. "This file contains details of the cottage you now inhabit, and your four mortgages—I include the fraudulent ones you concocted when your lady cohabitee lent you the title deeds."

"Those transactions are private," I said, hoarse.

"And illegal. I have great experience in handling louts, Lovejoy." Crumple, crumple. He passed me an envelope.

"Right." I cheered up, money at last. Then I sobered as I opened the flap. A single page of typescript. The notes on the circulating rumors he'd mentioned. "What about the gelt?"

"Two weeks' work will cancel your debts, Lovejoy." He passed a contract over. I scanned the terms. On paper they were lucrative, which only meant it was a tax dodge.

The phrase is "stick and carrot." I'd get two sticks, namely him and Sykes, but no carrot. Narked, I signed with a flourish. "It's a deal. And thank you for letting me see so many valuables close to." I nodded at the cacophony of antiques all around.

"Wait!" No crumpling now. I got the stone gaze instead. A

lot was happening in that brachycephalic skull of his at my smile. "Why the smirk?"

"Two things, Sir John. Go to the Pitti Palace in Florence. They too've collected everything they could lay hands on, and jammed it all together. Old mixes with new, good with bad. The arrangement's Randolph Hearst's cellar, poshed up. Same," I added happily, ready for the explosion, "as yours."

"And second?"

I kept moving. "The fake. Cheers."

Winstanley, embarrassed, was standing behind the hanging tapestry when I swished it aside. "A cautious man, Sir John," I said to him, opening the outer door. "But not antiques smart."

" *Which?*" Sir John and his serf spoke together, eyes all round the office.

It was worth a pause. "It'll cost you."

"Pay a wastrel like you?" His voice was like an underwater cartoon talks, in bubbles. "*Never!*"

"Then make a fool of yourself." I closed the door on their twin apoplexy, and beamed into Miss Minter's lovely eyes.

"Silly sods never learn," I said, to unglue her cherished illusions. "When he cools down tell him I said ta for the contract."

"What's the job, Lovejoy?" Tinker asked, opposite. I realized he had been staring at me for two pints' duration, three minutes flat.

"Look out an antique for a restaurant launch, Dogpits Farm. Then see if a Mrs. Ray of Dedham is an antique dealer on the sly. Then put the word round we're in the market for a genuine Roman bronze figurine."

"Jesus, Lovejoy! Where'd we get that kind of gelt?"

"Dunno," I said irritably. "That's tomorrow's problem. Then find who's buying erotica locally."

"Like George Prentiss, that book?"

"Exactly. Then find me Boothie the poacher. I want a word. Then find if Ben Cox is clean, in the Suffolk something trust

St. Edmundsbury way. Then anything to do with local finds, treasure trove, wrecks, tumuli, any damned thing. Then—"

"Then these lists, Lovejoy," said this lovely woman, sliding in beside me.

"Eh?" She had sheets of paper. Names, cars, florists, vicars. "You doing a survey, love? You've interrupted Lovejoy Antiques, Inc.'s board meeting—"

"Marriage. Saturday. Saint Mary the Virgin."

Obviously a loony. Tinker quickly sensed woman trouble and disappeared. "Well, thanks, love. I'm spoken for. I'll try and make it but—"

"You haven't forgotten?" Her limpid eyes filled. "You're our best man, Lovejoy."

A million gazes gleefully observed my appalled realization that here was Big Frank's intended. Hellfire, I'd clean forgotten. I patted her hand. "Oh, you're, erm, Jane!" I said brightly.

"Rowena."

"Of course! Rowena!" Where'd I heard that name lately? "Well, it's all in hand." I pretended relief. "Good heavens, Rowena! You did give me a start!"

"It is?"

I racked my brains for a wedding ceremonial's trappings. "Flowers, church, cars, everything. However," I added darkly, because a furrow of disbelief marked her pretty brow, "I'm a bit concerned about . . ."

"The photographer?" she breathed, going all anxious.

"Exactly," I said, taking on the frown. "It's just that you can't be too careful."

"Oh, that's so right, Lovejoy!" she cried. "But who?"

"Eh?" How the bloody hell should I know which photographer? "You just leave that side to me. You've plenty on your plate."

"Oh, I have, Lovejoy," she sighed. "Thank you for being so understanding. You're so sweet."

How true. I liked her for seeing through to my pure inner

core. "Just don't you worry, love. If I get in difficulties I'll phone. Bye, er, Rowena."

And she was gone, leaving a trace of Gonfalon struggling in the thick beer stench and me with a smile but a headache. I needed Fixer Pete. I felt worn out.

"Tinker," I bleated wearily. "Help, Tinker."

Funerals are lonely. Crowds can't make up for the one notable absentee, whose almost-presence compels mighty attention. Worse, there's no way to answer those unspoken questions coming your way from that coffin.

In our villages we walk to the churchyard. In town it's cars, motors, quite a cavalcade. For George Prentiss it didn't matter much. There weren't many people. Ledger came, like a tidy schoolmaster. Mrs. York, pale, interesting, comely in black; well, it had happened on her farm. Major Bentham didn't ride his horse; he wore tailored blacks, grays. A couple of blokes; I knew neither. The oldest scrutinized a wreath shaped like an electric bulb, probably an elderly workmate seeing the flowers had been sent right. That was it. No Mrs. Prentiss, widow of this parish. Mrs. York spoke with courteous brevity to the younger stranger; I guessed a remote cousin.

The priest was a portly mechanical toy. Word-perfect. His choir wasn't a patch on our village's, only four or five aged trillsters and a batty old organist squinting through impossible bottle glasses and misusing the middle flutes, as if anyone ever could. The grave was on the slope below St. Peter's. A minuscule acolyte held a gigantic brass crucifix in the wind. We all kept clear in case. Have you ever noticed, but prayers for the departed are the least convincing of all extant? Latin at least would obscure the grief, but times and sense have changed. You have just not to think of it.

Afterward, I hung back. The old man said yes, he knew George. He'd apprenticed him as a lad. Ledger was watching as we left the churchyard, heads canted against the wind.

"What was he like at work?"

"Same as most." He had the level stare of the skilled artisan. "You a friend?"

"Lovejoy. Antique dealer."

He half-smiled, nodded. "One of them, eh? I'm Smethurst. George was a good chap, but always doing foreigners. God rest him."

"Amen," I said. A foreigner is a piece of sly work, using the firm's resources. "Did his mate work there?" A Lovejoy flying header.

"Mate? Never knew he had one." Thud.

Slow in saying so-long to Smethurst, I was trapped by the major. He clapped my shoulder. I hate heartiness because it does the opposite of what's intended. Mind you, love sometimes does that. And death. And money. Everything?

"Ah, Lovejoy! There you are!" As if we'd happened across each other on an ice floe. He did a heel-rock or two. "Just a word. That, eh, episode. No hard feelings, hey? Misunderstanding."

Now friendliness. He was still repellent. I'd never seen a major more like a major. What age was he, thirty-four, thirty-six? "Maybe."

"So. Pals, hey?" He actually wrung my hand.

We said so long, one more uneasily than the other. I left and caught the bus. Ledger was leaning on the church gate as I passed. Neither of us waved, glared, or got arrested.

8

You'll never believe this, but when I got back to my cottage, quadruple mortgages and all, the water was on. I would have enjoyed it—no more dipping grotty water from my garden well—but it reminded me of Sir John's face as it imploded in another guffaw, at my expense.

Fried bread and tea later, I was examining a map. Ordnance survey, contour colors, and a key showing windmills and churches. I like old maps, always have. From the momentous ones, like Mercator's firsts, to those of Sir Walter Raleigh's Roanoke Colony in the New World, they've held fascination. They're great works of art. They betoken artistic creativity—which is more than you can say for anybody or anything since 1918.

I searched my area of the Eastern Hundreds for clues, landmarks, anything of significance, and drew a circle with my school compass, a derelict brass pivot aspiring to antiquehood. It included Dogpits Farm, site of poor George Prentiss's last stand, ancient long barrows the map marked as authentic—multo of these hereabouts—the ancient Brits' defense earthworks, anything. I started to spot in it major finds, from my store of newspaper clippings, scribbled rumors, inked queries on the local auctions.

I looked at it, and looked.

Five glasses of my homemade pear wine later, I was no wiser. Then Tinker phoned to say (a) Mrs. Ray of Dedham was no clandestine dealer, and (b) Mannie's complex life had taken a nasty turn, since a husband had learned of Mannie's unprecedented influence on his wife's nocturnal activities. "He's no reserve antiques left, Lovejoy. Even sold that white-faced enamel longcase clock he wuz always bragging about." I moaned, tears starting. These white-facers are almost unheard of, now that the known world's swamped by German repro brass-faced naffs.

"Any news on Ben Cox?"

"Nar, Lovejoy. Clean as a virgin's hankie, thank Gawd. I'm getting Fixer Pete like you asked. And Tom Booth, but he'll be night, o'course." He meant Boothie being a poacher. "'Ere, Lovejoy. That Mrs. Ryan."

"Eh?" Mrs. Ryan as well as the rest of East Anglia? "What'd she want?"

"Slipped me a quid in the Black Buoy, to tell you she wants your answer by tonight."

Oh, hell. Her neffie estate manager's job. I needed a manager of my own, not more labors. I told him well done and, knackered as I was, went for Toffee and started out to Ramparts Corner, home of our village's resident writer. He'd sent Ben Cox.

Billiam—his idea of a Christian name, nobody else's—lives in solitude interleaved with orgies. Our village is a puritanical old dump, yet everybody's thrilled whenever the strobes get going over Billiam Cutting's old barn. Villagers go about saying it never ought to be allowed and that, but are inwardly desperate to see those sinfully fleshpotty activities. He's Real Life. Women go out of their way to bump into him, even if it only means helping him to stagger home from the Treble Tile. Then they oh-so-casually let drop: Billiam said to me today . . . and set everybody wondering.

The farm—farm is a laugh—was somnolent when I plodded in. He's long since let his gates rot. Two of his three sheds have tumbled-in roofs. Windows gape. Birds saunter in and out through (repeat: through) walls. Fruit trees burgeon yearly, then scatter their bushels to fester among weeds. Billiam hardly notices the harvests. He's either sloshed, scribbling dementedly, or both. I found him snoring on a sack amid the agricultural debris and shook him awake.

"Bill. It's me. Lovejoy."

"Mmmmh?" He came awake slowly, chomping and swallowing and rubbing his face. He peered, pulled himself up, cast about and found a cobwebby bottle. Sighing and burping, he shared the wine. Last year's elderberry, too sweet by a mile. Idly I gazed around while his hooch blasted his brain back into its customary orbit. The place was a mess. Gruesome farm instruments rusted. Planks flaked. Disintegrating sacks, boxes unrectangled, plant pots in bent columns. Jubilant spiders festooned corners, spinning webs almost audibly. A few bulbs had hopefully shot green from a dissolving wheelbarrow. I let Toffee out. She started to roam, putting her feet down gingerly, with her nose going like a slumming rabbit.

"God, Bill. This is truly rural." I hate countryside. All these emblems of uncontrollable nature really depressed me, but there was a lovely old Suffolk scythe rusting on the wall. I'd try to talk him out of that, soon as I got a minute.

"You wouldn't think so, Lovejoy. Not with the goings-on round here in the black hours."

Ramparts is a few acres wedged in by Mrs. Ryan's estate, the dense ancient Pittsbury Wood, Dogpits Farm, and our village.

"Owls and foxes, eh?" I sympathized.

"People. If I'd been a crime writer I'd have gone out to watch."

"Still turning out bodice-rippers, eh?" Bill writes six romance novels a year, under six pseudonyms. He has it down to a fine art, his basic plots on wall charts.

"Why not?" Mention of his trade always makes him barbary. He gets a lot of hassle from posh writers. "What's wrong with simply entertaining people? Folk like romance. Soap beats eternal in the human breast. So literary nuts call my stuff breast-sellers? I outsell them by two million copies a year."

"Don't ballock me," I said, narked. "I'm swigging your rotten plonk, remember."

He mumbled a sorry, and with true writer's skill uncorked another dusty bottle with his teeth. I wish I could do that. "It was all right sending Ben Cox to you, wasn't it, Lovejoy? He was asking for somebody who knew the local antiquities game."

"Aye. That's what I came about." The fresh bottle was better, thank heavens. "Is he okay?"

"Ben? Straight as a die. Known him since school days, same class in St. Edmundsbury." He smiled, a bit shyly. "I ask him a few historical details for my romances. The authentic touch."

That settled, I now wanted my pen'orth. "So he wasn't anything to do with the night noises? I mean, Ledger's already had me in."

"Typical bobby. Doesn't he know you're a born townie?" He chuckled reminiscently. "No, Lovejoy. That was some blokes over Pittsbury Wood, playing silly sods. Probably badger-baiters. They were talking about them last night at the Treble Tile. Good wine, Eh?"

"Great," I said.

"Here, Lovejoy." He watched me persuade Toffee into her basket. "What do you think of Tanzie Heartsease for my new pseudonym?"

"Great," I said thinking, God.

"Lying sod." He went narked, really showed a flash of threat, gone as quickly as it arrived. "Still, Lovejoy. Your new lady-friend likes my books, if you don't."

"My who?" I was smiling at his merry banter, ready to leave with Toffee reclining like a princess on a palanquin.

"Mrs. Prentiss." He came with me, grinning. "I heard you were chatting her auntie up in her new restaurant."

Smiling at my most sincere, but now with difficulty, I cracked back that my acquaintances would rather read a train ticket than his gunge, but was so shaken I reeled in to the White Hart as soon as I was round the bend in the road. Billiam had left me the equation: Darling Candice equals newly widowed Mrs. George Prentiss. Couldn't be true . . . could it?

The antique that Mrs. York wanted suddenly deserved priority. Things were cobbling together to form a sinister picture, with me in the foreground, too near poor dead George.

"Hellfire, Toffee. Look at its size."

The bull heard and raised its gigantic head, giving me a stare. The field was huge, stuck to the north end of Pittsbury Wood. A thick hawthorn hedge rimmed the footpath that runs from the river path to the road half a mile off. A herd of cows noshed grass in the next field. I leaned on the gate, examining possibilities.

Toffee raised her head, yawned, settled back. She'd grown heavier as I'd walked from the White Hart—it's about a mile—so I stuck the basket on the ground. And saw Tom Booth. He grinned at my squawk of alarm.

"You stupid burke, Boothie." I was already nervy, out here a million leagues from civilization.

"I made enough din, Lovejoy."

The old devil had slunk up to scare me, his joke. He's a stocky man, pale and deep, not at all the wiry poacher of legend. I eyed him uneasily in case he was carrying dead. He's all bulging brown tweeds. This very moment he might be a walking gibbet, slain creatures dangling under that jacket. He's our village billiards champion. Of course not as good as Mary Queen of Scots—between love affairs she was actually the greatest billiards champ in history—but able on the table.

"It's all right, Lovejoy. I'm clean."

I'm not really squeamish. No, honestly. But life's important to a pheasant, isn't it? Bound to be. He takes orders at the Queen's Head.

"Admiring Charleston, are you?" Boothie spat expertly, lit a foul clay pipe. "Yon big bugger killt George Prentiss."

"Aye. What was George doing strolling across Charleston's field at night?"

"Dunno. I was seeing to the river, down Seven Arches."

"Which way was George going, Boothie?"

"Gawd, Lovejoy. I'd not thought of that." We looked at the terrain, thinking. The footpath crosses the field, then forks right through Pittsbury Wood; left brings you out at Dogpits. Well, so what? Round here, footpaths are free and literally thousands of years old.

"Was George coming or going?" I wondered aloud, keeping my voice even. "Message in a bottle if you can find out, Boothie, eh?" For all I know these old country wallahs might be able to tell from looking at the floor, like Red Indians.

"Right. I'll listen out. O'course," he added, ever so casually, "this isn't Charleston's usual run. He's normally in Little Tom."

Farmers give fields names. The biggest field on a farm is called Big Tom, the field we were looking at. So Little Tom was the one with the herd.

Odderer and odderer. "Did Charleston jump that far gate?" The five-barred gate between the two fields.

Boothie guffawed. "Him? Jump a gate? Yon bugger'd go through it, open or shut. Only thing he jumps is cows. Evil bastard."

The gate looked undamaged.

Boothie's gaze was serene. He nodded when he saw I'd got the point. The gate had been opened when George was halfway across, and Charleston had flattened him like a night express. God. I turned to see Boothie moving silently off at a languid lope, his trousers horribly baggy.

I called after him, "Does Ledger know somebody opened it?"

"Who'd tell him?" he said over his shoulder.

"Boothie." My tone must have done it. He paused while I asked, "Was it you making that racket in Pittsbury Wood last week?"

He laughed, knocked out his pipe and like a good countryman spat to fizz out the glowing ashes. "Ever heard a noisy poacher, Lovejoy?" He shook his head at the mystifying incomprehension of townsfolk.

"Campers, then?" I yelled after.

"None hereabouts since the major fetched hounds."

The sky was flooding darkness on a chiller wind. The woods began to make that near-whistling when the breeze stiffens off the sea estuary. The great bull was suddenly still, his massive head raised toward the trees. Had he heard something? The forest seemed to loom as the rain clouds lowered in an unpleasantly stealthy collision, a gathering of ominous strength.

"Here, Boothie," I said, intending a joke, but the track was empty. Gone. There was only me and the bull, standing in the path of something primeval and horrid. Meteorologists might describe it as a simple thunderstorm, but it was me standing alone out here, not them. I began whistling loudly and walked off at increasing pace.

"You're no bloody help," I muttered crossly at Toffee. She didn't even wake, idle little sod. Typical female, leaving me out here hurrying to get us both safe home from that eery shrilling darkening wood, and her safe under the blanket.

A tractor bloke pulling a cart laden with sugar beet gave me a lift to Bures. I know Don vaguely, a demon fast bowler who cracks the bravest—read daftest—skulls on our cricket team. He joked about doing it again next summer. They'd dropped me from the team after a fight with an umpire, honestly not my fault. I mean, umpires blind as a bat shouldn't be allowed, right? Don put me down at the old church by Bures crossroads to catch the bus to St. Edmundsbury. He thinks I'm odd. I think he's barmy.

"See you next Lammas, Lovejoy." Our cricket championship cup matches begin on Lammas Day, the old name for August First. He passed Toffee down. "If you've still got your cricket pitch, that is," he quipped. "Manor Farm's reclaiming your field. Mrs. Ryan, isn't it?"

"Reclaiming?"

"It's on lease, a peppercorn rent." He was sad-faced at the calamitous news.

"So what? There's that Long Tom field near Pittsbury Woods, big enough."

His face changed. "You'm orff yor 'eed, booy," he said, his dialect showing sudden stress. "Lammas Day's bad enough."

No pausing, no matter how I yelled what the hell was he on about. I watched him go. None of that made real sense. I crossed to wait for the bus, twenty minutes.

Nothing important of course—I ask you, village cricket—but odd. In East Anglia the cricket season's not long: April to October if the year's a record-breaker for fine weather. I waited, restless.

What had I just thought, that was so disturbing? The months of the year. What's worrisome about April? April? How innocent can you get? And October? October means soggy wet autumn, Michaelmas, All Saints, Harvest Festival at church with that bloody awful visiting organist from Wivenhoe making a right pig's ear of Purcell. But her breasts are lovely, and her smile sideways for us wavering warblers to start "Pilgrim," my favorite, would melt a sinner's heart. . . .

"Are you coming or not?"

"Eh?" I said, startled. The bus was here and the driver bawling down. "Don't yell your head off, Dick. You've woken my frigging cat."

Toffee grumbled all the way to St. Edmundsbury. Old dears gave her their undivided attention. She loved it. I got unanimous blame for feeding her wrong; she didn't say a word in my defense. Is that typical, or is that typical?

The Suffolk Independent Archeology Trust was not the massive building I'd led myself to expect. Think more of a broom cupboard. It was pure luck I found it (a notice by an old cobbler's announced a Grand Lecture by Ben Cox, M.A. The office address was given). Twenty minutes later I was clumping up the bare boards of a condemned terrace building to the third floor garret where Ben Cox sat working. His desk was half. I mean that literally; he'd sawn an old Victorian desk to get half of it in. The crude wall shelving was of suspiciously similar wood.

My expression must have given me away as usual. He nodded, smiling shyly. "Can we take for granted that I'm ashamed of practically everything in sight?" he suggested. A joyful welcome nonetheless. We dithered about whether to shake hands, decided it would be too forward.

"I admire your office," I said. "Well, you liked my cottage." He laughed, nodding. "Tit for tat, eh?" I sidled in, no mean feat. A stool, as in bar, was the only other resting place. I looked round, hung Toffee's basket behind the door.

"Ben," I said as he made coffee cackhanded in a roadmender's billycan. "You have no funds, a handful of burning-heart volunteers, and an eviction notice with the ink still wet. Right or no?"

"Right."

"To continue: Your repeated petitions to councillors have failed. You're broke. Mmmmh or nnnh?"

"Mmmmh."

"Furthermore you saw me on telly, and somebody told you I was maybe daft enough to help on spec. Another mmmh?"

He stirred the coffee agitatedly, red-faced. "Lovejoy. I don't think you're off your trolley. But if anybody needs a divvie it's us."

He sat, coffee-making forgotten. "We're losing the battle. The pillagers, the treasure-hunters. They hear of an ancient burial mound and go marauding in gangs, digging anywhere. It's these . . ." he hesitated, grasped the nettle, . . . "these antique dealers who've done it. They pay the earth . . ."

"Two lumps, please."

"Sorry." He meant for sounding off. He passed me a cup of foul brew nearly as bad as mine. "They make fortunes while our country's treasures are plundered wholesale."

"I've heard," I said wrily.

"Present company excepted." He gave a red-faced grin. "I get so angry. They're carrion."

"Who?" His eyes widened as I said, "Ben, you're an old soldier at this archeology game. I don't believe that you see a bloke misbehave on a ninth-rate telly show and suddenly decide to recruit him in your private war with a load of moonspenders."

"No. It's worse than that. We've had word of a big find." He became morose, pained. "One of our people intercepted a drawing of a bronze animal." He had it ready to hand, sly old dog— or maybe he simply wept over it all day long.

An outline drawing, not bad at that. A leopard or panther, something ferocious and leaping in feline grace, lovely. My throat had dried. Jesus, but if it was copied from a real bronze it . . .

"Intercepted how?"

"You won't believe it, Lovejoy. A relative in Australia answered a newspaper advert for an ancient Roman bronze. The wording's on the reverse."

Cut-out letters and words from newspapers, stuck to the card. *Roman bronze found Suffolk East Anglia this year price negotiable watch box column for contact.*

"The old game, eh?" Anybody who answers the advertiser's box number is a potential customer. The advertiser susses them out, ensures they don't include a troublesome percentage of Fraud Squaddies, then readvertises a price for "the advertised object." The undaunted buyers who write are then contacted by phone, the precious object is swapped under a pub table somewhere and lost to the so-called clean so-called aboveboard world forever. Believe me it's a hairy, scary voyage. Blood flows merrily in its churning wake. George Prentiss'll tell you.

"Don't tell me," I said. "You alerted Space Control, who did sod all."

"The Aussie police kept watch on the paper, but no further advert appeared." His eyes reproached me soulfully. "They really did try, Lovejoy."

"Or worse."

"Worse? What could be worse?"

He hadn't linked George's death with the problem, but I had. "Tipping them off's worse, Ben."

We agreed to meet the following day, when he'd bring all details of his area's recent alleged finds. His town librarian was anxious to help, an all-time first. Ben wouldn't let me keep the drawing, selfish swine, but gave me my bus fare out of a tobacco tin. Then he walked me to the bus stop, carrying Toffee's basket and bragging gently about the ancient town. He waved me off, balding head's wisps of hair blowing with the bus's wafting. As I made the rear seat, I mouthed a "Be careful" at him, feeling a sudden pang. As the bus cornered, for no reason I suddenly thought of his shopping bag of vegetables, cheaper at Ramparts crossroads.

Rotten epitaph.

• • •

The bus was jam-packed by Dedham. I left Toffee on deposit with the church curate there and walked down past the old flour mill to Sebastopol Cottages. My appearance wasn't too convincing for my scintillating con act. My shoes are always battered, and my shirts fray at the cuffs the minute I take them from the cellophane and pull all those pins out that threaten to stab you to death. On my plus side is the fact that appearances often deceive. Women know that more than anybody. Fortunately, they don't now that words *always* deceive. Let's hope they never learn.

So like a fool I was brimming with confidence when I reached No. 2 and knocked, transmuting myself into a buyer from America. I'm hopeless at accents, but would Sebastopol Cottages know that? The door opened. Casually I turned, smiling.

And froze.

"Lovejoy!" cried Rowena. "I was just trying to ring you!"

She hurried about, brewing up and shoveling biscuits. The house was snowflaked in lists, lists, lists. Trapped, I moved among them mesmerized, praying a bitter prayer.

"Did you contact the video man, Lovejoy? And the photographer? The florist? The vicar. . . ?"

"There's so little time, Rowena," I intoned, settling with what I hoped was an air of gravity. "Have you thought of the printers?" I racked my brains, but had the sense to start clearing the biscuits. A calorie in time saves nine. "Order of service I need to know too," I added reproachfully.

"Of course!" she squeaked, thrilled to be reprimanded in a good cause. "How sensible!"

Sweating relief, I listed possible wedding-day pitfalls. She cried agreement with every word.

"You see, Lovejoy," she revealed, innocently kneading my arm and sitting uncomfortably close. "Since Ernest, I've come to really rely on Francis." She rotated her luscious blue eyes, edged in closer for the punch line. "You don't think it unfair?"

"No." Inexplicably I needed more breath than usual. Odd, because no's such a short word. And who the hell were all these people, Ernest, Francis? Tinker, I'd throttle him. The stupid nerk should have realized. You don't get many Rowenas to the square yard in East Anglia.

"So Francis will have to pay for the wedding. You understand, Lovejoy?" Knead, knead.

"Naturally," I mumble-croaked. She wore a blue twin set, phony black pearls that swung rapturously in the best place on earth, and leaned across me to pour. Even in agony my survival instinct was on course. "Is there nothing you could, er, sell?"

Her hair brushed me as she stood and canted over, pearls on my face. God, I was distressed. Her slim waist, her curved flank, generated a terrible problem—to inhale biscuit crumbs and choke to death? Or exhale and reveal my lust in an unpreventable moan? Then she reached something down, between sexy butter-oozing muffins and the rampant teapot, and my moan came out anyway. It was a genuine Gardner piece, the sort I'd dreamed of for years. Gardner, the Michelangelo of porcelain, who in the eighteenth century went to create works of genius in Mother Russia's icy bosom. This gem was a tiny milkmaid, exquisite. My chest chimed in purest recognition as I sat. Mistily I turned. Rowena, I thought, gazing at the delicious innocent, may your vibes increase. The room was bright, like a lily in bloom. The vision raised her head, and with a look made of all sweet accord, breathed, "Of *course*, Lovejoy! *You're* interested in antiques, aren't you? Could you sell it? I found it in the attic. An American gentleman advertised—"

"Well," I said ruefully, "it's not valuable, love, but . . ." I glanced into her lakewide cerulean blues, then managed, all noble, "Right. I'll try. For you, Rowena." If that porcelain goddess hadn't been in my hands I'd have clutched the luscious Rowena. Touch and go.

"How sweet!" she cried, giving me a kiss. I helped her.

Meanwhile two more brain cells decided to make a go of reason and rhythmed: Francis equals ?Big Frank. "Does . . . Francis know of this, love?"

"No. He's too busy for silly old pots."

Pots? my mind screeched, but I didn't give her a thick ear. I can be very patient. "Then it'll be our little secret, eh?"

"And I can buy Francis a present!" She was excited, not alone as it happens.

Smiling, I said, "What a good idea!" We settled the agreement, taking our time over tea and crumpets.

Much later, I collected Toffee and went home, the exquisite Gardner porcelain sharing Toffee's trug. It was exactly right for Suzanne York's new restaurant. It would shame that costly modern palace, but that was her lookout. Meanwhile, a fortnight's bed rest, in traction, was called for. I was worn out.

Dusk was fast falling when I staggered into my tangled garden. But Mrs. Ryan clop-clopped in, just after I'd fed Toffee, to persuade me into her manager's job. Weakened by the day's exertions, I gave her my most sincere promise to fill in her form instantly. In bed, she told me she hoped I'd be as vigorous on the job as off it. I swore to try. Anyhow, I thought, dozing between her lovely breasts, I wasn't doing much these days.

What with Mrs. Ryan riding bareback, so to speak, I had no chance of a lift, so after she'd gone—very cloak and dagger, peering out for hidden watchers—I roused Jacko from the Treble Tile taproom and got him to drive me in his lorry to Dogpits. He demanded immediate payment. Some people. Serve him right if I never redeem my sheaf of IOUs.

Everything seen from the kitchen door looked horribly raw, so I stood there like a lemon, looking away, until a scullion fetched Suzanne. She seemed relieved I'd finally shown up.

"In the nick of time, Lovejoy!" she exclaimed on a waft of perfume. "We've billed your antique as a Great Mystery Prize." Very wise. She couldn't understand my reluctance to pass through those kitchen caverns of gore, but finally admitted me round the side. "You must write out an explanatory card, giving its value."

"I'm sorry," I said, going all soulful. "But my dinner's, er, basting in my microwave. I have to get back—"

Briskly she took charge. "That's easy, Lovejoy. Dine here."

"Oh, all right then," I conceded. I'm always doing these favors. "I hope your niece Mrs. Prentiss likes it," I said, another flyer.

"The point is that I do, Lovejoy."

About an hour later, my insides sloshing with wine and something called rossini something, I peeped through the curtains into the crowded candlelit restaurant. Business seemed great. Waiters sprinted. Music played. That lunatic major was wining and dining Candice, aka Mrs. Prentiss, the pretty woman who'd egged him on to exterminate me. Her eyes were brimful of excitement while he yakked and pigged himself in the trough. Not much mourning for poor George there.

As I watched, Suzanne made the announcement to a drumroll, reading from my card. She was in a side-split gold lamé evening dress, lovely and graceful. My exquisite porcelain was rotating on a stand. I was really proud. It looked delectable, a princess among subjects. I honestly had a lump in my throat. The orchestra punctuated her announcement tam-la-ta-taraamtaaah!

"And the lucky table," she was saying, "will win this beautiful antique treasure, worth . . ." She staggered a bit as she read my numbers, but recovered and gamely finished, a whiter shade of pale. Tata-taaam-tah! Applause!

Thoughtfully I let the curtain sink into place and let myself out among the zillion parked cars. Suzanne York was clearly a businesswoman, to think so fast on her feet. I admired her for that. Which reminded me I hadn't agreed my price for the porcelain gem. Still, a lovely woman from a rich county family wouldn't welsh, right? *Right?*

When I reached the end of the drive Jacko was gone. See what I mean about selfishness? I started out on the Long Trek. A night walk's restful—if the police don't pull you in after a hundred yards.

9

"No rest for the wicked, Lovejoy," Ledger said, putting a
small tablet into his police coffee and pulling a face to show me
he hated sweeteners (only the chemical kind, note). "You're
not pulling your whack, lad."

"Me?" I was annoyed. "I've done everything everybody's told
me."

"Wrong, Lovejoy." He tasted his coffee, sighed at the world's
slings and arrows. A familiar racking cough rose in the next
room. Tinker. They'd pulled him in as well. What for? Ledger
smiled a wintry nonsmile at my recognition. "I had hoped you'd
cooperate fully with the county constabulary. Yet not one scrap
of info."

"I'm no . . . *grass*." I'd heard it often in gangster series, and
now I'd said it under real authentic circumstances. I felt so
proud.

"Lovejoy, you're not trying."

"I am, Ledger. Honest."

His voice raised angrily. "Did you tell me about going over to

Bury and killing that poor bugger Ben Cox today, you rotten murderer?" He sipped, grued his face. "Phyllis. Who makes this bloody coffee?"

"Eh?" I said. "Ledger. What about Cox?"

The policewoman pinked prettily. "Me, sir."

I thought, I'm going off my frigging nut. "Ledger," I said, third go.

"I hope to God your promotion doesn't depend on it, Phyllis," Ledger said heavily to her. "You see, Lovejoy," he went on, pointing a stubby digit, "I asked you very politely: Simply give us a bell if any scam's on. And what happens? You bash poor Cox's head in without a word."

"No, Ledger," I croaked. "Just a minute."

"Can't we afford that Yankee stuff?" Ledger demanded irritably of Phyllis. "Granules."

"Afraid not, sir. Too expensive."

"When, Ledger?" Me, interrupting these affairs of state.

He eyed me morosely. "We aren't so daft we haven't traced your movements, Lovejoy. A busful of witnesses, the curate at Dedham minding your bloody cat. But I don't like it." He awarded me an ominous headshake. "Two down, Lovejoy. How many to go?"

"I've done nowt, Ledger. Honest."

"Don't muck me about, lad. Bodies all over my manor, you lurking in the foreground. Make us peelers look bad. Tell."

It would do no harm to reveal all, seeing I was at risk. "Well, I was asked for an antique by Mrs. York. Now I'm doing work for Mr. Sykes. And Sir John."

"Any particular work, Lovejoy?"

Sarcasm really hurts a failure. I coined quickly, "Paintings for Mr. Sykes, Chinese vases for Sir John." I added, "He saw me on telly."

"I forgot about that. Did you get a fee?"

"No," I said glumly. "I thought Sykie'd have . . ." I halted, scalp prickling. Ledger was smiling, having got what he wanted, knowing now it was Sykie who'd started me off.

"That'll be all, Lovejoy. But next time Sykie's goons bend you to their iron will, let me know, eh? *Before* things happen."

I chucked the sponge in. "Right, Ledger."

"And collect that filthy tramp of yours as you go. He louses up the place."

The police desk lot were still laughing at Ledger's crack as I left, dragging Tinker. He stank of booze.

"What's everything all about, Lovejoy?" he wheezed as the cold night air stabbed him to his vitals and his legs buckled. "Ledger kept asking if you topped some geezer today."

"Nothing to do with us, Tinker." I began lumbering him toward the Three Cups, our nearest haunt. This was all too much. Everybody wanted my help, but it's always me finishes up babbling nervously in front of magistrates. "Not any more. We're getting back to antiques and normality."

"Thank Gawd, Lovejoy." The thought of moral rectitude strengthened him to a brisk stagger past the war memorial.

"Here, Tinker," I puffed, trying to think up light conversation to keep him compos. "What's Lammas?"

We slammed into a parked car, blundered on. "Played half-back for Manchester United, I think. Afore you were born." I laughed and absolved myself everything. We went into the Three Cups with unburdened hearts. Makes you wonder if peace is oblivion.

Peace and oblivion? Next morning I was up having a bath early, as usual when alone. Then I brewed up and read local history—not for any skulduggery reason, just interest. Blissful peace. Until all Piccadilly trooped in, starting with a smart-suited chap who doffed his bowler and said he hoped he hadn't disturbed my breakfast. I peered at him with the door opened barely a crack.

"Are you a bailiff?"

He looked blank. "Certainly not."

"Debt collector? Magistrate's court?" Still blankness, so confidently I opened the door to ask him in and he served me with a writ. He was quite pleasant about it.

"Mrs. York. You've ruined her restaurant, Lovejoy."

"Peace," I said to him in pious thanks.

His anxious face cleared. "I'm delighted you've taken it so well. It's rather a lot of money. If I were you I'd try to make up with her. Lawyers are so expensive."

"I promise. When I've got a minute."

Second, a knock halfway through my first bread dip. I did my peer. Shoot-out or shared fried bread? I went through my interrogative litany, to responses of denial.

"Come in, then," I said, relaxing. "I've brewed up."

"I won't, thanks. Here." He gave me an envelope.

Gloom time. "A writ?"

"Mrs. Ryan. Default from her estate manager's post."

"Here," I called after him. "Thought you said you weren't a solicitor?"

"I lied, Lovejoy. 'Morning."

Third try at my glaciating breakfast. I managed a swig of tea before my old clapper bell—I got it from a demolished toffee shop—summoned me to do my portcullis act. Crack, squint, another catechism for another clone.

"Who's suing me?"

This one smiled. "Only a personal-delivery letter, Lovejoy. From Mr. Hilley."

"Who's Mr. Hilley?" Reassured, I signed for it.

"He's the gentleman whom Raymond Congreve conned with a fake Wedgwood. A blatant fraud that you financed, Lovejoy."

"I financed? Alone? Nobody else?"

"Mrs. Margaret Dainty and Big Frank proved they weren't implicated. 'Morning."

Next knock, I resignedly took my breakfast. Geoffrey, my

favourite constable, in uniform, puffing from having free-wheeled down the lane.

"How do, beau gendarme. Running me in?"

"No, Lovejoy." He took my pint of tea and swigged. I waited, feeling really down. This was clearly one of those days, if not several all at once. "Your case comes up next Tuesday. You're for it. Old Arthur's on the bench. Raymond's testified it was you arranged it, not him. Ledger's had you booked. Cheers." He returned my empty mug, plodded off.

"Cheers, Geoffrey." I noshed my fried bread where I was standing in the porch, to save bother. Old Arthur's a homely magistrate knocking ninety, with the forgiving qualities of Torquemada with gripe. For it, right enough.

Needless to say, birds thronged in from the bright blue yonder to scrounge. Blue tits drilled into the morning's milk while I was feeding them my fried bread, thieving little swine. I only had to wait five minutes, in the cold though, before a car zoomed in, size of a small liner. Here came Winstanley with guess what.

"Lovejoy?" He was uncomfortable as he handed me an envelope. Did an honest man's heart beat beneath that lazaroid exterior? Impossible; the nerk was an accountant.

"Good morning." He walked to the car, got in beside the chauffeur. Sir John beckoned from a rear seat. I brushed the robin off my plate and went indoors while he flew back to my Bramley apple tree and screeched his angry little head off—the robin, not Sir John.

Who entered, no knock, finding me rewarming my tomatoes, more in hopes than expectation.

"No results, Lovejoy." Why don't customers come pouring in when I've actually got some antiques?

"The contract's canceled, Sir John. You didn't pay up. In antiques, that's default. I have numerous writs to prove it. Find somebody else."

He almost sat, scanned the shambles, and changed his mind. "A man was killed yesterday."

"Aye. Ben Cox. They pulled me in for it."

"He was working for me, Lovejoy."

"Eh?" The frying pan congealed in fright.

"Like you. I owed him a retainer two days ago."

"Maybe not getting paid is a survival factor." No laugh from Sir John. I swallowed and asked the inevitable. "And was George Prentiss? His last stand was on your map."

He paused at the door. "Everything I know is summarized in the envelope, Lovejoy."

I was surprised he didn't charge me for it. "Send my check by post." I got a tea bag into the mug, my hand shaking. "Except Thursday. Our post girl steals everything Thursdays."

"Good luck, Lovejoy. Oh, one thing." I was turned away. So everybody seeking Roman bronzes for Sir John was getting buried these days. Me next? I thought, not bloody likely. I was getting out from under. "That forgery," Sir John continued, trying to be Noel Coward casual. "Is it the Girtin sketch?"

"Quite possibly," I said. "But possibly means possibly not. So don't chuck it away in case, will you?"

My porch door slammed enough to blow the cottage's reed thatch back to its parent marshes down the estuary. I grinned, got back to my grub, and mangled a whole mouthful, honestly. I was thrilled, sloshing it around and actually tasting the grub. Oh, relish! Sykes arrived at the second swallow. He was standing in the porch when wearily I opened the door and sagged there, all attention. Three somber goons stood in the background. It was that scene from *Alexander Nevsky*, macabre knights among the ruins.

"'Morning, Lovejoy. You've had a lot of visitors."

"'Morning, Sykie. Yes, a few."

"Lovejoy. No dropping out just because a bloke got topped in St. Edmundsbury. Right?"

"Right, Sykie."

"And no buggering about with all these tarts, old son. My lads say your pit's like a Saturday hair parlor. Get on with the job. Follow?"

"Yes, Sykie."

So much for resolution. Still, nothing wrong with failure, as long as you don't take it seriously. I mean, it was a failed insurance underwriter who in 1785 decided to found *The Times*.

They left, the goons giving me prolonged threatening stares. I had a splitting headache. The whole world was now goading me into a personal Barge of the Light Brigade. Well, maybe a Creep. I sighed lengthily. Nothing for it. I'd have to suppress my ingrained cowardice and raise my game. Dare to be surreptitious, Lovejoy, risk caution.

The phone was still on. "Sandy? Lovejoy."

The receiver squealed. I held it full arm's length and still heard Sandy's scream. "Ooooh! Mel, dearie! It's that *utter scoundrel* Bluebeard Lovejoy!"

Like I say, an embarrassment. I go red even when I'm on my own. "Cut it, Sandy. I've a job for you."

"Mel, dear," Sandy caroled sweetly. "Lovejoy *demands* our services. Thrills!"

"Money, Sandy," I said, to silence the maniac.

"He's said the magic word, Mel! Oh, what an absolutissimo cherub! Where, lovie?"

"Be in the Treble Tile, noon."

"Have the drinkies ready, cherub. Sweet lemonade for Mel, but no lemon unless it's genuine Seville. Gin and hormone for me. What's the job? No more Gold Coast tribal effigies, *please*. They turned Mel peculiar." I'd done a commission sale for them on an Ashanti shield, no later than 1880 but beautiful.

"A lady at Dogpits."

Sandy screamed. "You *sadist*! Double commission, then!"

Cradling my pintpot I let my head pulse unhindered. No aspirin. I'd cadge a couple from old Kate. She'd be cleaning the village chapel later.

The glimpse of my face in my cracked mirror depressed me no end: gaunt, unshaven, frightened. Nothing new there. I rose and shuffled among the chaos of Lovejoy Antiques, Inc., that writ-riddled enterprise. I was narked, what with Toffee miaowing for her grub, blue tits tapping on the window, the robin screeching at me. How did St. Francis keep his temper with his massive menagerie, much less get beatified? Or Byron write sublime verse with a zoo—bears, a camel—in his basement?

"One day I'll go on strike," I shouted, searching under the sink for the robin's minced bacon rind. "You see if I frigging don't."

But by noon I'd got a plan of action.

Fixer Pete caught me at the Olde Showrooms at Head Gate. This is a warehouse specializing in junk furniture, chuck-out stuff that even ragbone men can hardly be bothered with. It's run by Ridgway, a loud long-limbed bloke with sallow cachectic cheeks. He looks desperate, a real Mexico Pete. For years I've been telling him to turn to politics. They pay simpletons, and Ridgway's that all right.

"Lovejoy!" he thundered as I entered the glass porch. "What d'you think I've found?" He came clumping at me. Fixer Pete was upending some grottie old chairs over by the windows. He has more sense than rush over. A few old dears were ambling among the heaped dross. An old soldier snored peacably on a rotting chaise longue. I carefully didn't see Fixer.

I said wearily, "Another Rembrandt?" He's always just found another Rembrandt.

"No lies, Lovejoy. Scout's honor." Since Easter he's discovered a Turner, a Gainsborough and six van Goghs, he says. "Come and look," he pleaded. "It'll only take a second."

"Or less."

The painting was practically a black-brown wash. It could have passed for roofing felt. Nev bounced around it. He'd put it on an easel. "I'll make a fortune, Lovejoy. How old do you reckon?"

"Who cares?" I made to walk off but he caught at me.

"What's up? It's ancient!" He was appalled by my exasperation. I was justified. Everybody's got Shakespeare's secret last play or Michelangelo's missing sculpture *Sleeping Cupid* in some attic. It's not just once. It's ten times a frigging day.

"Nev, old pal." I'd felt no vibes in my chest. "Take any painting you like, hang it in total darkness, and it'll dowse. The colors blacken. Also, it's filthy." I spat on my hankie and caressed it. "See? You can't even tell what it is. Ship? Lovebirds? Landscape?" I didn't explain that sunlight will occasionally partly restore a dark-blackened oil painting to life. It's as if a painting knows its whole purpose is to be seen, and its little lamp simply goes out in despair when closeted in darkness. That's why I hate these investment companies and trade-union pension funds that hide paintings in vaults, the cruel sods. I'd rather have the Sir Johns of this world anytime, and that's saying a lot.

"Honest, Lovejoy? Sixty quid for it?" He saw my hesitation and pleaded, "The frame's worth that, for God's sake."

"Thirty." I scribbled an IOU, and called, "Fixer. Tell Tinker we've paid a fortune for this old blackboard."

"Okay, Lovejoy." Fixer Pete nodded, came along with me.

I left, with Nev grinning all over his face. I'd try the sunlight trick after cleaning it. He was right about the frame, but the painting was worth a try.

"What's the job, Lovejoy?" Fixer asked. He's a tiny smiley man with a tash off a silent film. His Chaplin walk is quite natural. I like him. He takes orphanage children on outings in his brother's taxi when the London cabbies convoy to Yarmouth. His own three kids are grown up.

"Fix a wedding, Pete. Somewhere posh; the George, say. It's Rowena's and Big Frank's."

"For how many?"

"Dunno."

"When for, Lovejoy?"

I rounded on him and yelled, "Fixer! I've given you the frigging job, now get frigging on with it."

A few fuming strides down Red Lion Alley and I was mercifully free of his wailed reproaches. Honestly, some people. Where's their self-reliance, for heaven's sake? Why do I always have to decide every bloody detail? No wonder you lose your rag, even a patient bloke like me.

Maybe it's associating with so many other antique dealers that makes me stupid, but it took time for the penny to drop about George Prentiss. I'd be wondering yet if it wasn't for meeting Clive as I came out of our local post office. He's our local "hanger." A hanger is an antiques con man who makes a well-heeled living from smuggling antiques (fakes included) into exhibitions. No, I haven't got that wrong and yes, I do mean he wangles things *in*. To be explicit, a hanger simply adds one. His only ally is our greed, so his scam works every time.

Clive is a flashy bloke with an air of being momentarily short of a chauffeur. Hangers are always rich.

"You don't change, Lovejoy," he said. "Saw you pinch that extra stamp book. Comb trick. Works every time."

"Eh? Not me, Clive."

"No, no," he said hastily, but still grinning. Well, the post office has the monopoly, so where's the harm? One lousy stamp book, for heaven's sake. "Glad we met, Lovejoy. Ready for a hanger job at the Minories?"

"What's to be hung?" We were in the High Street.

"A little nef, probably. Thought I'd ask you first." He saw my thoughtfulness. "There's time to arrange a buyer."

"You mean the Local Antiques?" The town gallery had been trumpeting its forthcoming exhibition. A nef's a little ship on wheels. Don't make the terrible mistake of thinking it's a

child's toy, as I've seen happen. It's a really valuable table ornament, usually gold or silver gilt. Lift the deck and you'll find
condiments or little spice holds inside. Some nefs have guns,
rigging, even musical boxes.

"Here's my bus, Lovejoy." Clive made it sound as if he'd
ordered the damned thing. "You in?"

"In," I said. "Only I'll decide what you hang, Clive. Right?"

"Great, Lovejoy." He bought the stamp book off me, half
price.

Carrying Toffee, ever heavier, I crossed the road among
hooting traffic to buy her horrible tinned muck with the
money. I'd tried to educate her palate to pasties but she was
basically a very unrefined cat and steadfastly turned up her conk
at my delectables. Nor would she eat custard, though I'd made
her two jugs of the bloody stuff. I'd concluded that moggies are
basically obstinate.

An idea was forming. The hanger con trick has mucked up
more exhibitions and auctions than you'd ever imagine. Clive
could be useful.

The hanger brings in an antique of his own and, by bribery,
stealth, the use of accomplices, or sleight of hand, installs it as
a proper exhibit, complete with notice card and number. Me
and Clive did a good one up Lavenham way a year back, insert-
ing a Sèvres porcelain standish—inkstand to us commoners—
into a manorial lord's exhibition. The catalog printer is bribed,
of course, to prepare half a dozen separate catalogs wherein the
mysterious addition is magically legitimized. I'd invited a Sèvres
collector from London that time, and he bought the standish a
month after the exhibition closed. If a hanger's any good, the
hanged item can be sold for twice, three times even, its street
value by virtue of being associated with a posh exhibition.
Mind you, I don't believe these people like Sykie, who claims
to have hangered Sotheby's and Christie's, though everything's
possible, no?

You can see the way my mind was going: Supposing Clive did

a hanger job using a bronze Roman figure—say, at random, a leopard with silver inlay—in the Minories exhibition. Big attraction for somebody.

Which, as Toffee and I left the market, set me thinking of excavating a Roman metal object buried in some field. For this you'd need a treasure-finder. My somnolent cerebrum voted with my feet, fetching me to our town's one metal-detector shop.

The window was crammed. Metal detectors can cost a king's ransom these days. Basically a detector's a disk at one end of a rod. They're only natty mine detectors, really. The shop was blazoned with lurid fluorescing notices: *Audio Ground Exclusion!!* and METER DISCRIMINATION PLUS!!! and suchlike specialist nonsense. Local treasure-hunters call them "bongers" because they perforate your eardrums if you walk the disk over any buried metal. But most call them mooners or moonies, not because of the disk's shape but because the game's one for night owls, the heroes we call moonspenders.

There were six blokes in the shop when I entered. I ambled about examining the instruments. Nine clubs had pinned notices up behind the door, I saw to my surprise. Ten different magazines were arrayed on a rack. The blokes talked in numbers and initials, like all elites, exchange a CS 411 for a VLF 990B and all that. I gaped affably. Customers came and went, a thriving business. The proprietor was in his element, fags at the ready and sheets of data stuck to the glass cabinets behind him. I'd never seen such useless technology outside an army.

"Help you, sir?" he said.

"Cost," I gave him sadly. "I've an old cheapo. I'm wondering whether to move upmarket."

"VDI?" he smiled shrewdly.

"Well . . ." My shrug led him into more initials. He showered me with pamphlets. I left in mild shock, promising to return. Technology's a killer, especially this sort. More particularly, it had done for George Prentiss. For another hour I watched the shop from across the road. All its customers were enthusiasts, with glazed eyeballs of madmen. But on the way home with Toffee I couldn't help thinking of the adverts on display. Half were from collectors inviting detector freaks to get in touch when selling detected finds. No help there, but they had all specified an interest in buying bronzes, gold, and silver, Roman and medieval especially, and said to contact the *Advertiser*.

Well, *nearly* no help.

10

Liza's our local news. Without her is made nothing that was made, as far as news goes. She runs the *Advertiser*, a rag issued free with everything. She's an underpaid stringer for the town's literary Hooray Henries, who oversee things from a pub called the Grapes. These print lordlings' Aston Martins are always parked at the boozer, while they gut democracy for every drachm. Needless to say, the effort's warped her. She dresses like a speedway rider, tight jeans, studs on her denim sleeves, leather carapace on her shoulders, jaunty cheesecutter.

"Lize," I said, knowing it annoys. "Unpaid and unstinting help immediately, please."

"Liza with a zed, not Lisa with an ess, you ignorant fascist chauvinist." We'd recently had a row, not my fault.

"Tough luck. The song's been written." While she laid up enormous sheets of paper I drank her coffee. Well, everybody else had swigged mine all morning. Fair's fair.

"And shift your frigging poxy basket, you." Lize gave Toffee a curious glance but said nothing, as if moggie-toting dealers were quite usual. I like her a lot, but not for news-making. As far as I'm concerned the less of it the better.

I asked, "Here, Lize. Do you keep addresses of all of us who place adverts?"

"Certainly not. I do too flaming much as it is. You know the system, Lovejoy. The boxes are in the foyer for the replies. Whoever takes them takes them."

So much for tracking the moonspenders through her. Any passing pedestrian can reach in for the sheaf of envelopes.

She shoved me off her stool and sat. "Right, you coffee-thieving bastard. What you want?"

"Anything about my village and adjacent countryside, love. Radius of three miles."

"Sodding frigging hell, Lovejoy." Her multichrome abuse is natural; she did sociology. "You don't ask much. How far back? A week? A month?"

"A year."

She went mad, calling me all the names she could lay tongue to. Humbly I heard her out. I'm pretty patient with women. If only they'd learn some patience from me.

"You've a nerve, Lovejoy. After standing me up in the Marquis."

"No, Lize," I said. "When I arrived you were already with a bloke."

Lize glared. "That 'bloke' was my dad."

"Eh?" I coughed for time to work up an escape clause.

"Didn't think I had one?" She slammed into her sheets. She could hardly speak.

"Your dad? Lize. I'm sorry. Most sincerely. Only he looked too young, compared with you I mean—"

"Out!" she screamed.

At William's bank I finally halted to get breath. Toffee was miaowing reproachfully. She hates being shaken. See what I mean? You pay them a compliment and what thanks do you get?

Sandy and Mel's gigantic Rover was at the Welcome Sailor. Once, it had been a respectable black. Now it dazzled even in dull November. Sequins patterned its bonnet, roof, fluorescent-handled doorways. A silver lamé fringe fluttered above the windows. Neon lights encircled each wheel, flashing even at rest. It played Vivaldi to itself as it waited. Chintz curtains, I noted, new, but vermilion chintz a possible mistake. I've seen quieter circuses. I drew breath and entered.

Sandy cried, "Oh *pancreas!*"

He was driving. His eyes, admiring himself in the adjusted mirror, had caught sight of the new restaurant.

"We're going home this very minute." They were the first words Mel had spoken since the pub. He and Sandy were in the middle of a tiff over their antique shop. It's actually a converted Suffolk barn where, as Sandy puts it, they live in sun. "It's *deformed*. Home, Sandra."

"You can't, lads," I begged desperately. "Just check whether this lady's decorated her restaurant right."

"Or not," Mel added spitefully.

Aggro, and we'd not even entered. I disembarked wearily. The car park was empty but for one saloon. Waiters lolled; nothing so doleful as a spare waiter, is there? Slump Towers, Ltd. Two lonely diners peered, possibly hoping for company.

"Patience, world." Sandy was doing his mascara, some glittery powder from a tiny pot. Lipstick, blush highlight, a quick check of his gold-luster earrings, done. He trilled, "Ready?"

"Ready," Mel caroled. I go red over this pantomime.

"Here I come, dear hearts!"

The driver's door opened. A small gilt staircase descended. The radiator grill churned out "You Were Never Lovelier," and here he came in a florentine-striped spencer jacket surmounted by a silver soprano cape, the burke. Lace gloves, high heels zigzag-welted in gold thread, ultramarine cavalier hat. Jesus but he looked ridiculous. He twirled.

"You like? Worship? Adore? Envy?"

Mel's stare dared me. "Er," I said, desperate and sweaty, "it's really, er, original."

Mel smiled. He's the quiet one. By the time we reached the entrance the kitchen staff, cleaners, and the band crowded the entrance, gaping. I felt a twerp following shamefaced in the wake of these two apparitions, trying to look like I wasn't with them. Sandy was chattering about the Rover's music: would "Yeoman of the Guard" be more appropriate? Then an outlandish scream made me jump a mile. Sandy had fainted spectacularly in the foyer, in instant pandemonium. Mel was suddenly screaming for doctors, Guy's Hospital, cardiac surgeons, oxygen. Waitresses were scampering, waiters yelling, all hell let loose. Wearily I crossed the spongy carpet and opened a bottle of wine. It was probably mine anyway, if I'd bankrupted the place. I sat to watch the riot.

Sandy was whimpering, threshing, amid the attention. No business like show business. Usually he begins yelping, a minute into Act One, Scene One. Suzanne, white-faced, pushed through the surging horde demanding what's the matter.

"You, Lovejoy! I might have known."

She made them carry him through, flailing like a ribbon in a gale, and lay him on a phony chaise longue. I took my bottle in while Mel screeched, "Give him air!" When the band had resumed playing and the chaos had dwindled, I went over and said, "Right, Sandy. On your feet."

"What are you saying?" Suzanne asked, bewildered.

I said acidly, "He's overcome by your restaurant's beauty, love."

Sandy instantaneously opted for life. "Lovejoy! Don't you *dare* that *mess* I mean poor people are expected to *eat* oh my God . . ." He saw the velvet lounge, screamed, and bonk, down he went comatose with Mel screeching was I trying to murder his poor cherub. I sighed and had another swig.

"Takes a few minutes," I told Suzanne consolingly. "Rubbish always affects him like this."

"*Rubbish*? It cost a mint," Suzanne whispered. "The very best designers . . ."

"Got a minute, love?" I took her hand and walked with her to the restaurant. The Gardner porcelain was still on its stand. "What actually happened last night?"

"Oh, Lovejoy. It was dreadful." Her eyes filled with tears. I thought, she's lovely. She wore a smart midday suit, pastel green, double string of pearls, and silver earrings. "We had a good crowd. Then suddenly people seemed to . . . well, drift. It was dreadful. And then they began phoning in, canceling. Cancel, cancel. Thirty-nine staff, two customers. Everything was all right until you came."

"Dry your eyes, love." I led her to a table. "Got a candle?" She snapped her fingers and black-tied serfs sprang forward. "Shut your band up, love. And pull the curtains."

She gave a puzzled nod and the waiters moved to obey. I had them draw all the tasseled drapes, extinguish the chandeliers. I crossed to the porcelain, smiling.

"All lamps out, folks. Just this one candle."

Everybody was becoming intrigued. The kitchen staff were crowding out. The band were looking.

"Off. Everybody quiet."

The switches clicked. I let my eyes accommodate to the candle's glimmer, then sat beside Suzanne.

"What's it for, Lovejoy?"

"Shhhh. Watch."

Shuffles, then stillness. A clink sounded from the band's dais, a gurgle. Seconds passed. A whole minute. Two. The quiet extended. Candlelight permeated the whole area. Shadows hitherto unborn slowly crept into being, cautiously at first, then with increasing confidence.

Another minute and the room had shrunk further. And the magic happened. The lovely suffusing glow of the flames danced out, moving around the exquisite porcelain in a golden penumbra. Mrs. York murmured, "Oh, God." It nearly broke my heart. No faith is born into this life but what some other belief dies the death. It's always piteous. I've seen it happen time and again; never any different. The tragic part is the pain of delivery, bidding farewell to all our pathetically modern assumptions. She sniffed, fumbled for a tissue.

Before us in the room the magic opalesence glowed. The porcelain was only a milkmaid, partly glazed, her head slightly downcast under the strain of carrying her yoke. Her arms were angelic along the yoke's bow, her pails slightly unleveled.

Yet her body was not sylphic; it was firm and curved, a realistic Russian peasant, a lovely woman accepting the duty of existence, hinting at sacrifice by the cruciform shadow she cast. I always get a lump in my throat, even me. Francis Gardner trudged penniless into Russia in 1767 and sprang beauty from between his hands like a magician does a dove. His color palette was simple Slav, but you'll never see—

"Lights, Pierre," Suzanne York said brokenly.

Click, and the room howled into consciousness with a crash-bang-wallop. She hurried out, a tissue to her face. The two diners, a young bloke and his bird, came over to stare at the delectable porcelain. Sandy and Mel were standing watching from the lounge entrance. For a minute I didn't recognize them because Sandy was silent. Then he started.

"The trouble with *you*, Lovejoy, is you do everything the *hard* way." He did his cosmetics thing, handbag mirror, lipstick. "Couldn't you simply *explain* to the poor bitch that your I mean *tremenduloso* porcelain would *expose* this oh my God costly *the earth* restaurant for the shithouse it is?"

"Sandy," I placated.

Mel interposed viciously, "How long will the silly cow have the vapors?"

"What I want is my drinkie-poos." Sandy tapped the impassive Pierre and rolled his eyes roguishly. "Cream sherry and Avondale water. Mel isn't allowed *any* for bad behavior."

"Very good, sir." Pierre sent a waiter hurtling. "Would you like a table?"

"I wouldn't be seen *moribund* at your table, darling, while these *horrid* colors positively *blitz* this *woebegone* carpet."

He swept grandly into the lounge, Mel trailing sulkily. I kept out of the way. This all meant he and Mel had accepted the job of redecorating the place. Time to leave.

Pierre's grave countenance smiled me out of the door.

"Your advice fell upon stony ground, eh?" I said.

"Mrs. York has had a great deal on her mind lately, sir." The soul of discretion. "May I, sir?" A waiter moved forward with a small box, two bottles of wine. "Barolo. A respectable vintage."

"Ta. You won't get into trouble?" I said.

"Not in the least, sir."

"Lovejoy." Mrs. York caught me outside and came with me. The strolling woman's side-to-side grace is so alluring. But no, she was determined to castigate herself. "Everybody else realized, didn't they, Lovejoy?"

"Not consciously, love. But once the milkmaid showed them loveliness, your posh restaurant was, well, tasteless. People sense more than they let themselves believe."

"But I'm good on design, fashion, style!" A wail.

"And beauty?" A decade-long pause while it sank in. "Modern's great if you like noise, loudness, slick formats, packaged ware." I felt sad myself having to say it. "Put all of it next a work of art . . ."

"And everybody simply walks away?"

"I'm sorry, love."

She stopped, facing me. "You feel it all the time, don't you? You don't need candles, the mystique, the silence."

"Never mind. Sandy and Mel'll scrap your furniture, color scheme, that god-awful cutlery, everything. They'll refurbish the rotten dump." I gazed at the restaurant's exterior. "But I warn you. Sandy will chuck tantrums on the hour. Mel will resign once a day. Yet a few days and you'll be back in business." I coughed, went red. "Sandy will, er, call you names, love. He doesn't mean it."

She was smiling. "Much. And how will I pay for all this, Lovejoy?"

"On tick. Profit share. Give Sandy exclusive rights to have a permanent antiques gallery in the lounge. Get in a dealer each night to give a twenty-minute show of genuine paintings, jewelry, antique dresses. Make it your theme. It'll go—if the restaurant's decor doesn't come off worst every time."

She was eyeing me, that searching look I never like from women. "And you, Lovejoy?"

"I'm busy," I said, "seeing my lawyer. Putting on the writs."

Underhand, that. She colored, her eyes bluer in swift contrast. "I apologize, Lovejoy. I'll withdraw it, of course."

"Don't help me, chuckie. I'm in enough trouble." I bussed her and left. At the curve of the drive I looked back. She was standing there, waving.

As I turned along the road to town I passed that gray-eyed homespun girl looking about to fray. She was examining a hedge in the lane.

"Flowers all present and correct, eh, Enid?" I joked, but only got a malign stare out of those remarkable eyes. I sighed and plodded on. I'd been a hero to her. Once.

A pleasant dark-suited bloke driving past in a gray saloon offered me a lift to town. It transpired he too was interested in antiques, and we talked all the way. He handed me a manila envelope as I stepped down. My heart sank.

"A writ?"

"Of course not." He chuckled. My heart soared. "It's three." My heart sank. "From somebody insignificant, I hope?"

"You could say that," he said. My heart soared. "The Central

Television Authority." My heart sank. "The Central Agency of
TV Presenters." A further sink. "And from Veronica Gold."
And again.

The saloon purred away. One thing, I thought, heading toward the town library, with writs cascading this fast I'd not be
short of fuel for the winter.

11

Everybody round here knows where the Eastern Hundreds spread to, but defining them is a rum job. Our town's gormless reference library lately sold most of its books off, "in the interests of efficiency," so you've to purchase all your own culture now. I rummaged in the remnants, confirming my worst fears. Some say a hundred's an area providing a hundred men, others a hundred hides of land. But an Old English hundred was 100, 112 or the "long" hundred of 120. A hide was 120 acres, or 80 or anything you liked. The more I searched the worse it got. An acre can be the modern measure, but different counties say it's anything up to 10,000 square yards. And a yard is only possibly a yard. Some say it's . . . Just short of delirium I gave up and caught the bus home.

Usually I daydream on buses, to avoid conversation. My old gran used to say that talk is the sound of brains emptying. She was right; silence is golden. So in silence I inspected the passing world.

Our land's undulant, flattish. On a good bright day the countryside appears friendly and pretty. It's not.

Leaving town, the bus levels across the old river and chugs
out past the station. Quite abruptly, as the bus coughs into its
third emphysematous gear, the scenery alters. Houses end.
You're between hedgerows, alone on a twirly country road
warmed only by a few skyline houses clustered nervously round
an old manor house. It's woods, valleys, fields, low rivers wearing long tree-lined hoods. Carry on and you run into a thin
scattering of postcard villages, all older than time, all appar-
ently friendly but underneath broodingly quiet. Legends
abound. Past feuds aren't past at all. Incomers are tolerated,
even liked, but somehow never see into local darknesses. Give
me towns any day.

The bus turned into our village. I said so long to the driver
and saw the chapel's graveyard gate standing open. Old Kate
was on her knees scrubbing the stone flags of the vestry. She's
our village wise woman, whose herbs mend broken ankles and
prevent pregnancy and all that. She has to like you or she tells
you wrong. Mind you, that's women all over, not just Old
Kate. She was using my kneeler, a thick fustian-filled Lancashire working pillow. I'd made it for her once because she's
got arthritis. For a few minutes I sat on the chapel elder's chair
and watched her go at it. God, these old birds really slog. If
only the rest of our kingdom's women worked half as hard.

"Cat got your tongue, Lovejoy?"

You have to smile. She talks exactly like my old gran. Local
people steer clear of Kate. I don't know why.

"Lammas," I said.

"The cricket club's only themselves to blame," she said,
making singulars plural in the manner of long-lived folk.

"They've done no harm, Kate."

"Much you know about it, Lovejoy," she said with an upward
glance. Her eyes were twinkling. There I go, faces again. But
it's a fact of life, that these old dears have really beautiful eyes,

as pert as any you'll ever get from a maid a quarter Kate's age. Baby girls can do it too, look from beyond eyelashes and set a man maudling.

"Give us a kiss, Kate."

She laughed, still scrubbing, shaking her head. "Mrs. Ryan not busy enough between your sheets, son?"

How do they do it? I've come to believe these old folks have a kind of a mental osmosis by which they imbibe gossip. But my brain went: On the other hand, Lovejoy, this owd biddie lives across the footpath from your garden, and a hedge-eating horse is a dead giveaway.

"I hardly know Mrs. Ryan," I said indignantly, and shrugged an apology at Kate's raised eyebrows. "Well, nearly hardly." I swung my feet. "Why don't the cricket club use one of the other fields, Kate?"

"There isn't another field, Lovejoy."

"Manor Farm has Long Tom by Pittsbury Wood. I saw it yesterday with Boothie. And I—"

"There isn't, son."

The barmy old coot wouldn't say more. She said to call in for a glass of her sloe gin. I gave her my most sincere Grade Four promise, and went down the lane thinking, no other field? How many had I counted? Eight? Nine? Still, a postponed cricket match isn't the end of civilization as we know it.

A bloke was waiting patiently in his motor by the cottage, the car radio playing. Even though by now I knew the drill I was pleased to see him. At least somewhere the nation's normality continued.

"Lovejoy isn't back yet," I said.

He checked my face against a photograph. "Sorry, Lovejoy. Here." A manila envelope. Oh, joy. "Wednesday fortnight, Suffolk Quarter Sessions."

"Who this time?"

"Major Bentham. Assault and battery. Obstructing a fox-hunt, inciting rabble. Grievous bodily harm." This was punishment for not teaming up with him and Candice.

"It isn't all bad news these days, is it? Swing right at the chapel for the main road."

Inside there was another summons from one Mrs. Candice Prentiss, widow; Chelmsford Court of Common Pleas or something, to answer charges of trespass and willful obstruction. It degenerated into incomprehensible heretofores and aforesaids after that, twenty wretched pages. Lawyers keep a robber's grip on law, the swine, so we can't use justice for its proper ends.

One good bit. There was a package from the *Advertiser* with a scrawled message: "Lovejoy. Open this, and you owe me. Liza X." I put the kettle on, and settled down to read the sheaf of cuttings.

Surprising how little we had figured in the world's consciousness. A whole year, and local newspapers had featured my village's segment less than fifty times. We might as well not have bothered to newsmake. Irritably I slung out an unfair report about an antique dealer who'd been in trouble with police, and an equally biased falsehood telling how the same dealer was mangled by the bankruptcy court. Swine. That Lize. One day I'll bite her ankles.

The rest slowly became two piles. The greater was rubbish, clearly recognizable as Lize's demented space-filling—Women's Guild Protests on Roadworks Issue. It's the sort of thing she prints when nowt's happened, simply copies any extinct news and changes the first line: "Anger flared today when irate villagers . . ." It's all based on a chance remark overheard at a bus stop anyway. The little pile, however, was more important.

On the whole we're a rum lot. I mean people. Our rehabilitation center, where hospital patients convalesce, had had its telephone switchboard damaged by fire. A truffle hunter, would you believe, had been offered a fortune for his dog. A fence had been repeatedly damaged on Manor Farm. Some nut had seen a UFO among some trees—the Air Ministry glibly implied the report was from lunatics. Young trees, stolen from a wood, were found in a lorry abandoned at Coggeshall. Thieves had stolen a pedigree hen; whatever next? A nocturnal cyclist had had an accident crossing the river footbridge, been treated in hospital. A conservationist spokeswoman threatened legal action against anybody, maybe everyone, if People Didn't Behave. There'd been a malicious fire in ruins out beyond Chapel Lane End. One headline was a winner: Local Constabulary Useless as Guardians of Root Crop Produce, Accuses Farmer. I decided to wait for the film. The new restaurant, of course. The fox hunt demo. Two footballers arguing over a team's beer money. An angler's car had been stolen—good old Ollie Hennessey, no less, and him pally with Clipper, who's probably the fastest resprayer of nicked motors in the east. I marked all these with a red blob.

A protracted think, then another shuffle-and-split sorting by dates. Four piles now. Significance? Well, we seemed to be in the news a little more often at certain times than others.

But things stick in your mind, don't they? Things like UFOs, a pointless fire, a nicked car, a complaining naturalist, and a damaged fence. And maybe a job such as estate manager, offered by a bedmate.

Winstanley knocked at four-thirty, with Roger's lad from our village garage. He had the keys of my ancient Austin Ruby. My old crate's 7-h.p. engine was raring to go.

As Roger's lad sauntered off, Winstanley said, "The bill will be charged against your fees, Lovejoy. There's also Sir John's message." He coughed apologetically. "He wants to know what you are doing."

"I'm having a quiet read, Winnie. Ta for the motor."

"But—"

Solitude's marvelous, isn't it? When you're thinking against time it's crucial but unnerving. I fried some bread and diced a piece of cheese. Nothing in the fridge, of course. Typical.

By six o'clock I'd sussed it out. Boothie, I thought, but first

Vanessa. Toffee was kipping in her basket so I could leave her. A swift crank of the Ruby's handle stirred the innards into a noisy wheeze. I could now comet around the globe to my heart's content. Only one trouble: It was dusk, night fast falling. Speed was called for.

With the Ruby's meager ccs beating maximum power, I notched a giddy 22 mph. One brief pause at the White Hart to light the crate's oil lamps, amid much ribaldry from boozers, and I puttered at a breakneck saunter into the Boxenford evening.

Vanessa and me met up yonks ago, over some mayhem down Pearlhanger. We were close. I stayed with her, but her healthy outdoor life proved detrimental. She's everything you see in the Olympics—yachting, hang-gliding, waterski racing, a real glass-bum. She had some idea of making me a permanent fixture. Never works, does it?

The airfield has a shed and a windsock, plus enthusiasts. Colin's the boss mechanic, a hefty youth with spatuloidal fingers. He collects recordings of engine noises; honest, it's true. In other words, Vanessa's team are maniacs. As I arrived they were examining an engine by floodlight. A generator muttered nearby.

"Swab, scalpel," I said. The lads laughed, knowing me.

Vanessa was delighted to see me. "Where've you been, Lovejoy?" she said, pulling to greet me privately in the hut. "You wretch. You promised to ring."

"My side's been playing up, love." I said. I'd forgotten to limp on the way in.

"It has?" She was all consternation. I gritted my teeth, smiled nobly.

"I've missed you, sweetheart." I went all misty, wishing she wouldn't wear overalls with spanners in every pouch. They ram your belly.

"Lovejoy." She cupped my face, searching. "You haven't come just because you want something?"

"Oh, I see." I said quietly, stung to the quick. "That's how you think of me."

"I'm sorry, darling." She embraced me. God, the spanners.

"Soon as I learned I was being sued I stayed away. Didn't want you involved, sweetheart."

"Oh, Lovejoy! How sweet!" Her eyes moistened.

Bravely I smiled, McClintock of the Mounties, leg shattered by a giant bear. "But as I was this way on, Vanessa, I thought of your brother." He's an antique dealer, he says. "There's a find, in Maldon. An almost perfect Dongware pot, fluted, wonderful, ivory-colored."

"Oh, darling." Tears filled her eyes. "You came to help my brother, and I suspected you of . . . I'm a beast."

"Everybody makes mistakes." We nearly burst into "Maid of the Mountains." My own eyes were stinging. I really believed me myself.

"Is there no way I could make it up to you, darling?"

"Certainly not!" I cried indignantly.

Later I prised Colin and his merry men from under my Ruby where they were wistfully contemplating incipient ruin, and rattled off toward civilization, with Vanessa's promise to cobble together all the aerial photographs of the Pittsbury area. Vanessa said would a couple of days be all right. I'd replied that it was surely too much trouble, and please could I pay her. She got mad at that, so I bowed to her will.

Finding a priceless Dongware bowl for her layabout brother was tomorrow's tough luck.

As dusk finally settled for darkness, I arrived at Boothie's.

In East Anglia not every house is a house, and not every cottage is a cottage. My own cottage is thatch, olde worlde wood, and plaster. Brick two-uppers, which abound hereabouts, are also called cottages. Such a one was Boothie's. He lives near Pittsbury Wood, the tip of a long isthmus of trees almost forming a separate copse. I'm making it sound open and in plain view, but it isn't. His cottage stands in a small fold, a tree-filled recess. I left the Ruby at thankful rest and, calling nervously because of the dark, made my way over the stile and down the thicket path. I took one of the Ruby's oil lanterns, leaving the old crate one-eyed up on the brow.

"Boothie," I called. "It's me. Lovejoy." No lights. I cleared my throat loudly. "Boothie. It's only Lovejoy."

The door stood ajar. I peered in doubtfully. Do poachers depart for the night leaving their doors open? Well, do they? Did Boothie have the electric, or was he an oil-and-candles man? The latter, by my recollection. I went and knocked. Silence. Some fool of a bird swished big wings past my head in a rush. Should be home minding its own business.

"Right, lads," I called in a strangled voice. "Surround the building." Wasn't that what the police say? "Right, sergeant. Search every corner."

In, feeling daft. My lamp threw its feeble glimmer into each of the four rooms. No Boothie. The back door was on the latch. I know because I tried it. Upstairs, in the pantry, the loo. No luck.

"Right, er, lads." Sillier still, certain there were no lurking footpads, but I felt my earlier performance'd earned it.

Decibel's kennel was there, the sack of gruesome biscuits Boothie makes him hanging from a little strut. I've seen Boothie do them, fat and oatmeal. What a sell. In a way I was disappointed. In fact I was halfway toward the Ruby's flickering lamp when I heard the whimpering.

"What's that?" I called, terror returning with a rush. My lamplight nervously gave up as soon as it hit the undergrowth. "Hello?"

A dog barked, and came at me. It was Boothie's hitherto

silent skulker Decibel, discovering a friend. We greeted each other in an orgy of relieved licks, pats, hugs.

"Where's Boothie?" I asked, like a fool, and instantly it was wriggling ahead into the vegetation, choosing a route that even I could follow. Every few paces it paused, showed me my flame in its eyes, and eeled on while I lumbered behind.

Nobody pays much attention to these low hollows. They're everywhere in the Hundreds. Useless, of course; hell to get into and hell to get out of. Usually there's a murky pool, and the brambles murder your face. This tanglewood had a slow ooze smearing its way from the fields higher up the valley's slope. It also had a man's body lying imprisoned under two great roots.

"Boothie? Christ Almighty."

Decibel was whimpering, pawing at the mud round the inert form. I couldn't tell if Boothie was breathing or not. He felt warmish, thank heavens, but stuck. I stood my lamp, grabbed him, and heaved, slithering into the sluggish stream with a thick splosh. Decibel wriggled, wanting to help but not quite knowing how. No good. Then I had the sense to feel. Boothie was wedged, actually wedged, under a big arched root. I heard a discreet tapping, which frightened me before I realized it was only coming rain. It would be quite a storm, judging from the big slow drops that began to whack down on the fold.

But Boothie. I knelt in the water, only inches shallow. His face lay about three inches from the swark. Lucky I came or he would have . . . Decibel was scrabbling like a mad thing. I yanked, cursing. All it needed was another inch or two and he'd not be able to breathe. The rain tumbled then, hissing and clapping above and about me. I sank back on my haunches for a breather.

"Steady, Decibel. We've got all night." Boothie seemed to have blood all over his temple.

The dog was berserk, scratching madly, its flung mud splatting. It was as if it was trying to tunnel beneath its master, and

I realized its wisdom. Scoop under him, and you could pull him clear. I shone the light to decide. Funny. It had seemed three inches deep. Now it was four. And that sleek drift was wrinkled, turbid, not so slow. Faster.

Then my mind yelped. Torrential rainstorm plus a shallow stream equaled a torrent. I tore into the mud, kneeling over Boothie and bawling for help. I rammed a shoe under his head to keep his nose clear of the water. The black water was running nastier and quick, fetching leaves and twigs down with it that piled up against Boothie's face.

When his arm finally did come clear I shoved myself back on the bank, hurting where the branches delved, grabbed Boothie's middle and dragged him clear, Decibel with its teeth pulling along, up among the brambles until we were a clear yard off that horrible muck. The rain was lashing down. God, I felt a mess. Decibel was wagging round Boothie's rag-doll form, licking his face—not a word of thanks to me, note. That's gratitude.

Whacked, a few paces at a time, I staggered with him to the cottage. The worst bit was laying him on his kitchen table. All right, I know it's not proper first aid, but I was in a worse state than he was. The only difference was that one of us was unconscious. Some poacher.

In the light of my lamp I inspected him. His head was battered. Not a beat of pulse, not an eddy of breath. Oh, God. I'd been handling a dead man; I'd rescued a corpse. I was alone in a storm with a dead man. I rushed into the rain with my lamp, one shoe missing.

"Guard him, Decibel," I bleated, and blundered up the path to the Ruby. A split minute and I was clattering away from that horrible dank copse toward the nearest police, Geoffrey's house at the next village crossroads.

"Tell me again, Lovejoy." Ledger was sitting on Boothie's wet table swigging coffee. They'd offered me none. Phyllis with her portable was typing reproachfully by torchlight. "Are you sure it was Booth? And his dog?"

"For God's sake, Ledger. Who took Decibel walks that time Boothie had pneumonia?"

"A poacher? Headfirst down in his own brook?" His eyes never left me. "Why no trail, Lovejoy?"

"Because it's raining cats and dogs. The bloody stuff runs downhill, you burke. Look." I pointed. "The table's wet where I laid him."

Ledger indicated the sash windows. "It's all wet, Lovejoy. Windows and doors open. Booth left his cottage agape. Sudden rainstorm blew rain inside. Common enough story."

I went through and looked at the back door. Ajar. I stooped by the kennel. Well, well.

"Then, Lovejoy, where is the corpse and its dog?"

"I don't know."

"Book him, Phyllis." Ledger rose, beckoned to the policeman outside. Three police cars swung their nasty blue blinders asynchronously beyond the copse.

"What for, Ledger?"

"Malicious misuse of police resources."

"Ledger," I said brokenly. "I won't—"

"Add resisting arrest, Phyllis. And bring our own coffee next time." He shoved his hands in his pockets and went to the door, judging the teeming rain.

"'Night, Ledger," I said dismally.

He glanced back, turning up his collar to make the dash. "Not you, Lovejoy. You're coming with us."

And I did, my Ruby puttering head-on into the rain behind the file of impatient police cars. But you can't help wondering what kind of murderer steals a corpse, and its loyal dog. And removes its personal dog biscuits. Ledger was right: poachers don't fall. They have to be pushed. And maybe they rise up and steal away.

12

Perhaps you don't know them much but a magistrate's court is a complete waste of space. They can be pretty informal. I've known one old duffer go on about fly-fishing till all the bobbies nodded off. Today's clown was a veteran, clearly bored to be working when he could be out burning peasants. He glared at me as I was led in. I'm on a right winner here, I thought, heart doing its customary dive at the spectacle of law.

"Lovejoy, sir," a bobby announced for me, in case I irresponsibly uttered fact.

"Why is he in such a state?"

Ledger had refused me permission to wash, my condition being part of his evidence. Hence I was still the monster from the black lagoon.

"Germane to the case, sir," my peeler said.

"It happened on my estate, sir," I said, building hassles in the sky. "I've not had time to change."

"Did he say on his estate?"

"Yessir. I'm estate manager. Manor Farm, sir." Ledger's

stricken stare hit me like a missile, but I was past caring. "I've had trouble with a poacher, sir, and . . ." Battles between poachers and estaters in East Anglia are background yawns. Nobody in his right mind lets them into court. The growsy old bloke erupted and sent us all scurrying for wasting the court's time. They released me after two phone calls, so I must have guessed right about the boundary. Boothie's cottage was on Manor Farm.

"Good one, Lovejoy." Ledger walked me to the steps. A bright fresh morning, cold as charity. "Gainfully employed, eh? A legend in your own lunchtime." Passing people stared at me, a symphony in gunge.

"Ha ha," I said dutifully. "My crate's in the pound."

Companionably he ordered the gate nerk to release my Ruby, me distrusting all this camaraderie. Police, like criminals, are determinants of social disorder. Their uniqueness lies in the fact that they apply the law by unswerving guesswork, whereas criminals follow form. Hence, Ledger's happiness was in inverse proportion to mine.

"You know our number, don't you? Ring any time." He grinned. "You see, Lovejoy, my lords and masters will go berserk if you get topped, after today's hilarious court proceedings. See my predicament?"

I hesitated. "You did believe me about Tom Booth?"

He laughed, genuinely laughed. "Only for public consumption, Lovejoy. Good luck."

Off he went, chuckling. I didn't like it. I mean, subtlety and peelers don't mix, Ledger being master of the single entendre. Yet he falls about at being foiled?

This clearly called for a visit to the convalescent home. The Ruby whined into complaining life and carried me there in thirty minutes flat, only two rests for breath. The exhilaration of speed. I felt like an astronaut.

The convalescence unit's at a crossroads outside the corner of Manor Farm's sprawling estate, with a good view of Constable country, rivers and such. It's lonely, but all right on a cold October day with white clouds racing to make the coast before the fenlands squeezed them into dry extinction.

The elderly stooping chief, Dr. Pryor, looked in sore need of a bit of convalescence himself, tired and gaunt.

"Before you say anything, doc, I lied to your nurse." I gave it half a second. "I'm not ill. I'm not a moaning relative. And I'm not a Health Service administrator whining about your colossal expenditure."

He sat back, not knowing quite what to think. "Our expenditure's not colossal."

"You're right, doc." When I grovel I go all the way.

He was smiling. "Reporter?"

"No. I boned up on the gallant defense you made in the local newspaper." Lize's photocopies. "So you'd show me round on trust."

He scanned me and nodded, scoring me harmless. "You must be on our side. NHS administrators can't read. Come on."

A rehabilitation unit's no picnic. Traction, splints, walking frames, it's all there. Ropes dangle. Pools steam. White-coated troglodytes have poor sickly people breathing desperately into piston machines. Fluorescent screens blip traces. Wires, flex, plugs, cables everywhere. Doc Pryor got in, "Lucky you've come when we've tidied," but I stayed close by him in case a machine grabbed me. There was the all-pervading NHS pong of cooking.

The old doctor noticed I was hanging back, squeamish.

"I see," he said laconically, and after that showed me only corridors, day rooms, the bleep system.

"Why's everybody happy, doc?" I asked. I'd counted several definite smiles. A young bloke wobbling ecstatically along in a frame thing even panted a cheery greeting.

"They're getting better." Pryor's tone announced that they'd improve or else.

A peculiar metronomic chanting lapped my ear. I asked what

it was. He swung open a door on a little girl about eleven, hair in bunches, syllabizing words to a metronome's beat. "So - the - horse - cant - ered - home - to - its - sta - ble - " Another smile and a thumbs-up sign.

We went on, me keeping an eye out for the corner turret room I wanted so badly to see, where the fire had been.

"Little Christine has a terrible stutter. Old-fashioned remedies do work sometimes."

"Stutter?" I halted.

He was pleased at my interest. "Yes. They start on the metronome. Then graduate to this." He showed me a little watch-shaped cylinder. "Orchestra conductors hold them." He pressed it into my palm. It tapped gently, a minimetronome. As we ascended the staircase I asked if it would work for a grown woman.

"Depends on the type of stutter," he was saying. "We use several different methods. But that one's usually worth a try. The trouble is stutterers think it's a cross they're simply born with. Society's unforgiving, no compassion. . . ."

I liked this irascible old man, flapping ahead in his grubby white coat, throwing out his accusations. We ascended stairs to the turret room. "Last and not most, here's Gerald, idle good-for-nothing. Tyrant of the turret room, bleep boss."

Gerald was a youngish bloke at a switchboard bank, ear-phones, mouthpiece. Metal flaps leapt from the old-fashioned console every time a green light buzzed. The room was a mess of ripped plaster. Its floorboards were exposed, stained, a few scorched by recent mayhem. Lize's newspaper had spoken the truth, an innovation. Plywood wall panels were partly burned away showing grubby tiles beneath. My spirits soared. Tile pictures. You get patches of decorative tile work in old hospital units like these. They're rare and valuable, so look before you ruin. Jesse Carter became the archetype when he started his Poole Pottery in 1873. A good stretch—say 300, of 15 tile pictures—will net you a blond, a world cruise, and still leave you enough to buy a new car. Many of these lovely old tile pictures are secret—like the four dozen incredible panels of nursery rhymes in the Royal Victoria Infirmary, Newcastle. Don't tell anyone. I came back to earth in the semiwrecked room.

"Wanted on three, doctor. Mrs. Hampson's son again."

Pryor grimaced. "Tell him to go to hell."

"Doctor Pryor says go to hell, Mr. Hampson," Gerald intoned.

The turret room was just that, a small room dominating the corner of the building. Like many of these National Health Service places, it had been an old family house once, its exterior displaying lovely ornamental brickwork. It set me thinking. The turret room commanded a view of Pittsbury Wood, the adjacent fields, the distant sea line, a gleam of estuary, an eave of Dogpits Farm, the stables at Manor Farm. I caught a glimpse of a tribe of red-coated hunters on brown smudges with white waggly dots shoaling ahead of them. Major Bentham's pack was out, the maniacs. Just before I opened my big mouth to ask about the view I spotted Gerald's cupped hand moving across the console. He was having to feel for the flap, not look at the green-light signal. Blind.

"This was where they did the damage, eh?"

"More newspaper talk?" Pryor smiled, looking about. "Yes. Three weeks gone. Smashed the windows. A fire, a night raid."

"Reasons?"

"Who knows?" he said despairingly. "The times we live in, I daresay. There's no money for repairs, so it'll have to come down."

"Hang on."

This place had once been a lovely old family house. Real people had talked and loved here for generations. It deserved better than being bulldozed, even if it was wilting under attack.

"Doc." I held out a coin. "Sell me a brick."

"Beg pardon?" Pryor was puzzled, but Gerald was smiling.

"Tell Lovejoy yes, doctor." Before I could reply the blind

man added, "I heard you, once, at a lecture about antiques. People told me about you."

I'd heard that the blind are unerring at voices.

"Very well." Pryor took the money warily.

"Right. Now sell me a tile." I thought of explaining how the Tile Society's burgeoned, but said nothing.

He was guarded. "You mean these?" He nodded at the exposed grubbiness.

"Aye. Now, doc. Sell me the lot?"

He cleaned his spectacles agitatedly. "They're not mine to sell, Lovejoy. They belong to the Health Service."

"Who will rubble them, and move your unit into a box."

"I don't understand, Lovejoy."

"Shut your cloth ears, Gerald," I said, "this is high finance." So, while Gerald—who'd long since got the point—chuckled and worked the phones, and I wondered how a clever old coot like Dr. Pryor could be so blinking dim, I explained in monosyllables the most routine of modern robberies.

"It's called the wall game," I said. "Get it? A building is, say, eighteenth century. By law it's sacrosanct. But builders want to cram pillboxes on the land for profit. So they secretly weaken the structure. The building becomes unsafe. In the interests of public safety, the council hires a builder—usually a most sincere friend—to destroy the lovely house, and everybody's happy, no?"

"But that's dishonest," Dr. Pryor said, frowning.

My headaches usually come on when honesty raises its head. You can only keep going. "The dishonesty is that the kingdom has lost a priceless treasure."

"But how can you buy every brick, Lovejoy?"

I thought, I honestly don't believe this. "Because," I said, as if to a child, "I've a builder of my own who'll remove this turret section before crooked councillors and cretinoidal NHS administrators can."

"But won't they notice?" He was all on edge. "And what can your builder do with a load of old bricks and beams?"

"Doc," I said, several headaches now rattling my skull. "Promise you'll never become an antique dealer. Okay?"

Gerald was grinning. "Mrs. Hampson's son is on again."

"Tell him to go to hell." The old saint explained, "Wretched man won't accept that his mother's fit to come home."

We left Gerald cheerily relaying the rebukes. "Play your cards right, doc," I promised, "and you'll finish up with a solidly rebuilt extension. You may have to ignore a certain amount of activity. Don't ask," I cut him off hurriedly. "Just accept."

"And if we don't?"

"I go to court. Don't worry," I said. "I know the way."

Outside, I checked. The turret windows were the only ones from which you could see over Pittsbury Wood. I left fairly optimistically, wondering which local builder wanted a knighthood.

On the way home I used the reassuring daylight to bump across that track and check Decibel's kennel, just to make sure the dog cakes had gone and not merely been shifted in the police search. I thought, Aha, where are you Boothie? And where's loyal little Decibel? I drove into the village whistling. I was so happy.

13

Women have a knack of all being stupid in exactly the same way. Ever noticed? This somehow frees them from original sin, so they can display infinite variance in everything else. On the other hand, we blokes go total in daftness; our emotional energies are dissipated by being so barmy in so many absorbing patterns that we've nothing left for anything else. Message: Birds are brilliant at the practicalities of life and love, whereas we males haven't a clue.

So you'll imagine my surprise to discover that Margaret Dainty had shelved blame onto me for good old Raymond's failed fiddle. She and I are marvelous friends, in the best way possible. She has that luster in her face you only see in eighteenth-century porcelain. That very luster, the "poor man's silver," which produced that dazzling luminescence, was actually solid platinum—the only metal that truly ensilvers in the kiln (silver itself goes a straw color). Margaret is exactly that lovely. What I don't like is that she protects me against myself, instead of against everybody else.

"Margaret," I said, pleased to have arrived at the Arcade just as she was starting her midday bite—two triangular crispbreads with a millionth of a sardine on each. Plenty of customers were around, taking their time. Always a good sign. In antiques two slow customers are worth ten harriers.

"Kevin," she called. "Get four pasties and some tea." Kevin's the tea lad.

The Arcade's a gauntlet of antique shops. Some are reasonable: Hal Freeman, silversmith; Gillian Ryder, a pretty alleged innocent dealer in Regency furniture; Lily of the woeful countenance and multiple lost lovers; Mannie the clock dealer, who lives on lentils and meals charitably provided by police when he gets done for fiddling social security. And Margaret.

"That's kind, love," I said, sitting on a patchwork dumpty. "Got much genuine stock in?" I was thinking of Suzanne's restaurant.

"Have I, Lovejoy?" she asked.

The chimes were moderate but sincere. I closed my eyes in bliss. "Pity about that secretaire." I nodded to the grand piece that dominated her nook, with its brass and tortoiseshell inlay, parquetry areas on the panels, and a heroic bust on each corner pillar. It looked right, but emitted not a single chime. "Fraud. Somebody been reading up their French *ébéniste* work, eh?"

She grimaced. "I wish you'd been around when I bought it."

Kevin came with the hot pasties. I fell on them, not a pretty sight, but soon I was going to burn through the Eastern Hundreds like a rocket, and there'd be no time for grub. Margaret watched approvingly. Real women get as much satisfaction seeing you eat as you do yourself. I can't understand why. I knew a bird once who lived on tastes, ate hardly enough to keep a sparrow feathered, yet used to work out menus like Watson and Crick planning molecules. Then she'd order, and quietly nick forkfuls, frowning and telling the waiters off while I got on the right side of every plateful. I used to ask her why she never had a proper meal. She just said don't be stupid. Chefs loved her, used to come out and spend ages arguing what kind of sauces with the veal and that. Where was I?

"It's signed JH Riesener, Lovejoy," Margaret protested.

"Spelled right, is it?"

My joke. (Fakers often misspell that most famous name, so always check.) Jean-Henri Riesener was no boring old eighteenth-century cabinetmaker. I'm really fond of him. His master was the great Oeben, a German of wonderful skill who became *ébéniste* to the French king and made *maître* without an apprenticeship. The scandal occurred when Oeben died. Jean-Henri and another workman scrapped over the attractive widow. Riesener won workshop, widow, and the guild mastership. But a good scandal never really lies down. To this day spite snipes in the world of antiques about Riesener. Rumor says that the delectable furniture he made for Marie Antoinette was really Oeben's work; that Riesener's superb mounts were made by Gouthière; that he and Mrs. Oeben were more than good friends; that Oeben was murdered . . .

"Come back, Lovejoy."

"Eh? Oh, aye. Why did you bubble me over Raymond?"

"So they'd arrest you, Lovejoy."

Half a pasty of contemplation later I asked, "Can an erstwhile lover request reasons?"

"So you'd be tried and found guilty, Lovejoy."

Well, consistency's reliable stuff, but this was no joke. She was looking at the floor. "Any particular logic, sunbeam? Be careful how you answer. I might not let you rape me any more."

"So they'd put you in jail, Lovejoy."

That did it. "Of all the frigging nerve!"

"You'd be safe in prison, dear," she pleaded. "And after it was all over I could make Raymond own up so they'd let you go."

See what I mean? Women land you in it, but it's for your own bloody good. "After what's over, for God's sake?"

She'd gone quite pale. I'd have clouted her with the pasty but I was starving.

"Everybody knows it's bad, Lovejoy. Sykes is at the George with his hoodlums. Major Bentham and that horrible Candice have their teeth into you. People dead. Police everywhere . . ."

Then an odd thing. I was so preoccupied I didn't notice the significance of it then. The gray-eyed Enid walked past down the Arcade. And Podge Howarth strolled past simultaneously. He definitely saw her, but they exchanged no sign of affection. Strange, that, because ex-lovers swap glances in a very definite way. In fact I'd swear they barely recognized each other.

"You're best out of it," Margaret was saying. "It's something horrid, darling." She only calls me that when she goes deadly serious, like now. "Evil, rotten. Out there in the woods. Poor George found that out. Then poor Ben Cox. And now Boothie. I want you to keep away."

Would-be helpers slay me. "Seriously?" I asked, going into my doubtful act.

"Seriously, darling. Please."

"Well," I said, doing my very purest persuaded-against-my-will gaze. "If you really think so, love. Only, Sykie and Sir John are—"

"Explain to them," she urged earnestly. "They'll understand."

"Right, love. I'll do what you say." I took her hand.

"Thank you, Lovejoy." Her eyes were brimming. "I'm so certain it's the right thing. I'll tell Big Frank to tell Mr. Ledger we made a mistake."

"Margaret, love," I said, all soulful. "You won't get into trouble?"

"No, darling." She dabbed her eyes. "I'm just so thankful. Bless you."

I struck. "You couldn't run to another pasty, could you, love? Only, I'm a bit peckish."

Ten minutes later I'd sprung from all that dangerous help and into vengeance. I finally raised the question of Lammas with someone who'd know.

"Lammas, Lovejoy?"

Reverend Woking's not a bad vicar, especially for a struggling parish like ours, but he is unnecessarily learned, a real scholiast, when we need somebody homely. For me, I don't mind him. Well, the only priests without faults are saints, and asking the bishop for one of those would be lengthening the odds somewhat, so our village blunders on turning ritual into habit, church observances into folklore. Nobody cares either way.

"Yes, reverend. What's Lammas actually mean?" I already knew, but had to get round to Lize's newspaper cutting somehow.

"Lammas? One of the old festival days. Quite pagan." He has all the hallmarks of the learned pedant: sherry for theology, tea for disputatious parishioners, fruitcake for little literary socials. "The gule of August, from gwyl, Old British language. Means a festival."

"What went on?"

"Oh, quite innocent celebrations." He hesitated with decanter poised, an Edwardian pressed-glass affair I hate. Some ecstatic auntie's ordination present, silly old crab. Why couldn't she have bought him a decent antique?

"Nothing sinister, then?"

"Certainly not." He chuckled, the very idea. "There are certain odd . . . coincidences about the day. Like the sacrificial lamb at York Minster. Folk assume all sorts—lamb-mass, you see, but quite wrong. 'Loaf-mass', really. A special little harvest celebration. Think Pancake Tuesday and you have it."

"About Saint Michael's," I said innocently.

"Saint Michael's?" he queried, just as innocently. The trouble with interrogating a priest is they've had millennia to learn clever replies. His glass refilled. Mine didn't. Some agitation was going on.

"Beyond the stile at Chapel Lane End," I said firmly, to keep him cornered.

"Oh, those old ruins? Good heavens, yes. I'd forgotten about those." He rose, paced, a really amateur send-up of a rector thinking hard. "Saint Michael's church is long since deconsecrated. Quite ploughed under now, I believe."

"The newspaper said somebody started a fire there."

"Tut-tut." He shook his head gravely. "Foolish prank, Lovejoy. All those valuable crops."

"Isn't it," I said. "It was on last Lammas eve."

He gave me quite a good gaze, not at all bad for a lying theologian. "Good heavens."

"And there was another fire. Same ruins. On May Day eve."

"More sherry, Lovejoy?"

"And the day before Candlemas."

"February—let me see—the first, is it?"

"Aye." Him forgetting Candlemas is like Tinker forgetting Derby Day.

"Terrible, terrible. Irresponsible." He did the whole pantomime; the sigh, the dolorous headshake. "It's probably nothing more than young louts, too much time on their hands."

"Only, aren't there the old, er, bad, days? There was something in the newspaper. Witches, the rural tradition . . ."

He laughed merrily. "Lovejoy, you deserve a medal for imaginings! The idea!"

I chuckled along. "Nothing in that Whalley Abbey business, then?"

He tried to look blank. "Whalley Abbey? Isn't that in the north. . . ?"

"Last year's official conference on witchcraft and black magic."

"Oh, that," he countered airily. "A few folklorists."

"A hundred parsons, plus the bishop's exorcist."

"And you suggest that here in dull old East Anglia. . . ? No, Lovejoy." His veteran's gaze met my innocent one. We both went tut-tut. "Mere fanciful foolery. If there was anything serious hereabouts I'd have heard, Lovejoy."

We talked a bit about music for All Saints, then he waved me off. Sir John's car was at the end of my lane as I drove in and Winstanley flagged me down. Sir John was reading the *Financial Times* or some other comic.

"Lovejoy," he announced, "this is irksome."

We agreed for once. I bawled over my clattering engine. "Another pricey visit, Sir John?"

"Don't think it isn't in your account, Lovejoy."

"Well, no news so far about any bronzes."

"I want a written report of your progress tomorrow noon at the latest, Lovejoy."

"Right." I'm cheerful when lying. It's the only time everything's predictable. I made to drive on, knowing he couldn't possibly resist asking.

"Oh, Lovejoy." Such studied casualness.

"Sir John?" I was poisonously hearty.

"That fake." He looked down at me from his monster vehicle, and I swear he actually tried to smile a winning smile. Like a prune with bellywark. "It's my Rembrandt print, isn't it?"

"Is it?"

He swallowed. I was close to being exterminated for insolence. Winstanley dithered in the road. I saw the chauffeur's eyes framed in the mirror. "I've had experts in, Lovejoy."

"Sack them. They're wrong. Your print's great." I gunned my revs to a slow drift. "One antique confirmed every visit, Sir John. At this rate you'll have to live to six hundred and eight to find the dud. Cheers."

"Tomorrow, Lovejoy!" As I chugged off he was leaning out of the window outraged and purple, yelling after me with Winstanley frantically trying to calm him down.

Mrs. Ryan was waiting at the cottage, in a worse fury still. I thought, what the hell, and went forward to give her a hug.

"Darling," I said, exhibiting sincere delight. "I heard you

were here and hurried after you. Come *on*. I don't want to be late."

"Heard? Late?" she said, rage suspended.

"Come *on*, my doowerlink," I urged. "Today's the day I start as your estate manager, isn't it?"

"You mean you're actually. . . ?"

"Of course! I've been looking for you all morning, slow coach." I leapt gaily back into the Ruby. "Race you."

"Wait, Lovejoy. There's something I must explain—"

"See you there, doowerlink." I swept the Ruby round and out. I wondered what an estate manager's pay was. Anything would be an improvement. With Sir John charging me for breathing I didn't know if I could afford one boss, let alone two. Still, I was quite happy, and sang Tallis's "Dies Irae" all the way over to Manor Farm.

Bad choice.

14

". . . All staff to give our new estate manager all possible assistance," Mrs. Ryan ended. We were in the yard, an acre of loaved cobble rimmed by barns.

The assembled mob managed not to break into rapt applause. I got a few nods, and a sly inspection from the females as they dispersed. One was luscious, a dark beauty given to giggles. It's difficult to imagine a woman in working clobber that isn't enticing, aprons, headscarves at the bakery, waitresses, nurses. There's a current vogue for collecting early photographs of working women. In fact photographers in 1875 got so hooked on girl coalface workers in Midland mining villages that . . . Hello, I thought, here's trouble. A young stalwart swaggered out. I'd noticed him hating me while Mrs. Ryan spoke her piece. Obviously displaced lover and/or promotion hopeful.

The diaspora stopped, except for Mrs. Ryan whose nag clopped away with her.

"The new boss, eh?" said Handsome Jack. "Know much about drainage, stetches, tree grafting, insecticides?"

"Not much, no."

"Lovejoy," he said, doing his smirk, "you're an ignorant bugger."

"Correct."

An old gaffer muttered a warning but Handsome Jack wanted a scrap. "He admits it!" The nerk must read the *Boys' Own*, and him a grown feller. He shoved me so I stepped back. He teased laughs from the girls, winking to show there was more subtle wit on the way. "At least old Munting wasn't an idiot." He crunched his knuckles. "I'm Sid Taft, B.Sc. in estate management." The punch line was coming. "Better qualifications than you, Lovejoy—shagging your way to the top."

"You're fired, Taft," I said, and asked the old farmhand who'd tried to make peace, "What was this cretin's job, dad?"

Then I hit Taft in the belly. He doubled with a whoosh, eyes goggling in disbelief. Reluctantly, because I knew it would hurt me, I bashed my fist into his left biceps. He used his next proper breath for a moan as the terrible ache spread through him. Then, with my hand smarting, into his right biceps. He'd be armless for a fortnight.

Nobody else moved so I pulled the antique giant knuckle-duster off my hand, going, "Ouch." They made very few of these heavy Victorian brass objects. It's wide, with a solid brass cylinder thick as a roll of coins. A knife projects four inches from the hypothenar side, but mercifully I hadn't needed that. They're valuable collector's items, especially when stamped with the name of a London ward like this, Cripplegate. It's hellish heavy, stings like hell. Taft was retching, on his knees.

I said, "You've made my hand really sting, pillock. Out. Now." I told two older blokes to get him home.

"What's your name, please, old 'un?"

"Robie, they call me." The wise old man had enjoyed it.

"Set everybody about their proper graft, then find me. I'll be in there having a cuppa, if yonder gossips know how to brew up."

Two elderly women watching from the doorstep of a white-washed building tutted inside as I left everybody to it and went to soak my hand. I felt really narked. I'd come to help Manor Farm. You try to show kindness, and what thanks do you get? I'm a martyr to generosity.

St. Michael's church ruins at Chapel Lane stood a yard proud from the field's contour. I climbed into the rectangular recess where the nave had been. Robie waited in biblical silhouette against the watery sun.

There's something really horrible about ruins. I don't mean the ruins themselves. They're splendid things, evidence of man's creativity. No, I mean what happens after a building has tumbled. Rain works steadily into cracks. Frost splits the stones. Moss slithers with hideous stealth over lovely stonework, and worms undermine. Soon, oblivion. All that remains is a paler shadow cast from the setting sun, a taller ring of standing wheat, an obscure legend. It isn't that lovely time-enrichment that ages women. With ruins it's sinister. I looked about.

"This on our farm, Robie?"

"Yes. Angel Field, it's called. Used to be good grazing land afore government subsidies."

"Who was Angel?"

He spat in derision. "Them as fly, you silly sod."

I'd not seen many hereabouts. "Why did the church finish?"

He nodded at remembered history. "My grandfather's day. Folk didn't like it. Still don't."

There was a black smudge against the old altar stones. East? I glanced around, trying to work out the way of the world. I'm no good at directions. They change too often for my liking. Now, you can't burn stone. And if they'd wanted to burn the crops they'd have started their fire outside the recess, right? Stupid vandals, or practiced nonvandals? I peered over at the field. Chapel Lane's copses and hedgerows were dark against the sky.

Beyond lay the village, my cottage's fawn thatch one of the distant cluster.

"Does Manor Farm get a lot of trouble from vandals, Robie?"

"Not much. There's ramblers. Them nature folk. Them . . ." He'd been about to jerk his head left toward the wood, but had stopped himself. "Poachers," he said.

He'd been going to say somebody else. Ta, Robie.

Up out of the ruins and we started for the edge of the field. This side, the estate boundary followed the river. On the far right the countryside descended in pallor toward the sea. Left, the trees shuffled close and became Pittsbury Wood.

"Wasn't it there some nerk saw a UFO?"

Robie chuckled. "Aye. Spaceship from Mars. They'm barmy."

"But nice countryside, eh, Robie?" I said.

"Some say," he answered. Silently I completed the old soldier's cynical rejoinder for him: *And others tell the truth.*

We trudged an hour, along paths by field margins, through thickets, across brooks. Old Robie led by the field where Charleston the bull stood frowning, then Little Tom Field where his herd ripped grass. The wood was always at our shoulder. Funny, but it made me uneasy. I felt as if the bloody thing was turning, watching us as we passed. Robie said nothing, except occasionally giving the names of fields.

"Dry Wells, good grazing. Yonder's Stonebreak, a bad wheat but good barley."

"What's in it?" It looked like wheat.

He spat. "Wheat, o'course. Subsidy." We eventually coursed round Billiam's patch at Ramparts Corner, to Pittsbury Wood, to the old gravel pits. At the top of the long slope was a dew pond. A few village lads have illicit swims in it. We'd done the whole perimeter.

The White Hart providentially crossed our path. Robie drank bitter, me anything wet.

"Eleven fields, Robie. All growing wrong stuff."

"Aye." He kept filling his pipe with black shag. "Government, Lovejoy. They pays us to grow daft."

"Could we make a profit, if we grew, er, not daft?"

"Maybe in part."

Food for thought. I rose to the bar for Robie's refill. Ted the barman had a million messages. Tinker was looking for me. Sandy and Mel had swept through in twin tempers. Big Frank wanted me urgently. Rowena Ray said please phone. Ledger had been in, smiling; ominous because nobody likes a happy bobby except in songs. Billiam Cutting, my writer friend, had asked for me urgently. Helen of the exquisite legs was in and waved to me with her fagholder, all symbolism. Liz Sandwell glowered punitively from the saloon bar—what had I done now? Margaret Dainty limped over to show me a faded box.

"Christmas crackers, Lovejoy. Dated. Hand-colored."

Robie watched me take her box. Ladies in bonnets, coaches, and Little Nell shops in the background. The six crackers were bleached by time—not much time, of course. The name of a Covent Garden printer adorned the label, 1840.

I said reluctantly, "Change the date to 1870 and you'll pass them off."

"Fake? Oh, dear." She sat despairingly.

"Christmas crackers were invented, love. They didn't grow like holly. Tom Smith did it, all on his little lone, 1847 or so."

"Oh, Lovejoy." She didn't quite fill up, but it was close. "We're going through a bad patch, aren't we?"

"Rubbish. There's always a good side." The bloody crackers couldn't sue me, for one. "George Manners in Brightlingsea'll alter the date for you, but he's an expensive old devil. Promise him a percentage."

"Thank you, Lovejoy." She paused for the woman's exit line. "Are you all right?"

"Fine, babbylink."

And there she went, all the grace of the older woman and

honest as the day is long. I knew she'd label her antique box, "Uncertain Date." Honesty's a nuisance.

Robie said sourly. "Too nice a lady to be in your trade, Lovejoy. It's all money."

"Like farming?" I said innocently, making him snort.

Yet he had a point. Greed. Money. It called to mind Sir John and the stealthy Winstanley. Money motivated Sykie. And Mrs. Suzanne York? And Mrs. Ryan? And the killer of George, Ben Cox, the attempted murder of old Boothie? I thought I'd hit on something.

"Robie," I said, watching him. "Was Manor Farm profitable?"

He harrumphed like old country men do, setting his head bouncing. "Not these ten years, son, since Mrs. Ryan owned it."

Ownership of Manor Farm a tax dodge? My anxiety eased. Greed's great. I love it. I mean, it's the banker's vitamin. It's erythrocytes to the vampire, the company man's throb for promotion. And in antiques it's that enzyme that makes swains of us all.

"All greed coincides somewhere." I'd said it aloud before I realized Robie was listening. No chatterbox, but not dim.

Money's odd stuff. It changes all the time, yet doesn't, if you follow. For instance, King Edward III actually bought Chaucer out of a French prison for sixteen pounds, whereas you'd not get a flyleaf from the original *Canterbury Tales* for that now. And all these would-be-rich women were too much for me, clouding the problems. So different, such extremes.

Sitting there, staring into the taproom fire, it was hard to see a pattern. One important thing: Brainy women are sensible, whereas brainy men are daft. Take the brilliant Mrs. Aphra Behn, for example. She reigned as the society hostess of seventeenth-century London while writing best-sellers—sensibly keeping up appearances, because she was the secret head of Charles II's spy ring. See what I mean?—a brainy woman's sensible. Yet Count Tolstoy's idea of a secret pilgrimage was to dress as a peasant—and have servants walking behind lugging suitcases of clean linen. See? Brainy but barmy.

Lesson: Either some clever woman was being sensible, or some brainy bloke was being daft. I cleared my throat to speak, but Robie got in first as Ted called time.

"What is all this, Lovejoy, you being manager?"

"Exactly," I said. "Words out of my mouth."

On our way back, two of our men were mending a fence by the old gravel pits. Robie swore some foul oath.

"Bloody fence been sliced again," one yelled across the pits. "Every sodding week."

It was the damage Lize had reported in the newspaper.

A Land Rover bounced across the field. Good old Major Bentham. I stepped nearer the edge of the gravel pit ready to take a dive if he drove at me. These pits are giant hollows filled with water. Anglers drown worms in them for hours at a time.

"What the hell are you doing here, Lovejoy?" He stepped down glaring. I'd never known a bloke like him for glaring.

"Keeping trespassers out," I said, "so sod off."

He hesitated. He wasn't practiced in hesitancy, so it took some time. Our fence-menders stopped work.

"You all right, sir?" one asked me.

"Ta," I called, eyes on the major. That "sir" was embarrassing for me, but worse for Bentham.

"I'm on my way to Councillor Ryan's," he said.

"Across our land? You're not. Never darken my moor again, varlet."

He went white. Blokes like him are the very opposite of transcendental meditation.

"Right, Lovejoy," he got out. "Right."

His exit was predictable—into the vehicle, an ugly swing nearly sending me and Robie flying, and across our field anyway. Mister Macho.

I said so long to the men and went down the footpath. "Who breaks the fence, Robie?"

"Village children. Lovers wanting quiet. Them poachers."

Still not telling, eh? Kids were possible but unlikely. Lovers, no because gravel pits are dangerous. Poachers, never in a million years.

We made the main drive to see Bentham and Councillor Ryan chatting amiably before the big house. The major said something after a glance our way and Ryan laughed. A clue? Well, it would have been but I'm thick so it went begging. I went and chatted up the giggly bird in the greenhouses. She was planting little plants in pots, a waste of time with all these fields lying about.

Late that afternoon Mrs. Ryan oh-so-accidentally met me as I left my grand office. This was a frightening shambles of files and charts with a pleasant plump woman, Mavis, hoping vainly for me to set tasks.

"Lovejoy. How was your first day?"

"Fine, ta," I said, smiling. She's so tiny that you talk to her crown unless you crouch a bit. She was wearing a pocket skirt of heavy flared material, a high-neck blouse, and a gathered jacket. She looked good enough to eat.

"You approve, darling?" she asked quietly.

"Sorry. Er, yes." I coughed. Ryan was on the terrace having a smoke. I said loudly for his benefit, "Er, well, Mrs. Ryan, I've been going over the, er, greenhouse work and the winter barley accounts." I hadn't, but still.

"Where do you think you're going, Lovejoy?" Still quietly.

"Eh? Home."

"The estate manager's house is your home."

"Ah, well, yes. I know that." I was thinking, God. Live here? "I'm going for my, er, things."

She smiled and the trap closed. "You haven't any things,

Lovejoy, except the clothes you stand up in." She lowered her voice further. "I'll settle you in."

"Right. Back about seven, Mrs. Ryan," I said loudly. "Once I've switched my electric off."

"And I'll be here to . . . receive you." Her eyelashes were long fans black on her cheeks. Truly lovely. I groaned a mental groan. Is there no end to sacrifice?

Which escape gave me time to meet Squadron Leader Edding about a UFO, and to be accosted by a naturalist about a daffodil, or something.

15

"Lovejoy. You are becoming tiresome." Sir John stood while I packed. Winstanley hovered. He cast about for somewhere to sit, then didn't. The place admittedly was a mess. He reeled at the spectacle of my kitchen alcove crammed with unwashed crockery. "This mess disgusts me, Lovejoy."

"Then don't come." My spare underpants weren't quite dry, but I'd have to sort that problem later. Into the bag they went. I was really ready, except for my old-fashioned nightshirt for when it's perishing—pyjamas are modern rubbish—but I wasn't going to rummage for that while he was here. He'd love a laugh at my expense. "The news is I'm still investigating."

"Lovejoy." I paused while he gauged me. Here it came, to-day's deliberate mistake. "It's my Etruscan mirror that's the fake, isn't it?"

"Is it?" I said, all innocence. "Well, they make superb reproductions in Florence." The Borgo San Jacopo's at the wrong end of the Ponte Vecchio, and down there they turn out "Etruscan" bronzes like Ford cars—horses, mirrors, figurines, rings. They'll even add that patina of long-buried bronzes while you wait, believe it or not.

Sir John made a gagging noise. I watched, interested, then guessed right: anger. "You'll pay for this sadism, Lovejoy!"

"What with?" I called as the door slammed. Bloody nerve.

Toffee was getting fed up with all this coming and going. I loaded up her blanket and took her to Henry. She was welcomed like a sailor.

"Oh, I'm so glad, Lovejoy!" Eleanor cried. "They really love each other."

"Oh, aye?" The big greeting seemed to consist of Henry yanking Toffee's fur in handfuls, and Toffee chinning Henry's tufty little head. Henry ogled and puffed. Toffee purred.

"That it?" I asked, disappointed.

"Aren't they lovely together?" She was all misty.

"Great. Just see they survive, okay?"

All three gave me assurances, differently phrased. I drove to Nettleholme at an exhilarating 14 mph, the wind being slightly against. By seven I was telling a skeptical sentry that I had an appointment.

"No, sir," the sentry told the phone distastefully when it asked. "He's civilian."

Well, I've been called worse.

Edding was a calm man, unsurprisable. Good schooling skillfully concealed in light banter. His type never ages beyond forty-five or needs spectacles. They have several hobbies at which they excel, speak Swahili and Serbo-Croat. They quote Dr. Johnson.

"It's that UFO business, eh?" Edding smiled.

"Over Pittsbury Wood way, yes."

"That what it's called?" He relaxed in his swivel chair, feet up. I wasn't taken in. This bloke knew the map coordinates to a square inch, playing ignorance his game. "What date was it?" He called for a file. "Never understand these bloody forms," he said, not really looking, then chucking the file aside as a bad job. "Well, we sent up a kite on recce."

"Is a kite still an airplane?"

He grinned, no offense intended. "Sorry. Slang." He grew wistful. "They took the old Hawker Hunters off us. Never could lift the bloody nose, but lovely old bag. We have these new Harrier things. The lads love 'em, o' course."

"See anything?"

"Not a sausage, I'm afraid. A UFO's always good for a laugh. The lads love a scramble."

"How far did they search?"

"Oh, Orford Ness. Then inland to Huntingdon, give or take a furlong. Flight leader reckoned it was just the lighthouse."

"Was the area put under military surveillance?"

Another disarming grin. He had a pub pianist's cheerfulness: Don't take any of my stuff seriously, folks, I'm not Franz Listz. "True and untrue, Lovejoy. The public like an official response."

"What response exactly?"

He didn't quite stifle a yawn, but his reply was that level of intensity. "Oh, a couple of land vehicles. It pleased the maiden aunties and the UFO fanatics along the route." Feet off the desk, a casual chuck of the file to me. "Read the report if you like."

A bloke named Harold Ayliffe, thirty-two, address in Bures, Suffolk, had phoned in a sighting, a sky glow settling in the woods soon after 2:00 A.M. He was a photographer, trying to snap a badger at its night prowl. Naturally he had run out of film.

Edding said, "You'll know it's confidential, being Manor Farm's estate manager?"

"Of course." I thanked him as he saw me out. "So nothing I need worry about, eh? You can understand my anxiety."

"Quite. A good sound recce," he said, pleased. "Invaluable.

One thing might help, Lovejoy. Post a man or two round that wood for a few nights. Keep control."

"Good idea." I knew there'd be a full transcript of our conversation, plus a photograph of me, at their next security briefing, but that was okay. I drove off with an inner smile.

Harold Ayliffe, wildlife photographer, was the name of that cyclist who'd hurt himself on the river bridge. Queerer and odderer. Harold was probably a moonspender. I'll bet I know who his girlfriend was, too.

One thing I always get wrong is people, who they really are, what they're after. Not just women but men as well. Maybe that's why I play a daft game. It goes: With that name, what sort of bloke is he going to be? I visualized Ayliffe on the way to the clinic, and decided he'd be cheerful, with a natty taste in suiting.

Wrong.

The clinic sister showed me a morose, tubby middle-ager floundering in a plunge. Six or seven other patients splashed in aquatic disarray, to an old Biederbecke record. I noticed they were all at one end. Ayliffe with his gammy leg exercised at the other. The place echoed, its tiles giving watery ripples of reflection.

"I've got a bad leg too," I told the sister. "Can I join?"

She laughed. "After the surgeon's set it you can."

Some days you get no cooperation. "Are all nurses shapely, or is it your starchy apron just breasts you out?"

"Cheek."

Ayliffe gave a sort of derision. "You'll get nowhere with her, mate," he said. "She's a cruel bitch."

"You contaminated down this end?" I asked.

"Them miserable buggers," was all he'd say about his isolation. "What you after, besides her?"

"Nothing much, Harold." I was urbanity itself. "I dig any old thing, if you know what I mean." He grunted, but maybe from exertion, holding on to the edge and frog-kicking. "Sorry you got hurt, incidentally." It was all supposition, but a nocturnal angler/cyclist/wildlife enthusiast rolled into one was too much. Therefore he was a moonspender, maybe even the one that killed people. He slowed, looking up at me. The physio lass hand-clapped, exhorting her gasping shoal to think they were beautiful dolphins, poems of motion. Silly cow.

Ayliffe checked she'd momentarily forgotten him, then said, low, "I said nothing. Tell the councillor. Honest. I only reported a UFO—"

I crouched down. "—to the authorities to protect yourself. Harold, we know."

Agony seeped into his gaze, nothing to do with exercising. "Put in a word, mate. Only I was scared they'd top me for treasure-hunting at the wrong time."

"Well." I shrugged helplessly. "I'll give it a try, Harold." I rose, trying for a bit of George Raft threat. "But the big man's had me appointed Mrs. Ryan's estate manager, to ensure there's no repetition."

"Honest, mate. I said nothing. He knows that." His head-jerk pulled me closer. "The same goes for my bird."

Proof, lovely proof. On the way out I chatted the sister up and asked her if she had any old stethoscopes, doctors' lamps, any of those gruesome tools in her storeroom. I promised her clinic's welfare fund three percent of the profit. She said seventy—that's seven oh—percent. Laughing, she came down to fifty. Bitter, I concurred and left disgruntled at the cynicism of women. I'm really fed up with lost innocence. There's too much of it around.

The white post on the river bridge showed one miserable scratch, that's all. No, it hadn't been repainted. Also, you'd have to be on the wrong side of the road to hit it when coming from the alleged direction. Bad planning, Harold. While manking about with the clinic sister, I'd asked after Ayliffe's lady. The sister said Enid visited Mr. Ayliffe almost every day. Enid. I was right. The admissions girl gave me Ayliffe's address. By the time I reached the village I knew more about Harold than his dad did.

Farms are quiet at night, but I clattered up in my old Ruby with all the gentility of rush hour. I was thinking women, but not because I'm a rabid luster; I mean to say, all the scrapes I get into are women's fault, not mine. It was just that Sid Taft B.Sc. (Est. Man.) had got it right. Mrs. Ryan didn't employ a scruffy antique dealer to run the estate from altruism. So my noise was a useful adjunct, because I badly wanted to plumb Mrs. Ryan's depths, so to speak, in solitude. My mating call, courtesy of the extinct Austin firm of motor makers.

She was there, talking in the yard. Two stable girls called good nights as I arrived.

"Ah, Lovejoy," she called loudly, as if I'd lurked. "Did Mrs. Benedict show you to your house? No?" She added, forestalling any troublesome independence, "I'll walk you over." Mrs. Benedict was farm cook.

The estate manager's place was set obliquely behind the manor house. By a lucky fluke Mrs. Ryan had the key. She went ahead, switching lights on: "And there's a built-in cupboard . . ." sort of thing, all for a chance eavesdropper's benefit. I tried to interrupt, daft because I'd only my canvas bag. Mrs. Ryan shushed me, not looking, pursing her lovely mouth. "Walls have ears, darling," she whispered, then loudly: "The upstairs bathroom is . . ." I followed meekly. That Walls Have Ears poster from World War II is worth a fortune, mint. Dillon's do dangerously good copies.

"There, Lovejoy!" We were in the bedroom. Her eyes were bright, her tiny figure poised. "Satisfied?" Pause. We drew breath to speak, didn't. "Isn't this where you offer me a drink, Lovejoy?"

"I've got none, love."

"The downstairs bureau." She extinguished the lights and marched away. She seemed exasperated.

She said with asperity as we settled carefully in opposite arm-chairs, "The farm staff will observe that we are having a living-room talk about your duties over a welcoming drink, Lovejoy."

"Er, about duties, Mrs. Ryan."

She crossed her legs, enjoying herself. A foot dangled its shoe, a slight high-heeled affair with one aslant strap. And a slimming dark blue fitted velvet dress. Was this how ladies strolled farmyards? "Don't you know those, darling?"

"Well, er, there's an orchard I haven't seen. And cultivated blackberries." Asparagus was also rumored to be beavering away out here, hard at it.

"The estate, Lovejoy?" She spoke dismissively. The subject bored, enterprise could go to the dogs.

"What'll Councillor Ryan say if we go broke?"

My worried words prized her eyes wider. "He concurs, darling."

"And Sid Taft, God's gift to agriculture?"

She stretched with delicious enjoyment. "Need you have damaged him, darling?"

"Yes. Do I meet Councillor Ryan?" I'm so resolute.

Her glass was empty. "Not yet a while, darling." She rose, carefully not glancing at the window's parted curtains. "You, ah, meet his wife instead—in the large bedroom. No lights."

"Look, Mrs. Ryan," I tried. "I'm scared of bankrupting your estate. Shouldn't we talk over a plan of action?"

"What a good idea," she murmured. She didn't break step on her way upstairs.

Getting on for ten o'clock that night I was explaining over a leisurely pint with Tinker. The estate manager bit set him off coughing. He ended on crescendo, hawking phlegm into a spent mug. Two ladies over by the log fire went green and reeled out. The old devil glued himself together, wiping his stubble on his grease-stained mitten, his rheumy old eyes streaming merriment.

"Great, Lovejoy!" he graveled out between cackles "Keep shagging her arse off and we can take Ryan to the cleaners!" He has this elegant turn of phrase.

"No, Tinker. I'm there to get out of being sued. And because of what you're going to tell me."

Once he starts grumbling he never stops, the miserable old sod. "Everybody is chiseling the estate, Lovejoy. It won't last long."

"Eh?" That made me all ears. The sly old wretch saw he'd miraculously scored a point and gazed piteously into his glass. I flagged Ted to keep them coming. "You mean go bust?"

He scratched, rose to reach his fresh pint over. A sickening slurp, a fetid gasp, and he was ready. God, he was a mess. "Everybody knows that."

I gaped at him. "Do they?"

"'Course. Old Munting said it often, miserable bugger." His criticism probably meant that my predecessor was too wily to be fooled by staff or poachers. Or employers? Tinker cackled reminiscently. "Always having rows with Ryan hisself."

"How did he die, Tinker?"

He stared at me, then his small frame convulsed in its disheveled greatcoat. I waited impatiently. A laugh usually takes a minute, then two more for coughs. Then another minute to roll a fag with one of those hand machines that never work, though the early prototypes are collectible items. You can still get them for nothing; folk chuck them out.

"Lovejoy." Billiam slid into the seat next to Tinker with a waft of turpentine, a shopsoiled rainbow. Between literary masterpieces he does portraits on oil paper. They're pathetic. "Caught you."

"You heard about Boothie?" I asked. "And I'm sorry about your pal Cox."

He was on edge, fidgety. "Yes. I'm scared, Lovejoy. First George Prentiss. Then Ben. Now Booth. Lovejoy, Ramparts Corner's miles from anywhere." It's not really, but I knew what he meant.

"Sorry, Bill, but what the hell can I do?"

"You're the estate manager. Send a couple of blokes. My ground rent's paid to the estate."

"Hang on." My brain whirred as logic entered in. "Your house? On the estate, like Boothie's?"

"Since before the Conquest," Billiam said scathingly.

"Look, Billiam. I'm in enough trouble. Send farmhands to hold your hand? They'd laugh me off the place."

"Only . . ." Billiam jumped in panic as the taproom door crashed open and a noisy mob of football lads shoved in. "Lovejoy, I'm too feared. I might clear off."

"Very wise, Billiam." He was making me feel uneasy. I didn't want the population thinned round Pittsbury Wood. I wanted more allies, even loony writers like him.

"I'll remember this, Lovejoy." He left, blaming me.

But what could I do? I was at least as scared as him. "I'm back, Tinker," I said. "The joke being. . . ?"

"How old Munting died." He struck a match and fired his latest creation. I leant away from the carcinogens. "Munting's playing darts behind you, Lovejoy. He'll miss double twenty."

My astonishment set him off falling about. I turned and inspected the thickset elderly man on his last arrow. A pipe-smoker in an Aran, twill trousers.

He missed double top, like Tinker said.

Tinker's last watering hole is the Stranded Barque on East Hill, where they drink longer after their legal closing time than before it. I ran him over there in the Ruby as he finished his report.

"It's funny, Lovejoy. There's no local things."

"Why not?"

"Dunno. Word is Sykie or somebody's soaking it up. And everybody's shifty-scared." He hawked, spat at the gutter, reached only to the half-door. He blotted the phlegm with his sleeve.

At least I could make the farm lads give the Ruby a good clean tomorrow. "Odd we never noticed it." I pulled in at the pub.

"Not really, Lovejoy. There's plenty of antiques about. It's only local stuff that's gone missing." He meant that new finds were vanishing before sale. "It's like . . ." his alcohol-soaked mind searched for analogy . . . "like we lived in Australia, somewhere the bleeding Romans, old Brits, and them never got to." He hawked again. I elbowed him out onto the pavement to narrow the dirty old devil's range. He graveled, spat, missed. "Odd, seeing everybody in the Eastern Hundreds is out moonspending all frigging hours. Know what I think, Lovejoy?" He blinked up at me in the street light, his tatty old beret askew.

"No. What?"

"I reckons somebody's got everybody nobbled."

From Tinker this was Napierian logarithms. "But who's got that much gelt?"

"Aye. True." He sighed a thirsty sigh. I shelled out a note.

"Keep sussing, Tinker. Bronzes, iron, anything. Get into yon boozer and start ferreting."

He squared his shoulders and said, a real martyr, "Right, Lovejoy."

Toffee had gone to kip when I arrived at Henry's, but I collected her on principle. Cats and farms seem to go together in nursery rhymes. Why not in real life?

When I phoned the White Hart Sandy and Mel were in. I told them to redesign the exterior of Suzanne York's grand restaurant in Victorian Gothic decorative brickwork. I cut short Sandy's squeals of delight, and had an important think—my last resort. Came midnight and Councillor Ryan's big Rolls hadn't returned to the big house, so as an act of self-preservation I shut everything off and drove home to my cottage. I had too many plans on the front burner to risk Ryan catching his missus and me in Position One. A lucky decision, this, because an early visitor called in defense of all living things. She excluded me, quite typical.

16

The telly went off about one in the morning, leaving its hypnotic little dot whining away. I brewed up, put the radio on. A chap talking nineteen to the dozen over pop music, never letting records run full length.

Once Toffee had settled I was restless. The novel I'd got from our library van—no mean feat—proved dull, full of CIA and KGB, big themes in limerick. I nodded off. It slipped from my grasp. Toffee raised her head irritably at the thud. I sang, "Jesu, Joy of Man's Desiring" but got the pitch wrong and finished up breathless and annoyed before the end. Then Mrs. Ryan returned, which made me breathless and annoyed before the beginning, as it were. She left in great stealth about three o'clock, saying things like Oh God, do I have to return to that and so on, the usual, which is time-consuming and unproductive but par for the course. I made the necessary rejoinder, Be careful, doowerlink, and till tomorrow, switart. My lips felt a foot thick from work soreness. Night tea needs sugar, I find. Daytime tea can do without. Odd, that. I ought to ask Doc Lancaster if I'd made a fantastic medical discovery, but he's a bad-tempered swine who wants me to exercise. He smokes and drinks like a fish.

I thought some more. What did I have?

George Prentiss, electrician, feeble collector, and scared of the dark, is gored to death in a field. He carries a cheap erotic book. Enter Ben Cox, archeologist. He's worried sick about his county being robbed blind of its treasures, especially ancient bronzes. In particular, a Roman feline. He gets done; his matchbox office is pillaged.

Meanwhile, back home, that wise poacher Tom Booth is found query dead, query. And vanishes. I get the blame—normal, since Ledger blames me for solar eclipses and weather. Leaving aside various impending lawsuits, and the minor problem of Billiam's terror at Rampart Corner, Mrs. Ryan's tiring need of me as estate manager, Councillor Ryan's financial fiddling, and Rowena's forthcoming marriage to Big Frank, there was the problem of me. Because I figured in the bad bits.

For example Sir John and Sykie, that lopsided partnership of equity and the beast, who shared interests in local archeological finds. I was the link in the chain there, for reasons Sykie'd explained. That's the trouble with rich collectors—sooner or later they have to trust somebody. Sir John had decided to trust Sykes, the London antiques middleman, who of course would be amply paid after each deal. Sykie I know is not a bad bloke inside. He simply thinks double. I'm just glad he's not a politician. In this fiasco, Sir John was the mark, the one who'd get rooked, and Sykie would be that much richer. Simple, no?

Certainly, if you forget George, Cox, and Boothie, RIP cubed. The rest—Rowena's decision to be Mrs. Big Frank VIII, Suzanne York's posh caff, my current battle with Goldie of telly quiz fame—could hardly be blamed on the local yokels. Equally, I thought with feeling, they weren't my bloody fault either.

Having sorted out absolutely nothing, I read Clark on civilisation. He always cheers me up, because he gives top marks to Erasmus, my hero. Now, there was a bloke who was always troubled by localities—I mean having to leave Holland because the Dutch were always boozed blotto, flitting about England and Europe one breathless step ahead of the black death. I knew how he felt. No longer alone, I slept the sleep of the just.

When gray-eyed Enid called, six-thirty, I was up feeding the robin.

It was one of those windswept days. Today women's stocking seams would be askew, their hair uncontrollable. Men would realize for the first time that they could no longer bear the chill. All football teams would lose seven-nil.

"That's wrong," Enid said, sitting on my wall.

"Feeding the robin?" I was amazed. "He'd starve."

"There's worms. We must maintain nature's balance."

"Ah, well. I'm weaning him off worms. Tea's up."

A minute later, her hands were round a hot mug. I sat in the porch out of the gale.

She was an open, rather dreamy looker. Today's mode was jeans, muddy boots still ruined by blackened leaves at the welt, and a hooded duffle. The frontier image. A stoned doll dressed as Trapper Jim.

Irritably I moved the milk. Speedy Gonzales had slipped in and neatly drilled the foil cap. "Blue tits," I explained. What with the robin, the spadges, Speedy, and the morose Enid, it promised a spirit-sapping day.

"You visited my Harold. You're the new estate manager?" A blackbird came ascrounging, perched on my shoulder. I like him, but he sings down your earhole. I'll be deaf that side before I'm much older. "We need your help."

Toffee emerged to coil round my ankle. She'll do anything for warmth. "As long as it doesn't lead to a lawsuit." Enid did her opal stare. "I've had a few bad encounters lately."

She nodded understandingly. "Those fox-hunters. We believe you're empathic to our cause." Toffee leapt on my other side. Blackbird on one shoulder, black cat on my other; no wonder Enid looked apprehensive.

"What you want me to do, love?"

"Keep intruders away from the retreats."

I looked my question: What the hell's a retreat?

"Places where wild flowers grow, where we gather and ritualize. Do you know that the world is exterminating ten species a day?" These statistics slide off me like snow from a duck. She grew vehement. "It's your duty to protect Pittsbury Wood and Earth Mother, Lovejoy!"

Toffee raised herself, arching and hissing. Mildly I looked about. Usually she only does that for dogs. I told her to shut it. She subsided but stared at Enid with undisguised hate. Well, females never hit it off. "How?" I asked Enid.

"Put your gamekeepers round the perimeter. We've had birds' egg collectors, nature photographers, badger-hunters, all sorts of predators."

Everybody suddenly wants me to post guards round the countryside. I'd only been gaffer a day.

"Look," I said, deliberately goading to suss her out. I just didn't believe in Enid, not after finding she was Harold Ayliffe's bird. "There's only two gamekeepers. I'm no saint, Enid—"

"Saint?" She was suddenly bitter, furious. "Saints, Lovejoy? If women were Devil's Advocate no saint would ever be beatified—"

Toffee sprang down and raked Enid's hand, spitting. Blood started along Enid's skin in parallel lines. Enid yelped and rose. Toffee streaked onto the wall clawing Enid's neck. Enid screamed, recoiling with blood everywhere. Toffee was all ready for another go but I yelled her name angrily. She returned at smug stroll, quite unfazed.

"Gormless moggie," I said, threatened her. She sniffed my fist. "I'll thump you. Sorry, Enid. She's never done that before, not even with field mice. Toffee, no breakfast for that. Burke."

Toffee licked her paws. I'd never seen her so satisfied. She knows I've not the heart not to feed her. Like all women she takes advantage. Enid was staring at Toffee, at me.

She said, "Doesn't she attack them?" She meant the chiselers currently eating me out of house and home.

"The birds are friends." It came out before I realized. "Er, Enid. One thing. Tell me about George." She halted at my words, cast a gray glance. She was still blotting her neck and hands.

"George is dead." Words flat as a board.

"Then use the past tense."

"George was nothing to do with us. He should have stayed at home. Like the rest of them."

What a lot of plurals. I watched her go, out through the gap in the hedge and up the lane, a small indomitable figure. I fed Earth Mother's assorted scroungers, then had my fried bread and drove to work. I took the aerial photos Vanessa had delivered, to examine when I had a minute.

At the manor house Councillor Ryan was alone having his breakfast, a runny egg with Worcester sauce. His thickened mottled face revealed what his shape did not, nights of council arguments and the big-belly lunches. I swear the years fell off him when I entered.

"'Morning, Lovejoy. Settled in?"

"Yes, sir."

He beckoned me in and gave me his wife's coffee cup. I stood. "Good to see you. Problems?"

"No, sir. An offer."

His hand stilled, slowly lowered the coffee pot. It was Royal Doulton, Edwardian vintage but pristine. Sensible spending, that. A real antique set costs a fortune. As things stand, you can easily make up an oldish Wedgwood or Royal Doulton set for a quarter of the price of new.

"Money, Lovejoy?" He thrilled to the possible.

"No, sir. Money plus prestige."

He laughed then, shaking his head. "No, no, Lovejoy. Prestige *costs* money."

"Make a profit my way, and you'll be near a knighthood."

"Knighthood? For a confidence trick, Lovejoy?"

His coffee was great, but then I've no culinary record to compare. "Your building firm at Seven Elm Green."

"Yes. It's an honest business."

With colossal exercise of will power I didn't guffaw. "Transfer some brickwork from Point A to Point B and you'll rescue a health unit from closure."

"Who pays?" He knew the unit I meant.

"Point B." Well, cross that bridge.

He lit a fag and thoughtfully polluted the dining room. "Sit down, Lovejoy. Have you had your breakfast?"

"No," I lied, settling down near the toast. "Thanks. This is it: Set your brickies dismantling the unit's exterior while repairing the interior damage. A, er, man called Sandy will organize its reinstallation elsewhere. I've already arranged the finance. Payment on the nail."

"What guarantee, Lovejoy?"

"My job," I said. "You're the boss, not me."

"True." He blew a smoke noose, watching me. "Do you always eat that hungry, Lovejoy?"

"Eh? I didn't think you wanted your eggs." He'd invited me for breakfast, for God's sake.

"Is it worth a press announcement, Lovejoy?"

"No." I get narked by little coffee cups, hardly a swig in the damned things. "I've a friend runs the *Advertiser*. After it's done we accidentally leak to the press . . ." I hesitated. Mrs. Ryan was there in the doorway being amazed at the spectacle of spouse and lover noshing a merry repast. "We don't mention your profit." I rose. "Morning, Mrs. Ryan. Forgive the intrusion."

She swept in. "Stay, Lovejoy. There's much to discuss."

"Right," I said, sadly scanning the bare plates. She rang for more grub. Ryan was due at the town hall, which meant I'd be able to refuel in peace, so to speak. I smiled at him when he rose and said yes, stay and finish.

"If you're sure, sir," I said obediently.

About black magic, superstition, witchcraft.

I'm not at all superstitious. I never get spooked. No, honestly. It was just coincidental that I decided to broach these questions in broad daylight. I got the Ruby parked in the tangle of motors that thrombose the shopping mall and made Moran's Music Shop in good time.

Not many two-manual harpsichords play during working hours, so the music led me to Dorothy, my favorite witch. Actually I don't know any others, but even if I did she'd be a contender. You know what I mean. Dorothy is Moran's resident musical talent, strings and keyboard, to pull the crowd.

"John Dowland?" I guessed. She plays in the foyer, forever complaining about the cold.

"A pavan from his *Lachrymae*, Lovejoy." Dorothy is always dreamy, playing. The passion's always a Dowland giveaway, like lust in John Donne's religious poems.

"Lovely, Dorothy." I scanned the crowd, maybe twenty people. Not the right time for confidences about black magic.

Dorothy could see my expression in the window glass, and gracefully improvised a coda to the pavan. Her instrument was a kit assembly, based on an early seventeenth century Flemish maker called Ruckers. New, it costs half the price of a new car.

"Break time, folks," I announced, shuffling people into the street. They clapped a bit, moved out. Her jealous husband Les glowered from the side window. I grinned and pulled the chain so his roller shutter descended on his distress.

"About witchcraft, Dorothy. You still one?"

"Are you serious, Lovejoy?" She was curious but muted her voice. "What on earth are you asking things like that for?"

"Are you. . . ?" What the hell do you call a witch? Do they go in leagues, like football? . . . "you all the same, love?"

Passing shoppers gazed into the foyer. I pretended to be a sober harpsichord purchaser. If Ledger heard I was boning up on witchcraft in the High Street he'd have me certified.

"Of course not, Lovejoy. There are four white covens locally. If you want a black coven the nearest's beyond Wormingford—"

"Hang on. White? Black?"

"White roughly equals good. Black equals—"

A nod shut her up. "Where do you meet, love?"

"Plesae don't ask me any more." She closed the keyboard and rose. I grabbed her arm.

"Dorothy. Please, love." I was in agony. "Answer me one question." She hesitated. I cast about, put my hand on the imitation Ruckers harpsichord. "I swear I'm on your side; on Dowland's original keyboard."

Out stormed Les to sling me out of his grottie foyer. "Piss off, Lovejoy, or I'll—"

"Dorothy. Please." My eyes held hers. "Is it in Pittsbury Wood, on the four old days? Lammas? Candlemas—?"

She hesitated, gave a discreet nod. I kissed her coldish cheek and left, an inch nearer truth.

17

Oliver Hennessey was the bloke I'd seen in Woody's caff with Clipper the gypsy. He's proprietor of Vesco's supermarket. I caught him supervising the checkout tills.

"Only four girls turned up today," he said bitterly, giving a girl a tin of pineapple chunks. "Put that through a few times, Tracy."

"Yes, Mr. Hennessey." She mouthed to a pop tune wafting over the hubbub, rolled her eyes at me in mock exasperation. The put-through is the checkout con trick. I watched Tracy for a minute, for old time's sake. She rattled customers' figures into the till then, with a casual, "This yours, love?" got a denial, lifted the tin to one side and carried on. But the price of the chunks would be on the shopper's bill. The old dears pay up unthinkingly. At the end of the day Ollie keeps the extra. It's always the tills nearest the walls where the put-through is worked, so beware. It only takes new girls three attempts to become perfect con merchants. Says a lot for mankind.

"Any old tills, Ollie?" I asked in his office. "Old adding machines?" They chuck them out free. Form a small collection and in a year or so you'll be able to sell them at a convincing profit. It's not antiques, but it's bread.

"Mmmmh." He stared morosely at the mayhem of people smashing into each others' heaped wheelies. "Thought you were on the scrounge. Coupla quid each? They're in the stores."

"Ta. I'll collect them on the way out." I went to stare with him. God, I hate shopping. Whichever way I put my plastic bags down they fall over. A proper pre-Edwardian shopping bag stands up on its own. Our ancestors weren't thick. It takes modern civilization like us to be gormless to the highest degree of efficiency. You might say we've raised incompetence to a modern art.

I said, "Here, Ollie. Did you get your car back? I heard it was nicked down by the river while you were fishing."

He started then, as I knew he would, snapping right out of his gloomy inspection and really seeing me for the first time. "Who told you?"

"In the paper. Only, I thought I saw it yesterday, Manor Farm way."

"Blue Cortina?" he asked, too casually.

"No. An old Montego. Light red, four-door?"

"You didn't report it or anything?"

"Your business, Ollie, not the peelers'."

"Thanks, Lovejoy." Desperately he began maneuvering me out. "Take two old tills. Tracy'll show you where."

"Ta, Ollie. Oh, still at the old hobby?"

Another start, but more deeply shocked this time. He looked stricken. When he heard I was Mrs. Ryan's estate manager he'd have to do something. Him and his nongypsy mates, that is. I gave him a knowing wink.

"Fishing?" he said, meaning something different.

"Yes," I said, meaning what he meant.

"No, Lovejoy. Too busy."

We parted in mutual apprehension, me to raid his stores and chat up the succulent Tracy, him to phone his mates and say I signified trouble. I drove to see Clipper. Start as you mean to go on.

Driving to the gypsy site with six obsolete electronic calculators and three old mechanical spring-tills in the Ruby, I should have been pleased. I wasn't. Tracy had turned out to be simply what she seemed, an all-time first for womankind. She was an ordinary checkout lass. No special relationship with Ollie—in fact she thought him a worm. I'd learned nothing new, but fixed a date with her at the sports club, Saturday. Any port in a storm, and life's one long storm.

Our local gypsies are distinguished by being nongypsies. They neither sow, spin, reap, nor tinker. They couldn't mend a kettle to save their lives. Mostly they exist on social security supplemented by nicking anything metal. They masquerade as poor downtrodden vagrants so they can plead victimization if anybody threatens to stop their many illegal scams.

Clipper was predictably surprised to see me.

"Good scrap in Woody's, Lovejoy." He laughed, but watchful. "Over that stuttering whore."

I didn't rise to his goading. "Down to a mere ten cars, eh, Clipper?" Four or five caravans and a scattered herd of semi-derelict cars. "Catch much the other night?"

"What other night?" he asked, cutting a stick into the fire and not looking.

"You and Ollie Hennessey. Going fishing."

"Better than selling hankies." He was inspecting my Ruby. "Sixty quid for that crate of yours?"

"Ollie's motor no good, then?"

"None of your cracks, Lovejoy." He stared up angrily. He could make three of me.

"Only a joke, Clipper." I waved him down.

"You're big for your boots, gaffer."

A man nearby snickered. There were four of them talking over a battered car. Clipper meant my new job. A few children ran wild. A woman hung out washing on an improvised line. No red Montego was among the motors.

Deciding on a guess, not quite random, I said, "That's what I came about, Clipper. I heard your mates were sniffing around the end of Pittsbury Wood."

The air stilled. Clipper looked at his hands. Of a sudden his knife seemed a foot longer. His patch is near the railway station. Traffic was nudging past a hundred yards off. Broad daylight, so I felt under no threat. Not much.

"Doing no harm even if we were," Clipper said evenly. "Which we weren't."

"No. Course not." I smiled pacifically at his mates. "But my job's got responsibilities, Clipper. The nature conservancy people are complaining about you lot killing wild birds, uprooting flowers and whatnot."

Clipper relaxed. "Everybody's got a down on us poor gyppos, Lovejoy. You know that." His mates laughed.

"Well, just be warned. I'm setting a gamekeeper by the gravel pits for the next few nights. Cheers."

I'd done well. Clipper called after me, "Ta, Lovejoy. I owe you a favor."

To keep up the deception I laughed along and called back, "Aye. Tell any real gypsies you meet to let me have some caravan ware." Caravan ware is the type of metal buckets, tins, pans, and suchlike, graphically painted in florals and rustic scenes. You will see them on canal longboats, and occasionally genuine gypsies will sell you one.

I drove off in high good humor. Two of the men even waved, all friendly. My hands were damp. I was certain that over the past two or three days I'd spoken with the killer, and I was still breathing.

At the farm Mavis had a phone message. "Councillor Ryan agreed to the proposed building project." I phoned Suzanne

York to prepare for invaders that afternoon. Then I warned Doc Pryor at the rehabilitation unit that he was not to notice if suddenly a gang of navvies gently stole the facing brickwork of his building.

"Are you serious, Lovejoy?" he asked.

"They'll replace it with new, Doc, and repair your damage."

"But, Lovejoy," he tried. I talked over him.

"Don't worry, Doc. It's complicated, but it all comes right in the end." Fingers crossed.

Before Mrs. Ryan dragged me into the woods and wreaked her sordid lusts on my poor defenseless body, I summoned Robie. I had Mavis digging through the files for notable public criticisms of Manor Farm over the past year, and got the district map out.

Robie said, just short of outrage, "I should be with the herd, Lovejoy; south pasture. You're another of them, doing wrong by the land."

I'd had enough. "Shut up, you miserable old bugger. See this map?"

He was really miffed. "I don't need no map."

"But I do. Which farms are productive?"

His wizened face split in a grin. "All on um, Lovejoy."

"Except us?"

"Aye. We're mostly Grade Two land. There's only bits of the farm country Grade One. They can grow anything along there."

"Why can't we?"

"You'm an idiot, son. This land's goodhearted, till you mess it about. Now it costs a fortune in fertilizer chemicals and we get a big yield—of idiot subsidy crops. You're a jack-in-office, lad. Not a clue."

"But you have?"

That staunched him. "Aye."

"Suppose I set you to grow old-fashioned on ten acres, Robie."

"The councillor'd scupper it."

"Never mind him. Where would you choose?"

He pointed to the field abutting Pittsbury Wood's northern boundary. "There."

"New Black field. Why there, Robie?"

"Black earth, not the local red. It'd grow anything, New Black."

"Has it always?"

"Not been there long, lad. Barely two hundred years."

"That can't be true." The farms in the Eastern Hundreds have been the same shapes since before Domesday Book was written by William the Bastard's one patient scribe. Robie saw my disbelief and tapped the map.

"Till then it was part of Pittsbury Wood. Trees mulched that field since time began."

It was a quadrilateral extending between our wood and the estate's apple orchards. Where they killed poor George Prentiss. They'd then carried his body half a mile, to be gored by Charleston the bull. A good way of shifting the blame.

"Robie. Think up a list of best crops. You'll grow nine-tenths for public sale, and one-tenth special stuff."

"What special stuff?"

I lost my rag and yelled, "How the hell do I know?" People expect me to do every bleeding thing. "Get gone. Fetch your crop list to the Treble Tile about nine."

"Right, gaffer." He was looking at me. Just then Mavis came trotting in with some files.

"But, Lovejoy," Mavis wailed, "Sir John's secretary's just phoned a supper invitation for tonight and—"

I took her shoulders. I was due to meet Mrs. Ryan for a woodland rape or else, and suddenly everybody wants to chat. No wonder you get narked. "Mavis, doowerlink. Your job depends on my performance during the next hour. Contain yourself till I return."

"What does he mean?" I heard her asking Robie as I hit the road. He didn't answer either. He'd now got problems of his own. High time.

Mrs. Ryan lay over me, penciling my features with a grass blade. Tiny women often do this, I've noticed. Heavier, taller women lie and give horizontal pillow glances. I suppose there are statistics somewhere. But all talk afterward. Why? I was away in the dozy death, so tragically full of dismay, which affects the man's detumescent soul. Women think a man just nods off. But if ever one senses that terrible grief and knows the right thing to do, she can have me for life. I'd love her for nowt.

"Lovejoy?"

Here we go. "Mmmmh?"

"You've had a lot of women, haven't you?"

"You made that blade of grass a corpse. No wonder conservationists are out to get me."

She laughed, her breasts shaking. Her blouse was over her shoulders, agape, like her jacket. A cynic would have said she'd come prepared, pleated plaid riding skirt so's not to show a crumple from being rucked up. We were deep in Pittsbury Wood. I'd sent the two gamekeepers along the river on some wild goose chase.

"Tell me about your other women."

This called for my purest lie. "You're my first, Mrs. Ryan. I was a virgin until you."

Another laugh, an admonitory tap on my face. "You're an innocent, Lovejoy. But feral. Therianthropic. A born theriac."

What was the woman on about? "One day I'll nick a dictionary and give you a mouthful back, Mrs. Ryan."

She prized my eye open to see in. Her indignation was genuine. "You see? You never call me anything but Mrs. Ryan."

"You told me to."

Another minislap, this time more impact. "That was ages ago." A pause. Cunningly I slid my eye shut. "Lovejoy. What's my Christian name?"

"Erm. Jane?"

Silence. Well, bound to be close. "Jean?" Silence, but with

threat. "Joan? Joanne?" Maybe it didn't begin with J. "Florence?"

"It's Dora." Dora? I could have sworn . . . "Naturally I took the precaution of saying always be formal. James is so quick. A single slip and . . . and . . ." She gave a moan of exasperation and rolled over. "You see, Lovejoy, it's not only James. It's women too." As she spoke I came to, leaned up and gazed thoughtfully across her lovely form. The ground swelled where we lay, rose in a great sweeping curve through the wood. How wide its diameter, if you completed the half-circle to a full one? A mile? She was prattling on, but tardily and with sorrow. "It's different for a woman, Lovejoy. All other women are at her heels. They'd be on me like wolves if this got out."

Well, women have these wars. I let her talk, ooohing and aahing to show I was all ears while I thought about this wood. The great King Cunobelin, Shakespeare's Cymbeline, lived here before the Roman emperor, that clever idiot god Claudius, decided to dust us over. I've no illusions about these earthworks that mark our countryside. They were probably nothing more than cattle compounds, though they're called all sorts of fanciful names: ramparts—hence Billiam's Ramparts Corner—dikes, walls. We just don't know. Archeologists don't know most of all. This particular "rampart" on which we lay runs in an enormous half-circle through the wood. Ten feet high, sloping sides, about twelve feet or more thick. Trees grow thickly on and by it, and the undergrowth is densest about its slopes. Robie'd said the New Black Field was formed by clearing the wood and leveling that part of the great ring that continued out there. Mrs. Ryan and I had made love lying on the ridge's slope. We'd kept dry in the autumnal cool on her riding cloak. Her horse was knocking about somewhere.

". . . not enough any longer, Lovejoy."

"Eh?" Some ominous tone had snuck in.

"James lives a marvelous life—business, great suppers, council work. For me, it's second."

Thank God I'd come to. This line of reflection was playing into my hands. "But you've got everything," cunning old Lovejoy said, full of thoughtful concern. "You run the estate. You ride, entertain. And then," I added as if I knew everything about everything, "there's your special interest, isn't there?"

Her head turned, tense. "Special interest, Lovejoy?"

"Me, Mrs. Ryan."

She laughed, that disturbing tension easing. "Promise me you'll stay, Lovejoy."

"I'm not planning a move."

"I don't mean that, darling." She pulled me down to her throat. Her skin felt cold. She talked softly over my nape. "I'm not stupid. I know you're only between wrongdoings. You'll leave as soon as it suits, back to your silly old furniture and vases."

Silly old furniture? She was off her nut. I told her so. She didn't laugh this time, just drew the fold of her cloak over my bare shoulder.

"Promise me you'll stay, Lovejoy." She sounded so sad. "Even if you don't mean it. Promise."

"Why me?" I don't really care for this sort of talk. The words are the same as always, but it takes more out of you.

"Because you do what you will, no matter what."

Oddest reason I've ever heard for a promise, but here goes. "I promise, love."

"Thank you, darling." She was still speaking misty-eyed as she raised my head so she could peer into me. "Now seal it. I won't mind if you hurt."

Yet only last week she'd played merry hell because I'd left a mark on her thigh, which quite honestly couldn't be helped and I mean that most sincerely. I was especially obedient as I complied, because I was sure now that Mrs. Ryan wasn't an enemy. Which was far, far more than I could say for most.

And now I knew what to do. It'd lead to more lawsuits, but hang the expense.

Then I sent word to Winstanley that I'd got wind of a possible Roman bronze found locally. Then phoned Sykie's sons with the same lie. Then I told Mrs. Ryan and Robie that I had to visit the farm employers' federation office—fervently hoping there was such a thing because I made the name up—and went to Gimbert's auction on East Hill.

18

Tinker was waiting for me in the delectable aroma of paradise: sweat, dust, and centuries of humanity's grime. Add greed, and it's the nearest to heaven we'll ever get. It's honestly moved me to tears before now.

The auction had been going about twenty minutes. Old Spurrier was on the rostrum because our regular gaveler was sick. He's precise and slow, for like all auctioneers he has no cerebral cortex. People—meaning dealers—had barely arrived. Auctioneers start with rubbish, saving the best wine for last, so to speak. Only a few adrenalin-drenched hopefuls were breathlessly penciling minuscule bids in their offset catalogs. The current flavor of the month however was jubilation. I was among my own kind, within arm's reach of antiques.

"Tinker," I said joyously. "Today we do our friends a favor." And our enemies, though I didn't say so.

He nearly swallowed his fag. "You off yer bleedin' head, Lovejoy?" Sometimes I wonder about Tinker's cigarettes, those he rolls. They start off as twiggy scraps. So how do they finish up ash a foot long? Spontaneous generation or something.

"It's unlike us, Tinker, I agree. But it's in the script, see?" I was walking round, upending tables, sliding drawers to see the wear, touching brooches, everting hems of so-say William IV frock coats and Victorian dresses. Among other tricks, always feel in pockets. It's astonishing how often vendors overlook documents, coins, rings even, jewels, love tokens, keepsakes. I once found a child's amber pendant in a lady's reticule, down Maldon way. It wasn't mentioned in the catalog, so I offed it and lived on the proceeds for a fortnight. Sold it to a local museum.

Nothing free today, though, and the whizzers—auctioneers' assistants who haunt these gatherings like woodworm—seemed especially vigilant, so I got us a cup of tea. We watched the auction blunder on and chatted. An old Victorian harmonium looked likely, so I told Tinker to try a bid. Like I keep saying, buy old and wise.

"Bid? Where'll I get the money, Lovejoy?"

Irritably I gave him the bent eye. "Shut up about bloody gelt. I'm fetching it from the bank or something, our usual tale. You've done it often enough, for God's sake." Some days folk lose all sense. I let my eyes roam, checking distances, as if I didn't want any skulking barkers overhearing the next bit. "And let go that I've landed a local bronze, genuine Roman."

He gaped. "You clever bleeder, Lovejoy. Where'd you get it?"

"We haven't really got one, Tinker." I thought, give me strength. "We're pretending, see?"

He cackled, nodding. "What's it like?" Give the old devil his due; once he's grasped an idea, however abstract, he's hundred percent.

"It's a leopard. Six inches long. Foliage-pattern base."

"Lovely," he said, admiring it. "Any inlay?"

Good point. "Yes. Silver. Don't be more specific than that."
I'd try for vine leaves.

"Do we take layers on it?"

Difficult, this. "Let me think a mo."

While Tinker rolled another fag to cough himself senseless I worked out pros and cons. In antiques there's a thing known as a "layer," a provisional deposit. It can be real cash, an IOU, or a simple promise. If I said yes to Tinker, he'd start taking layers for our mythical Roman bronze from dealers, a dozen if he liked, until I told him to stop. And all this with no price as yet fixed for the prized object. Sooner or later, though, I'd have to produce the valuable piece, and negotiate with those who'd dropped layers on it. It's first come first served. Unscrupulous dealers make a living out of these penciled deposits. Seeing that rogues outnumber us honest souls by infinity to one, the layer system is fraught with hazards. Whole wars break out when a dealer layers on a desirable antique, then finds that some rival has gone and "bought under"—that is, actually honored his deposit and paid in full, the scoundrel.

"Better not," I said reluctantly.

Tinker's face fell. "Shame. Oh. I fetched Fixer Pete."

"Eh?" My memory couldn't blip so I asked what I'd wanted Fixer for.

"Dunno. Happen that new tart of Big Frank's?"

"Hell. Where is he?" The wedding. I'd forgotten.

"The Ship. Any message?" Tinker's face was wistful at the thought of Fixer getting sloshed unaided.

"Aye. Tell him to fix cars, photographers, nosh, cards, and that for a Saturday wedding. And a vicar who doesn't count divorces." I slipped him a note as he stared. "Not for me, you silly old sod."

"How many for, Lovejoy?"

"How the hell should I know?"

"Frocks as well? And what's to go on the invitations?"

I gave him one of my most malevolent gazes and pointed a finger. He went, coughing and chuckling. I felt really worn out. I mean, here was I with an antiques auction going on before my very own eyes and people were always wanting me to wave a magic wand over the entire frigging universe. Weddings. I ask you.

Momentarily free of the world's cares I went to Joe Quilp, more to calm him down than in response to his frantic signaling. Joe claims to be George I to IV furniture and continental porcelain. His trouble is that he possesses—I use the term loosely—Varlene. Mrs. Quilp is of stupendous beauty, and sails through life with a cool disregard for bank balances and marriage vows. She drives Joe to distraction. Varlene was just arriving outside in a grand hired Daimler.

"Yes, Joe?"

"Just look at her, Lovejoy." His lips go purple when he sees Varlene sowing debt for yet another thirty-day harvest of manila envelopes. "That motor *costs.*"

"I'm not into marital counseling, Joe."

"Sorry," he whispered as Varlene swept in. "That wheel thing. Scientific, is it?"

The door clanked its ancient bell. Even that sounded randy as Varlene adjusted her mink and strolled with voluptuous languor among us, silencing the auction. She flounced closer, all of her on the go and only old Mr. Spurrier not noticeably lusting force ten. I wonder if opposites attract in people, like magnets. I mean, here was Joe, a drably thin scarecrow. And here's Varlene, linked to him till death do them part, a luscious pneumatic spender-bender.

"Lovejoy darling!" she shrieked, embracing me in copious mounds of undulant fur-covered flesh. Freud would have loved her, a mine of symbolism. I sneezed the fur from my nostrils. "And helping my darling Joesy-Woesy!"

Joe goes all soppy when she's in range. This is what I mean

by women sending you mental. He blinked adoringly. "Hello, Varlene."

"Be a pet, Joesy," she gushed. "Pay the car. I'm *exhausted.*"

With blown kisses she swept through to the auctioneer's office. Joe bleated, "Er, don't buy anything, dearest, until I . . ." Gone.

"That wheel, Joe," I said in an undertone. "It'll go for a song. Buy it." It resembled a slender cartwheel, with two brass rods joining its short axle. A rocking-horse handle and a dial at the join completed it. "It's a Victorian pedometer, a distance gauge. Cartographers and the military used them. You push the thing like a wheelbarrow. That mechanism'll be marked in miles."

"It's a clock," he said obstinately.

"It's not got twelve numerals, only ten. Ramsden's manufacture, at a guess." I couldn't stalk across to have a closer look or others would leap to conclusions.

"Ta, Lovejoy." He sounded miserable as sin. "But I can't now. I'll have to pay that bloody car off."

"I'll postpone it for you, Joe. Good luck. Oh." I paused, clumsy theater. "Keep it quiet, Joe, but I'll have a Roman bronze in the next auction. Nod as good as a wink, eh?"

He said a pathetically optimistic so-long as I went and got into the great Daimler.

"Dogpits Farm, please," I told the chauffeur, adding, "Mrs. Quilp will just have to catch up. This is the second board meeting she's made me late for."

"Very good, sir," he said. Now if he'd been an ordinary taxi he'd have told me to get stuffed because taxis are mostly straight. It's the self-drive firms that are always corrupt. I like people who're deep in deception. I sat back, pleased. My loyal old Ruby might as well corrode on East Hill as anywhere else. I wished Sir John could see me now.

Meanwhile, Joe Quilp trying to form a secret syndicate for a valuable Roman bronze was a real laugh. As secret as a three-column spread in *The Times*.

The Daimler reached the restaurant forecourt. I signed the chauffeur's paper with a forger's flourish, and stood awestruck at the spectaacle. Sandy came trotting.

"Lovejoy!" he squealed. "I'll *not* have it!"

"Lovejoy?" The foreman also came, smoking an urn of black shag. I moved upwind. "I'm Gorham, Ryan's builder. Get this poofter off my neck. I've wagons of brickwork hauling in from six o'clock tonight. And I won't have bleedin' pansies chucking tantrums."

The restaurant was gutted. Even some of the windows were gone. Doors were slabbed up against trees. Plasterwork, bricks, rubble, those absurdly pretentious aluminum struts, all lay in heaps. It looked bombed. Inside, hammers sounded. Concrete mixers battled with trannies. Workmen sang, called, bawled. Planks were everywhere; why? They never use the damned things, only have to burn them when they leave. For the first time in my life I felt nearly sorry for a modern building. It had lasted a day. Served it right for being new, mind you.

"Lovejoy!" Sandy was near to another collapse. "Your barbarian *lout* is threatening me!"

"Lovejoy." The foreman builder had a voice that suited. It carried like a color sergeant's. "This queer's in my way. My orders are to exterior this place in ornamental brickwork. Forthwith."

I wondered if exterior was a verb. "Look, lads—"

Sandy shrieked, pointing to a van, all windows. Two men sat at drawing boards. One was on the forecourt with a theodolite. A girl was making rapid sketches of the restaurant facing. "See, Lovejoy! He's already started!"

"Lovejoy!" A bark from Gorham. "I'm warning you. My men've orders to reface whoever gets in the way." He strode ahead of his smokescreen to the van.

Sandy started to sway. "I just can't go on. "It's . . . over, Lovejoy." He staggered, stretched out an arm. His voice became a whisper. "Today is the end of civilization. Is this how life ends. . . ?" Et tiresome cetera. It's actually from a silent film, Lillian Gish or somebody. Sandy runs them on an old moviola in his barn, mouthing their words. I wonder why he didn't take up melodrama as a career—though maybe he has. I had to nip this in the bud because this particular speech lasts an hour and ends with a near-fatal coma.

Lies to the rescue. "Doesn't Mr. Gorham conceal his real feelings well!" I heard myself exclaim. "You'd never think he was so keen."

"Keen?"

I got up steam. Lies do a lot for eloquence. "Gorham asked if it really was you two who designed the minstrel gallery at the Tolbooth before he agreed to do this job."

Sandy's fury evaporated in the warmth of self-esteem. "He did?"

"Mmmmh. You know how it is, Sandy. A leader of workmen. He won't allow himself to be seen as sensitive, with high aesthetic values . . ."

"He *liked* my gallery? *Really*, Lovejoy?"

"Would I lie? He raved. Out of this world."

"Of course," Sandy said sweetly, "it was mostly *me*. I mean goodness to gumdrops Mel was hardly *there* while I sweated absolute *serum* everybody said Michelangelo'd have absolutely *rejoiced*—"

"Aye, well," I interrupted. "Mr. Gorham is a real fan of your work." I became furtive. "Not a word, though."

"Naturally!" Sandy squealed. *"I'm exactly the same!* I mean I'm soft as putty under all this real butch showiness. . . . So it's all a front?"

"He has an artist's soul, Sandy," I said, profound.

Sandy was in tears of self-compassion. "So much to do. So

little time." He tittered suddenly, did his eyes in his handbag mirror. "I'll just pop over and tell Mel."

Relieved, I crossed to the van. I was sweat through. Gorham smoked in a glower. "Have you got that bloody pansy into line, Lovejoy? Or is it a dustup between his decorators and my brickies? Because—"

Honesty seemed called for. "I've talked him round. Told him you admired his minstrel gallery."

"That fucking monstrosity at the Tolbooth?" He spat on the gravel. "So he's the pillock, is he?"

"Gorham," I said wearily. "Pretend, eh, mate? It costs nowt."

Mrs. York was inside, in a pink costume with raised 1948 shoulders and high heels. She looked lovely. Pearls for pink, fashioneers say. She had baroque pearl earrings, my favorite if they're done right. She seemed extraordinarily glad to see me, little girl at a party.

"You heard about the gothicky brickwork?" I asked.

"Amazing, Lovejoy! It's absolutely thrilling!" Her lovely eyes were shining as she drew me by the hand, showing me how the flooring would be replaced tiered, where floodlights would dangle and sprout.

"Great," I said. "I'm not big on technology, love."

"But you are on finance?" Major Bentham came beside us, spoiling my day. He was in his benign phase again. Really odd. I'd met him four times: one attempted horsewhipping, one prayerful talk, one attempted rundown in a Land Rover, and today's casual chitchat. What motivated the bloke?

"Oh, Christopher!" Suzanne said crossly. "Don't spoil it! Lovejoy has everything in hand."

"I'm sure." He smiled after an inward wrestle. "Could he explain it?" He tapped a riding crop against his calf. Nerks like him are born Sturmbahnführers.

"Okay," I said. "The brickwork's free. The rebuilding's financed by Mrs. York plus Sandy and Mel. Repayment to

Suzanne's on the drip-feed from takings and tax on the restaurant takings. Sandy and Mel get exclusive commission rights on antiques sales here."

Another desperate smile. Candice had appeared at his shoulder, in a simple knitted dress, waistcoated to show fetching innocence. A simple diamond clasp emphasized differences in local poverty levels.

"Doesn't that assume the restaurant will actually have a clientele?" Bentham asked with that dangerous smile.

"I'll get it a clientele."

"Like you did before?" dearest Candice quipped.

"Stop it, Candice," Suzanne commanded. "I won't have all this bad feeling. Lovejoy's trustworthy."

Obviously a genius as well as bonny. I smiled a trustworthy smile as Mel came to the rescue with a complaint about food. Suzanne was all instant concern.

"That whipped half-cream again?" She uttered a soft cry, gave me a quick peck in farewell and together she and Mel rushed away. Between Candice and Bentham I felt in a plastic wallet. Togetherness time.

"Lovejoy." Candice had her hands together, as if about to treat us to a soprano solo. "What exactly is it you want?"

"Me?" I stared blankly. They waited with the hard faces of dealers. "Nowt."

"Come, Lovejoy." Bentham even took my arm, friendly. "This place of Suzanne's isn't much, really. A few acres, ponds, a river. Land that's no longer arable. Grazing leased for a herd or two. I could make it a viable proposition—if Suzanne could be persuaded to stop this ridiculous restaurant scheme. Naturally there'd be a financial . . . shall we say, consideration, for whoever gives Suzanne the right advice."

I shrugged my arm free. "She's worth ten of you two," I heard myself say, and thought oh hell, that's torn it. "You're right, of course, Major. Dogpits Farm's none of my business. And God knows I could do without the hassle. I'm helping because she's a woman struggling to do something lovely. Whereas you two are like everybody nowadays—you'd do anything to change the numbers in some bank. It's a sickness."

"Is that why *you're* East Anglia's greatest failure, Lovejoy?" Candice, sweet as ever.

For almost a full minute I pondered while they seethed hate. Only one answer. "Aye, love." And walked off.

Into a shoal of messages and orders, the most interesting of which was that Goldie was at the Red Lion, wanting to see me "without delay." I thought, about bloody time. Women always take an age to come, when you're in a hurry yourself. Ever noticed that?

19

"Mister Munting?" I was at the corner in the dark. The thickset man stopped. Blokes were leaving the pub, shouting goodnights. "I'm Lovejoy. Chance of a word?"

"Walk with me. Where's your scruff?"

So he'd spotted us that time. "Tinker's gone." We fell in step. "Any tips, like, how to make a farm solvent?"

We crossed the road by the flour mill. It was coming on to drizzle, the night breeze stiffening. "You're in antiques, Lovejoy, so you know. Everything's income."

"Manor Farm's not got enough, eh?" I gave us a few paces before adding, "Unlike others locally."

He paused us on the river bridge to light his pipe. Cars passed with nocturnal sluggishness. We put elbows on the parapet staring upriver into the darkness.

"Land's beautiful," the elderly man reflected. "Its simplicity's God-given. Take a farm, lad. An acre of good-hearted ground costs so little, yet she'll repay care for generations."

I yawned. He chuckled.

"But money men don't think so, Lovejoy. They see land—cared for over three thousand years, like Manor Farm—as a commodity. A money man isn't interested in its spirit. He only wants a license to cover that precious land with offices."

"But the council . . ."

He punctured the night with a match puffed at his bowl. "You've guessed, Lovejoy. The council gives building licenses. Councillor Ryan would have no difficulty."

"They daren't give building permission for a farm."

"No," he agreed. "Only if it's losing money."

I thought, he thought, we thought. "Could it be solvent?" I asked finally.

"Easily. It was solvent before Ryan came. We had an unholy row, so he slung me out."

"So Ryan's doing it deliberately? I hate asking."

"What would you do, Lovejoy?" I didn't know how to answer. He snorted and replied for me. "You'd sack your manager, and instead hire a dud: you. You'd buy a local building firm and keep it handy. You'd get elected to the council. Ryan's done all that."

"That's still not proof." I had to be sure because lives hinged on it, mostly mine.

Sad now. "There's two proofs, Lovejoy. One is to put forward an efficient plan. You'll be fired."

That wouldn't do; I had to stay in situ. "The other?"

Even more sad. "Let Ryan get on with it."

There wasn't anything else. Much. "These lassies who come to the wood. You let them?"

He shrugged. A motorbike swept past, a roaring searchlight. "They're like Tom Booth. They're part of the land. Always were."

"Witches? Part of the land?"

A chuckle. "Come, son. Nobody believes that. Ritual's in church, in play, in politics. So a few girls, women, sing funny flower songs in the dark of the day. Where's the harm 's long as they don't set the wood afire?"

If he said so. "But you *did* mind the treasure-hunters?"

"Aye. I always gave orders to run them buggers off."

We talked more, just this and that. I felt quite rested now I'd found the enemy. I trusted Munting, and believed his interpretation. As we separated, he said something on that curved bridge.

"You'll not stop him, son." He sounded so defeated. "Folk like Ryan allus win because they don't care about things, the way you and me do. But good luck with your try anyway."

For a long hour I sat alone in the Ruby while the town's activity charred lights into black and silence crept out of the stonework.

Munting was right, but hadn't gone far enough. The moonspenders were the problem. Ryan's plan actually was complete.

In the Eastern Hundreds, every builder lives in terror—of archeology. When a bulldozer breaks ground, the sight of a Roman tile or mosaic, or an ancient earthenware beaker, strikes fear into the builder. Reason? The dreaded restraint order. All site construction stops while wandering tribes of archeologists inspect the unearthed treasures. The builders sob and complain to Parliament, but they always lose. Culture comes first and wins hands down. Good, eh?

No. In fact, bad.

Builders don't like paying men to stand idle while waiting for archeologists—not famed for speed—to excavate one tiny Romano-Celtic amphora. So they slip a few quid to their workmen to say nothing about a find. If the discovery is a mound of ancient silver coins, then extra bribes are called for. Plus, the builder sells the treasure on the sly and splits the proceeds with the finder.

Hereabouts, builders' men call it silence money.

You may think this is hyping up the ultimate long shot. It isn't. In one unexceptional year over 300 finds were made in our ten square miles. Most are minor—Roman coins, buckles from the Great Civil War. But two were tombs, and one was a temple, plus, unbelievably, a Roman oyster bar. The great bronze head of Claudius the god came from a local river bed. And gold circlets of Celtic kings whose lineages were old before Rome was born. You get the idea. It's even worse than I've made it sound, because law's involved, and law's always wrong. The law of treasure trove only applies to precious metal. It therefore covers one debased hammered silver coin, but not that exquisite Anglo-Saxon bronze horse-furniture found in Buckinghamshire, which London auctioneers sold to a German collector for a fortune. Worse still is that the poor coroner *has to guess why the object's in the ground!* God's truth. The law, you see, only covers gold or silver *accidentally* lost, not burials, or hidden caches. Ever heard of anything so daft? You couldn't invent a loonier law if you tried. Hence, the chances of treasure entering the record books is slight to say the least. Moonspenders, remember, are hunters. And to a hunter all killings must be fast. Courts take a year to make up their cumbersome minds. Okay, so concealment's illegal, but moonspenders say finders keepers.

Which is where Ryan was one step ahead of Mr. Munting. Simple for Ryan to tell his dedicated estate manager to wage war on all moonspenders—then only give him two gamekeepers to combat them. And each night slip out word where the gamekeepers would patrol. . . .

Easy when you own the land. Ryan's clandestine arrangement with the moonspenders was immediate cash for any item found. Naturally, they'd swarm to the estate like wasps to honey. Manor Farm would become Aladdin's cave, Eldorado. Do it systematically enough, and the whole estate would be cleaned out, making a fortune. Ryan, Mister Methodical, would have the moonspenders hunting section by section, like sappers with mine detectors, the swine.

No impediment to building permits then, eh? And clever old Ryan would net Fortune No. 2. Who'd winked an eye at his wife's indiscretions—all in a good cause. Anything to keep the farm in a state of financial ruin while the moonspenders searched and dug and stole and pillaged. I felt sickened.

"Your try," Munting had called my involvement. Stuff that for a lark. I got out, cranked the old Ruby awake, and clattered off. Try, indeed. I'd frigging succeed. And one reason was that Veronica Gold was waiting at the Red Lion.

20

Veronica Gold was wearing sun specs—this in autumnal East Anglia. Two men paced irritably about her, smoking fags and refilling glasses. An anxious girl in trendy dishevelment scribbled utterances for posterity. I'd been admitted to the room like it was Hernando's Hideaway, three knocks and ask for Millie.

"If you want me to beg, the answer's no." I'd refused to sit. I was hoping they couldn't really afford a lawsuit. I'd only lose money I'd not got.

She looked drained. "Drink, Lovejoy?" Her voice said cut the cackle.

"Tea, please, if you've got any. What's the incognito bit?"

"There'd be hundreds here, ogling. The public's a mob. You just don't know." This to an antique dealer? "I always travel in secrecy."

"Why travel?" I was very reasonable.

"I'm here to resolve this ridiculous situation."

Her and her rotten situations. "You mean lawsuits."

She was already on the gin and tonic. "You caused them."

I could afford magnanimity. "Then I forgive you, Goldie."

"No, Lovejoy." She didn't hope for too much from her story, but did her best. "You misunderstand. I'm here to ask what's in it for me, to get you off the hook."

A short apparent think. "Nothing, love."

"What?" they all yelped together, outraged.

"It's not worth my while." I took the tea from the girl scribbler. "Ta, love."

Goldie silenced her aides with a gesture. "Why not?"

"BBC Sues Penniless Pauper." I was thinking of Lize. Her headlines would reach an all-time grammatical low. "Media Mammoth Marmalizes Minion."

"Daydreams, Lovejoy."

"Come on, Veronica," I said. "Since when does a cosmic superstar have time to come zooming round the sealands?"

"Listen, lout," a nerk interposed angrily, but Goldie closed her eyes and shook her head.

"I'm calling the lawsuits off, Lovejoy," she said.

"Ta," I said, elated. "What's your proposition?"

A nerk began, "Who the hell d'you—?"

"Shut up, Boysie! Can't you see he suspects?" Veronica's voice was a rasp. We all jumped. My cup slopped. I said sorry, because women go berserk if you spill things. She lit a cigarette and puffed a plume with a head-jerk. I gazed admiringly. Women's actions. "If we educate you, Lovejoy, we might be able to use you."

"That game thing? No, ta." The nerks shuffled agitatedly. The scribess hesitated.

"We've had a certain amount of rather weird interest," Veronica explained, testy. "It could be worth exploiting." So people had written in about that lunatic antique dealer she'd had on last week's program, boosting her ratings. I felt a surge of cheer.

"No thanks."

"There's a fee," Goldie said in her metallic monotone. Relief. Five more minutes and I'd be shaky, hands cold and voice wobbling.

"Keep your fees, love." I shook the teapot, barely a splash. You can't win them all. The dregs dribbled into the cup. "Promise more tea and I'll talk to you alone."

She smiled suddenly, possibly her first real one since she'd been a girl. "Algie, Boysie. All of you down to the bar."

They left in various degrees of outrage. We did that curious seated ritual dancing, ahemming and pretending not to be ready for a scrap. Finally she broke.

"What are you up to?" she asked. "I can't agree to anything illegal. I'm bound by the broadcasting mandate."

I went, "Tut-tut. That old thing."

Her smile was broad, brilliantly full in the lips. If ever this harridan really learned to smile, a bloke would have to be on his guard. I found myself smiling back, fool.

"About your program, Veronica," I began. "Listen . . ."

Lize was delighted at the scoop. I tapped it out on her typewriter while she fired questions. Yes, I conceded reluctantly, I'd made the marvelous find on the exact spot where poor George Prentiss had met his death. We worried over the wording.

"It sounds . . . deliberate, Lovejoy," she said.

"Like murder? Yes, I suppose it does."

She drew a sharp breath. "Do you mean it?"

"Aye, love. But I only want you to hint."

Then I drew from memory Ben Cox's sketch of that Roman leopard, and let Lize have it.

"That's it; scoop number one. I'll give you two if you promise not to be rough when ravishing me after supper tonight."

"Supper? I promise."

"Scoop two. Lovejoy, now manager of Ryan's Manor Farm

estates, revealed today that in the interests of conservation all campers, ramblers, and vandals will be banned."

"True or false?"

I said airily, "Add a few paragraphs about Ryan's determination to help animals and plants, him being an environmentalist." Ryan'd go puce when he read that. It would stop his hiring out acres for hunting and duck shoots. Still, you can't make omelets without a cracked shell or two. And this way Enid and her crew would find out by tonight. "Want scoop three?"

"Do I!" She was jubilant.

"Because Lovejoy's heart is in the right place, he will rebury that precious object at the exact death spot, Saturday night. A memento for poor old George, his friend."

She sat back on her heels. "Are you serious?"

"One other thing. Is your car mechanic bloke, er. . . ?"

"Not tonight, Lovejoy." She started to smile.

"Well," I said. She finishes the day's paper about five. I was meeting somebody—was it Mrs. Ryan?—at ten. Time for at least a quarter of all I planned.

Brainwaves come easy. The difficulty is carrying the ideas out to good effect. I proved this by doing a bad thing. Like most such, it was based on a totally good and benevolent assumption. I reasoned: Harold Ayliffe had been punished by Ryan, boss of the local moonspenders, because he'd disobeyed orders. On a dark night he'd disobediently gone out with his electronic miracle stick hunting for archeological morsels without Ryan's express permission. He is discovered. He is beaten up by the boss's minions.

So far so normal. These gang tiffs are like street-prostitute arguments—this area belongs to one group, so other prostitutes steer clear or else. Ayliffe had naughtily jumped the gun, so no wonder he'd finished up in hospital. Things were coming together. Like, what if Clipper, the nongypsy treasure-hunter, had found some common Civil War artifact? Ollie Hennessey, that Civil War enthusiast, simply allows Clipper to "steal" his car in payment. The police'd stand no chance of finding the motor, not after Clipper's lads pulled a disguise job.

Ayliffe being safe in that clinic, I could easily prove Ryan the nameless bossman. How? Why, simply threaten everybody by phone, and the one who motored round to Harold's house in haste was boss, right? I'd simply wait, watch, take his number. Naturally, I'd like it to be that goon of a major, but he was too thick.

With a pocketful of coins, I started dialing. My voice isn't particularly easy to disguise, so I was a slithery Lebanese, then a basso profundo Russian. Sir John got a falsetto Prussian.

"Messich fur Sur Chone," I chanted to his cold but delectable secretary. "Harolt siz cum tonicht or he vill reveal alles. Repeat messich, pleess."

She told me it was already recorded and rang off, ice. I sighed and dialed the hotel for Sykie. I told the entire known world to call round at Harold's house tonight, or else. That was my good idea.

The bad thing was the result.

Ayliffe's house was small and terraced in a street of endless doors.

The trouble with these old-fashioned streets is there's nowhere to loiter. Lamps aren't those thin towering concrete pillars. They're the gas sort you can climb up, Benjamin Hicks 1820s pattern, which posh executives buy to ornament their barbecue pits. No front gardens, either, so you can't hide. Walk down once and you're just an evening stroller. Come back, and chintz twitches while some heavy constable gets off his bike and feels your collar. No, it's no joke. This modern spate of burglaries isn't due to social factors, folks. It's the design of our modern streets. Old streets have a thousand eyes. I got there about eight. A singer in a nearby tavern was wrestling a pop song into a premature grave. I needed a super brainwave.

A pathetic substitute came in a flash—lurk in the yard! No lights meant Enid was out stalking snapdragons, so I did the old rag-and-bone man's trick of counting the front doors going up the street, the yard doors going down the back alley. Then a quick glance at those houses showing lights, and into Harold's yard with miraculous stealth. I fell over a bloody clothes prop, the untidy swine, and walked into a bucket to set some dog growling. Panicking and sweaty I got in, by rattling the tumblers over with a small crochet hook I happened to have handy.

A car grumbling its way along the street, tires slow and squeaking. I heard it and thought aha. I shuffled eagerly along the hallway hoping to peer through the front door's letterbox to identify it. I was praising myself for brilliant planning when I noticed two things simultaneously, all in an instant. One was a woman's voice chanting upstairs to a vague thumping. Ayliffe's old mum, perhaps?

The second thing I detected with my razor-sharp senses was all hell let loose from this firebomb breaking the window and exploding in the front room. I fell over, shoved against the wall by the blast, and slumped for a second, winded. There was one nasty cough of foul petrol-fumed breath, and flame whooshed into the hallway behind me. Slowly I climbed erect, stunned and wobbling. I remember thinking, Where's that come from, for heaven's sake?

Then a car's tires really screeched and its engine thrummed. Unbelievably, another cocktail splashed in a shower of glass into the room. Lucky I was in the hallway, but even so heat stretched my cheeks and hands. Fire shot along the floor into the hall after me. I heard myself squeal, and in a mist found myself clawing at the front door. It wouldn't move. Locked. I panicked, then tried to elbow the vestibule glass but failed, damned near broke my bone on the safety glass, impenetrable. A second ago, stealth. Now this pandemonium of flames and noise. It'd have to be a leap across the fire now spreading along the walls—

I heard a scream from upstairs, a high screech of terror. The stair side was aflame, a sickening bluish business, all swift aggression with hardly a glimmer of yellow to light a coward's way out. I heard an answering scream, me, and swore, cursing my festering luck to be here, and upended my jacket over my head to blunder up. The stairs went on for ever, took a lifetime. My voice was booming out "Ow ow ow . . ." as I charged, knees and feet everywhere. I actually crashed the door open with my head and hands together, always the idiot.

Enid was in the front bedroom screaming, when I battered my way in still going "Ow ow ow." I stopped it from embarrassment and gaped. We gaped at each other. Another whumph from downstairs as the creeping blue fire got hold of something. She stepped away, hands out protectively. Mind you, I must have looked mad, crashing in with my hands horned up by my head, hooded in my jacket, with watery flames flickering behind me. But she looked odder.

She was gowned to the floor in midnight blue. A dark candle stank the place rotten. No bed here, only marks on the floor. Spangles, shiny radii, a kind of writing. Oddly she held a stick and a scroll. A voice yelled outside in the street. A door slammed.

"The bloody place is on fire," I shouted, countertenor. She didn't move, staring.

"Come on, you silly cow," was my next contribution to constructive discourse. No movement, so I slapped her stupid wand aside, stepped among those daft scribbles, kicking them all over the place, and dragged her to the top of the stairs.

A roar met us. Smoke gouged my lungs and scraped sight from my eyes. I recoiled. Every staircase hides a hellhole that stores paint, vacuum cleaners, brushes, and the flames had reached it. The noise increased. I was badly frightened now and dragged Enid by her hair into the back bedroom, slamming the door behind us on that huthering heat. Smoke seeped quite pleasantly up from the floorboards. I tried the light switch. The bulb lit for a second, exploded. The window.

It was the old sash-and-sill sort, thank God. I hauled Enid onto the sill, her legs dangling. Opening the window had set the fire roaring like in an old draw chimney. Flames were actually tonguing under the door, horrible swines. Smoke clouded out over our shoulders. We set to coughing, having to hunch over to breathe.

My streaming eyes cleared enough to see how close safety actually was. I was so elated that, before I thought, I'd reached, swung round the drainpipe to stand on the tiled roofing over the back door, and dangled joyously down to the ground in a trembling sweat.

"Please," I heard some pest scream.

Crazy Enid was still sitting up there, smoke billowing out around her. She was choking, swaying to breathe. I yelled a mouthful of obscenities and rushed about dragging buckets, a wheelbarrow, anything to stand on to climb back on to that decorative tiling. I grabbed the drainpipe to keep myself safe—it was only about fifteen feet to fall—and extended a hand. She tried to reach but failed. She recoiled, clutching the sill and spluttering.

"Enid," I said to the silly bitch, calm now I was safe. "Enid. Let go. Grab my hand as you fall."

"I can't." She was weeping. "I'm not that degree of perfection, Lovejoy."

"Eh?" Degree of perfection? I thought, she really is off her nut. She was going to get burnt to fucking death in a few seconds. I could hear the bloody fire growling, gathering itself. A pane beneath us exploded as the obscene glow of unstoppable flames diffused over the yard. We'd all go any minute, and here she was nattering balderdash. How the hell do you talk to a mad woman? Join them.

"Indeed you are not, Enid," I agreed calmly. "But I am. Jump. You will fly—"

The silly cow took me literally, closed her eyes and leapt sideways, arms and legs wrapping me in a spider-hold that tore the drainpipe off its mountings and tumbled us both down the tiles, me cursing. I wedged a foot in the gutter and stopped us plunging headfirst miles to our doom—well, a few feet, maybe even more. I prized her free and lowered her, followed, and cracked her across the face. "You stupid bitch!"

People were everywhere now, fire engines with bells, gongs, the whole paraphernalia of hysteria mixed with nuisance. Enid was gaping at me, but smiling in her gape, if you know what I mean. Lights were going on. Sirens came closer.

"Magister. Your anger is just." Enid spoke with the fire reflected on her face. She wore an expression of exaltation mixed with, well, I'd say awe if I had to choose a word. Doubtless some trip she'd been on. High as a kite. I mean, in her nightie singing to a candle?

She gazed rapturously at the house with that demented smile. Flames were gusting out of the upstairs window. The frames were spurting, blistering, sagging. I shook her hand off and edged away. I hadn't realized fires were so noisy, the force so tremendous. The damned wall might fall on me. I moved further, faster. The firemen arrived as I reached the gate, bursting in with axes and grim intent.

"Magister." Loony Enid was trotting alongside.

"Anybody inside?" a yellow-helmeted officer man yelled at me.

"Dunno," I said. "She'll tell you."

"No one," Enid said.

He gestured his men forward. "How'd it start?"

Blame raised its ugly head. Blame, legal penalties, and menacing manila envelopes. I looked at Enid, and brightened. She was gazing devotedly at me. A way out. Enid'd get off scot free, being totally barmy, right?

"It was her," I said, and commanded, "Tell him, Enid."

"You?" The fire officer stepped over a trailing hose. It swelled obscenely as water rushed. I'd never seen so many people in a single yard before.

"It was I," Enid said in a calm monotone.

I was delighted. "Tell him it was your candle, Enid."

"It was my candle."

"Tell him how you knocked it over."

Her worshiping eyes never left me. "I knocked my candle over."

"She's in shock," the officer decided. "Who're you?"

"Just passing," I said. A couple of women came up with blankets for Enid. None for me, note.

"You help her to get out?" the officer said.

I drew breath, but Enid was too quick. "He walked unscathed through the flames and brought me safe." She was quiet, adoring.

"Good chap. How'd you get down?"

"We flew," Enid said.

Abruptly I decided to use the breath for muscular power instead, and quickly eeled out among the assembling spectators. The fire officer shouted but I kept going. Enid could manage on her bloody own from now on.

Well, fair's fair. Women never take enough blame.

This escapade I tell in detail because it has a bearing on forthcoming deaths and survivals, and was the cause of several new bills from Sir John. Winstanley delivered these to me in the Treble Tile late that evening. He was really apologetic that the next lot of subpoenas wouldn't be ready until the morning.

"You're forgiven, Winstanley." I'm always kindly about delays of that kind. "Er, incidentally. . . ?" I was having a cough-splattered session with Tinker and Liz Sandwell. She was vastly amused at my sheaf of envelopes.

"The reason for the invoices?" He stood there, neat with the menace of the subordinate who loves his niche. Among us mob of antique dealers he looked a right prat. "Your default. Don't you remember? You and Sir John were to have dinner. We incurred costs. You were reminded on five occasions . . ."

"I hope those expenses are included," I said severely.

He frowned, actually checked. "Yes. Envelope seven."

Liz said indignantly, "Why've I never thought of that? He's stood me up time and again!"

"Shut it, Liz. Right, Winnie. Tell Sir John ta."

A grave good evening, and off he trod through the taproom smoke. Isn't loyalty great?

"And him an ex-dealer, too!" Liz patted my hand consolingly, rose to buy the next round.

"Eh? Winstanley was an antique dealer?"

"Mmmh. He used to partner some woman, frosty but quite a looker."

"Name of Minter?"

"That's it. They both went into business. Very wise."

I lusted mildly after Liz's lovely haunches through the fug, thinking at last one piece of the puzzle was in place. I should have been more interested, but I had to phone Beryl at her museum. I plugged my free ear and told Beryl her problems were over.

"Over?" she asked. "Lovejoy, are you drunk?"

Mistrustful cow. "No, love. I'm not in a pub. Honest. I'm ringing from the, er, football match. Listen. You know the garments in your long gallery? Display Sixteen?" That was the wedding scenario. "Well, get them ready for people."

She cried in panic, "Real people? It's impossible—"

"Cheers, love." I rang off, hearing her cry my name despairingly. Anyway, I'd shot my bolt. She could either come along or I'd raid the bloody place and nick Display Sixteen myself. Friends really nark me. They don't try. I slammed out, ignoring Liz's annoyed call. I had a horrible night ahead.

21

That night I stood alone in the wood. I honestly wasn't scared. No, I really wasn't. I'd arrived about eleven-thirty and positioned myelf under some tree near the great earthwork. I'd no light. I wasn't cold, having fetched a thermos of hot tea and a couple of pasties, everything planned for once. I even wore a sheepskin thing I'd found at Manor Farm. I leaned against the tree trunk and watched the blackness. It watched me. We watched each other, through the minutes up to midnight. Then through that witching hour. Then one o'clock.

About twoish it turned cold. The wind rose to whipping onshore gusts, yet stayed dank and seeming more an emanation from earth than movements of air. I stood there like a spare tool, not really knowing what I was doing. Me being me, I'd swigged the tea and noshed the pasties as soon as I'd got into position, which didn't help. Ten minutes and I was starving again. A few creatures shuffled, coughed, rustled. Badgers, I supposed. Or night birds? I'd heard of owls getting nasty with your eyes.

Not that I was worried, even. I mean to say, a grown man in among a few trees, and a stone's throw from his own cottage?

About three hours into my vigil I heard a short whine, as of an old man's hearing aid. It cut. I listened, having difficulty with the branches whooshing above. I thought I heard it once more, two short bleeps, but that was it. An electronic scanner. The moonspenders were about.

Time passed. Then I heard a faint near-hiss, the sort children make learning to whistle through fingers, and I grinned into the witchwood. I almost laughed and called out, but thank God I didn't.

Then the wood gathered itself back into silence, a lady who'd burped in company. And nothing. No lights, no engines. No eerie witches' covens frolicking round fires. If Enid's coven came to Pittsbury for woodland jollies they were being bloody quiet about it. No bonfire, no flying broomsticks. Nowt. If there'd been a crowd I could have sold some hankies if I'd had some hankies.

The train line runs along our valley. From countless sleepless nights I knew that the Royal Mail about four o'clock gives a prolonged shriek to rouse young Cecil, Harry Bateman's lad who keeps the level crossing at Chitts Hill. That long whistle absolved me from my night guardianship. Dawn was upon us. I unstiffened and creaked off as quietly as I could, trying to move as I'd seen Boothie, in short drifty paces. The Ramparts Corner crossroads when I climbed the perimeter fence was scumbled by moonlight. Billiam was presumably resting his artist's muse in drunken snores. Over half a moon. From there it was easy. Safe home. Toffee was kipping in her basket. She didn't even notice me return, selfish sod. I wish all females were like her.

"Nothing in the wood," I thought. It'd be different next time. When, say, the moon had stretched to fullness and the ancient world's great equinox reached completion. But by that witch night I hoped to have help.

Silly me.

Speaking of fakes, bronze is funny old stuff. Once I'd finished the plaster model of my Roman leopard in my workshop I was in the hands of experts—always dangerous. The model itself was no problem. Anyone with a tin of Plasticine or a bag of plaster of Paris is in business. When the object's tiny, like Cox's little leopard, simply slop a glug of plaster or Polyfilla, whatever's left over from some previous work of creative genius, into a rectangle between bricks. (Don't do it on your wife's best Doulton plate because plaster will fix it solid.) Let it dry. Then carve your plaster brick. You need no special tools. A nail file'll do if you've got time.

Bronze casting's a lost art and likely to remain so. What, you cry, in this technological age? When every country on earth's firing old mangles into orbit cluttering up space? Yes, afraid so. Look at *Boy Praying* in that Berlin museum, and ask yourself who can cast metal that thin. Answer: nobody. So why don't we struggle to relearn? Because there's a million polyresins and coldcasts we can use instead. Look-alikes, but not test-alikes.

Brendan Fernoy's our local casting man. He'll do anything— engine parts, silverware, jewelry—for the right price, with a cheerful disregard of patent law. You have to run one terrible gauntlet, though. She's his wife Denise. She's addicted to flowers, and despairingly tries to grow them in her tiny garden. No problem? Well, actually, her tiny garden is the problem, because it's been converted into Bren's minifoundry. I arrived without warning, wise tactics.

"Is that you, Lovejoy?" she yelled. She was upstairs doing the bedrooms. "Don't you dare make Brendan do stinkworks!"

"Er, hello, Denise," I called up her staircase. "No, just these bulbs he wanted."

"Bulbs? *Flower* bulbs?" She came clattering downstairs, lovely legs but no chest—worn out screaming at Bren, I expect.

"Yes." I saw Brendan gaping from the parlor and pretended dismay. "Wasn't I supposed to say. . . ? Oh, hell!" I'd a little sack of double white daffodil bulbs, though I prefer yellow King Alfreds myself. I feigned exasperation, no difficulty. "Sorry, Bren. Was it meant to be a surprise?"

"Surprise?" Denise said, still suspicious.

"When you asked me to bring them," I told Bren. He was quite blank. God, the effort of duplicity. You'd think one lie'd be simple, for God's sake.

Denise looked at Bren. "You bought me some bulbs?" Her eyes filled.

"Sorry, Bren," I said. "Clumsy me."

Bren was still gasping as Denise said, "That's a beautiful thing to do, dear."

She was so overcome that I had to blow my nose. I felt really romantic as I made my departure. Bren would be in clover—until he started up his foundry and wrecked Denise's struggling attempts at cultivation. The work I usually leave for him in a biscuit tin at the bottom of his neighbor's yard, with a quid for the neighbor's trouble. Now I'd have to keep out of Denise's way for a few months. If only women were more cooperative.

22

The compulsory supper turned out to be a banquet. Sir John and I dined in solitary regal splendor at the George in a private room. It wasn't boring, Sir John being a murder suspect times three, and a collector. Inevitably I was on my guard. Antique dealers and collectors are like Israel and Ireland, would-be opposites yet basically the same. I had no illusions. And now I knew Winstanley was an ex-dealer I wanted to judge him anew. Winstanley hovered—how did he do it? I was almost convinced the blighter actually floated—at the door, presumably sampling grub for poison like a Roman emperor's food-taster.

Sir John was in diplomat attire. I wore my suit. We noshed in decorous silence, apart from platitudes. A faint din rose from the saloon bars.

He'd thoughtfully crammed the room with a good two dozen antiques from his suite at Castor Chemical Industries. I recognized three small paintings, a mahogany whatnot, four Lancashire chairs with their lovely straight backs, even his display of twifflers—these are eight-inch plates; every pottery made them, but they're special to collectors. I really felt sympathy. I mean, the poor mites hadn't done anything wrong except be beautiful, and this rich cretin was trundling them out for inspection. Shameful. I feel the same at cattle shows. The silly sod even had a tiny veilleuse, Lambeth delft of 1760. He saw me looking during pudding and struck, the delicacy of a falling chimney.

"You like my Lambeth footwarmer, Lovejoy?"

"Mmmmh?" I said absently through a mouthful of some sweet amorphous gunge. "Oh, that." I gave the precious early piece a mental apology. I was in raptures. The word means night-lamp, but it's actually a pottery cylinder for keeping dishes warm. The godet, container for your floating wick, was missing. The veilleuse's delightful blue flowers and leaves on white were outlined in green, a trick no Dutchman ever used. Actually it was too small to be a proper dishwarmer. *Veiller* means to keep a night vigil, so we were being treated to that special rarity, a bedside drink-warmer, perhaps for an infant's nightly gruel. I could have strangled the avaricious old sod, humiliating a prize like that.

"You hate me, Lovejoy," Sir John said calmly.

"No. Collectors are the only criterion of civilization."

He served brandy from a Rodney decanter. Well, he snapped his fingers and Winstanley sprinted over to pour. The name is Admiral Rodney's, the splayed base made so the decanters couldn't topple while riding out hurricanes at sea. This had the true concentric steps down its sloping sides, indicating that it was an officer's. True Rodneys are post-1782, the year of his great victory.

"Hatred is based on envy, Lovejoy."

Well, I laughed at that. These folk have no idea. Of course I want to own all antiques, but I'm not so barmy that I take myself seriously.

"You've served your purpose tonight, Lovejoy," he said,

smug. "You've proved that the antiques I brought are genuine. You're unable to conceal your elation at each."

"Only a few hundred to go, then."

Anger rippled to his brandy. "You'll divvie—that word's correct?—for me soon, Lovejoy."

"All right. It's a deal."

His financier's mind sent rapid signals to block his exclamation of joy. "At what price, Lovejoy? You have very little to bargain with. You're arraigned in a dozen courts at my behest."

"Wrong, Sir John." Behest. Get that.

To my admiration he waited before answering. Sundry serfs served sweets on late Regency muffin plates. I'd have settled for the porcelain and missed the toffees, but I started on them from politeness.

"I fail to see, Lovejoy."

"I've pieced it together. I know what happened. Everything. Ledger'll go berserk. And there'll be trouble in the antiques mobs. In fact," I added nastily, "I'll be bloody glad to be out of it. Safe in jail." I let that sink in and added piously, "Deo gratias."

Seeing that formidable intellect suddenly zoom into ultra-drive was an experience. He froze. His gaze rayed me. I shivered. No wonder he'd made more money than religion.

"You know everything? Who's been preventing me from buying the archeological finds? And how they did it?"

"Oh, aye."

"Who? How? And why?" He was scarcely audible. I'd hate to be his banker on a wet Monday. "There's simply no means . . ." The outrage finally got to him and he sipped through cyanotic lips from a Stuart glass.

You can't help being sorry. It's people, isn't it. I mean, here was a man at the pinnacle of achievement—knighthood for services to industry, serfs leaping on every whim, rich as what-sisname. Yet too thick to comprehend anything outside a bank balance. Sadly, I told him.

"You thought you'd got it sewn up by offering to fund Ben Cox, by bribing George Prentiss to inform on the moonspenders. Both ends neatly tied—the legitimates and skulduggers."

He whispered, "I promised them a fortune, Lovejoy." He looked paper mashey he was so white.

"There's forces bigger than money," I said, feeling pity. "Ben loved the art. George used your pay to buy a rare kind word from a woman he loved." He flinched, literally flinched in his lovely slab-back chair as if I'd lashed him. Pain's painful. "Dogmas die, Sir John."

"Impossible, Lovejoy." A whisper. He roused to do battle for the one true faith. "If that were true, Lovejoy, exterminators would merely procreate their victims."

"Don't they?" I went innocent. "In 1794 the Jesuits fled the holy continent to safety—in the sinful stews of Regency London." I'm delighted about this, because they brought the delectable Stonyhurst Gospel. History's nothing but similar examples.

"But money is power," he pleaded.

"True," I admitted, kindly now I really knew he couldn't hurt a fly. "As long as subordinates believe it."

"They have to!" It was an anguished cry. The poor man said, "Nothing on earth can destroy faith in money."

I got up. "Ta for the grub, Sir John."

"Wait!" He struggled, motionless, then finally managed, "What forces, Lovejoy?"

"Two," I said. "One's love." I hadn't known of the other until recently. "The other's belief in anything a human being damned well wants to believe in. Romance, mysticism, witchcraft, anything."

"Please," he called piteously. I didn't pause.

"Am I right, Winstanley?" I said pleasantly, stepping past him into a corridor thronged with trolleys and waitresses.

"If you say so, sir," Winstanley murmured.

Get that. A "please" from Sir John, a "sir" from Winstanley. Funny how nightmares affect people.

On the way downstairs I was accosted by Mr. Pitlochry. He's a twerp, the George's manager. Out he came like a Byzantine knifer from the hangings.

"Ah, Lovejoy," he said, smiling a smile in which malice figured large. "This Saturday wedding arrangement."

I remembered Big Frank. "Yes?"

"It's off."

Which actually did make me pause. Had Big Frank seen the light? Or Rowena the dark?

"I'm canceling it, Lovejoy." He shot his cuffs. "I won't have this establishment used by your ilk. This is a respectable hotel. You and your sordid acquaintances—"

Hate always brings out the facts in me. I said loudly, "This building was a brothel in the thirteenth century. It was a plague-house in the black death. It's been a charnel-house, a haunt of footpads. It's been a smuggler's exchange, a prison, headquarters of traitors, a penny alehouse, a chapel, and a mortuary." Passing guests paused aghast on the landing.

Pitlochry's assurance faded. "Enough of that, Lovejoy."

"It's been a public lavatory, a fever hospital, a military whorehouse." I raised my voice. "I wouldn't hold my friend's wedding reception here if you paid me. Avaunt, scoundrel."

Ledger was drinking at the bar as I passed. "Nice one, Lovejoy," he called.

"How do, Ledger." I felt sheepish.

"Good supper with Sir John?" That turned a few more heads.

"Dunno. It was all in French. I told him about Saturday, though."

"Saturday? What about Saturday?" He was enjoying the attention until I gave him my parting line.

"We settle up then. You, me. And the poor dead souls you let die, Ledger. 'Night."

I opened the street door and left. This bloody wedding thing was getting on my nerves, just when I wanted to see a ghost about a dog. Some days it's just all frigging go.

23

The White Hart was crammed like on Grand National night. I'd never seen so many of us together. Even Jessica was in, plying Lennie her thick son-in-law with gin and instructions, her perfume overcoming the aroma of six centuries of booze. I racked my brains, wondering why I'd wanted a word. Something Tinker had said, it seemed years ago. I pushed through, yelling abuse to the catcalls directed my way, and collared Tinker. We sat over a lake of ale. He said Fixer Pete was in.

My mind was fevered. There was suddenly so little time. Only three days, and October would end. Saturday would be on us—the wedding and its now-canceled reception, the plot I'd hatched with Veronica Gold and her traveling television weirdos. The restaurant at Dogpits Farm would reopen, to giddy triumph or yet another Lovejoy-engendered tragedy. And killers would roam in that same day's lantern hours. Enough problems to be going on with, you'd think, but the gods deemed otherwise. Liz Sandwell showed me a brooch.

"No, Liz," I said, a little abstracted. "It's genuine." She's the pretty lass I've mentioned from Dragonsdale.

"But the pattern, Lovejoy," she complained. "Garnet between emerald and amethyst?"

"Spell it, love." The stones were a crescent, set in gold. Maybe only a century old, but the pin firm as a rock.

"Ruby, emerald, garnet . . ." She ticked the stones off.

"Amethyst, ruby, diamond." She still hadn't got it. "The initial letters spell REGARD, Liz."

"So they do!" She was delighted.

"You get DEAR, LOVE and others. It's a lover's ploy, from an age when people actually believed in romance."

"How clever, Lovejoy!" Liz went off, happy. It would be marked up 400 percent now, even though it was a "young" antique, as we say. The good buy young. Still, her luck proved that God's chances, though not much of one, now were a definite hundred-to-eight.

"You should have charged her, Lovejoy," Tinker complained. He's always on about other dealers cadging my expertise.

"Boothie," I said. "He had a sister somewhere."

"Tom? Aye, Woodbridge way. Her husband's deep sea."

Then Fixer arrived, shoulders shrugging, fingers rippling, feet tapping. He dances to a distant beat.

"I heard about Pitlochry, Lovejoy." Disaster makes Fixer jaunty. "Don't worry. Troubles need fixing."

"I've already done it, Fixer."

He clearly disbelieved that anything could be transacted without him. "Balls. Cheers."

"Cheers," I said mechanically. "You know the Minories Gallery?"

"Beryl's old museum?" Fixer shook his head. "Nar, Lovejoy. You couldn't hold a wedding reception there."

"True. But it's a folk museum. Clothes, household items,

cooking utensils down the ages from 500 B.C. Have a couple of pantechnicons call, late Friday."

"The thirtieth?" He eyed me, worried. "Here, Lovejoy. I'm not going to nick a folk museum."

Tinker gave a cackle, shaking his head. He never has a clue what I'm up to, but he looks wise in ignorance—same as the rest of us.

"All legitimate, Fixer. You settle the rate."

"Right." He sent Tinker for another pint. He drinks as fast as any barker. I'm not as fast, a feature of my character that Tinker much admires.

"And don't forget the buses to take the guests from the George. Have something printed, fancy, showy."

He grinned. "Everybody rolls up to the George, then I whisk them off to a mystery destination? I like it." He had his book out, scribbling. "Here, Lovejoy. You're not usually this keen on things, unless there's antiques involved."

"I'm reformed," I lied. "Just don't forget the coach."

He looked sideways. "Coach? As in Charles Dickens?"

One thing about Fixer is he never asks what for. "At the Minories, thirty minutes after the wedding starts."

"If you say so." He sipped his ale, embarrassed. "One thing, Lovejoy. Er, the vicar wants an advance. . . ."

Money. "Draw a third deposit from Ryan's farm office tomorrow, Fixer." I raised my voice and called, "I'm in to Fixer Pete for a frigging fortune." The dealers reflexively gave ironic cheers. Our way of gaining witness.

"I knew you were okay for it, Lovejoy," he said, ashamed.

"Don't worry, Pete." I was quite magnanimous. "Keep guzzling, the two of you." I left Tinker a note and gave him the bent eye as I rose. I had to arrange what I'd already lied had been done. Falsehood's tricky, unless you believe in it at the moment of delivery, like I do.

Dogpits Farm was still ablaze with lights but now all harmonious. It was like Bonfire Night, with oxyacetylenes for fireworks. Scaffolding, floodlights, the noise of generators. Lorries obstructed the forecourt so I left the Ruby halfway up the drive and walked, guided by the gravelly chunter of cement mixers.

Inside was a shambles too, except behind dustsheets. Ropes showed where you could walk. Men's faces cast pallor against subterranean gloom as they slogged. It was ten o'clock at night, but the pace was frantic.

Mel and two besuited blokes were having supper in the long foyer. The kitchens were all aclatter. They all looked tired out.

"Yoohoo, Lovejoy!" Sandy was in tableau in a small alcove adorned with orange lanterns. He announced, "Ask me how Mel's behaving."

"How's Mel behaving, Sandy?"

"Don't ask, cherub!" He lowered his voice conspiratorially. "I'm pretending I've fallen for somebody." His screech of laughter made me jump a mile.

"All this looks a . . ." I paused. His eyes glinted warningly. . . . "A, er, so active everywhere."

He relaxed. "We'll be *perfectly* serene by Friday."

"You will? Three days?"

He turned maliciously toward Mel. "Except," he called, "for a difference of opinion over the entrance furnishings!"

The two foremen groaned, recognizing the symptoms. Mel rose, white-faced. "If that positively *wicked* remark's intended for me, then Lovejoy please remind a certain person that it wasn't me who makes *ghastly* mistakes with seersucker!"

"There!" Sandy screamed. "Lovejoy, if you think that I'll continue sacrificing I mean my very *blood* . . ."

Etcetera.

An hour later Sandy was sharing a bottle of wine with me, which is to say he was drinking it and I was being allowed to watch. Mel and the foremen were back at work. The progress made was phenomenal. The restaurant really would be ready. Its decor would be weird, from what I could figure out, but I trusted their judgment.

"Great, Sandy," I praised, the umpteenth time. I'd rehearsed wistfulness in the crate coming over. "If only everything else was." I sighed, having rehearsed sighs too.

"Trouble?" He quivered with anticipatory glee. "Tell!"

Another sigh. You can't overdo melodrama where Sandy's concerned. "It's this wedding. I'd planned something really special. An antique wedding, Queen Victoria's dress, with Rowena secretly changing at the Minories, then here in a coach-and-four."

"An antique wedding? Real?"

"Well," I said bravely. "You've worked so hard, and I wanted a terrific opening night . . ."

"So you planned to divert Big Frank's reception from the George to here?" His eyes shone. "Tremenduloso, Lovejoy!" He was thrilled. "Like Cinderella! Mind you, Queen Vicky's dinkie twenty-five inch waist!" He smirked. "Like mine. Ro's a gasworks! She'll need cantilevering . . ." He paused. "What's the matter, Lovejoy?"

Time to put the boot in. Head bowed in sorrow, I said, "It's too late, Sandy." I'm good at dismay and used every erg; I needed Sandy because Beryl had said it was impossible. "There isn't anybody with the command of dress sense." I timed it perfectly, adding, "Except you."

I heard the purr in his voice. "So true, Lovejoy dearissimo, but it can't be done. I'm just I mean positively *too drained* to dress that porky cow Rowena I mean the lace alone—"

"Aye. The television crew will be desolate." I did my sigh.

His voice whipped, "Cameramen?" Smugness vanished. He caught my arm, bangles and bead rings clanging. "Television? Here?"

"Mmmh? Oh, didn't I tell you?" I shrugged regret. "I promised Goldie a sensation, so the whole BBC—"

He rose in an ecstasy of devoted self-love. "Brilliantissimo! They'll worship me!"

"Look, Sandy . . ." I was determined to stay forlorn until he'd bitten the bait.

He clasped his hands in rapture. "And everybody absolutely positively adoring me!" His eyes moistened. "Little me, who started life in a poor fisherman's cottage on this kingdom's most barren coast, hardly a crust . . ."

"Aye," I said sardonically. His family owns half Strathclyde. "Well, it's off."

He practically spat with hate. "*Off?*"

"Nobody to dress the happy couple in Victorian."

"Oh, that!" He smiled, unclipped his handbag, and selected a mirror. "Rotund Rowena and Forgetful Frankie? Fear not, cherub. A mere bagatelle." He took my arm, which I disengaged. "What should I wear, Lovejoy? I have a positively *idyllic* salmon and torquoise blouse, but aren't shoes *hell?*"

"Must I send Fixer over? He's done things so far."

"Certainly not! Have you *seen* his *nails?*" He stopped with a clatter of bracelets. His earrings were a foot long. "Oh, Lovejoy. What's that Goldie cow's TV rating?"

"Audience? Fifteen million on one channel, plus—"

He sighed blissfully, eyelashes fluttering. "All for me!"

Touch and go, but I'd finally cracked it. It was a late hour, I know, but I had one last job at Dogpits Farm. On the way over I'd phoned to make sure Candice and the mad major weren't in. I wanted Suzanne York for a long, long chat. Of all the people involved, I felt she was practically nearly virtually trustworthy. Almost.

The night was solid, its moon knittled by dark cloud, when I drove boldly into Woodbridge. It's a pleasant small town, handicapped by fervent nature-lovers and arty photographers. Now, it rushed silence around me as my Ruby wheezed to a halt. Nobody about, no lights apart from two on the tide-mill's locks; they use the sea tide for grinding corn. I was knackered, so I was beyond tiptoeing. I walked behind the lovely black-and-white Tudor house, and whistled "The Lincolnshire Poacher."

The house had leaded windows, faintly sheening when I moved my head. Then, suddenly, once when I wasn't moving at all. I said softly, "Boothie?"

"Evening, Lovejoy."

Jesus, but it scares me every time. That he was officially dead made it worse. I heard Decibel's rapid soft panting as my belly returned from the superstrata. The dog nudged my leg, friendly. I remembered Jo's rule of pats and strokes, and patted.

"I heard you in the wood, Tom."

"Aye," His disembodied voice said drily. "I decoyed Clipper's gyppos off, to save you."

"You saw me?" I was disappointed. I thought I'd been really skillful, Hereward the Wake.

"You looked a pillock, standing there. Come on in. Kettle's on. I kept our Elsie up, to give you some of her steak-and-kidney. We expected you an hour since."

I followed, head hanging. I'd thought I was streets ahead of the game. But there was no stopping now the whole world was teed up.

Next day, Brendan dropped the leopard off into the Arcade, big in sacking and labeled, "Ceramics with Care." The long envelope taped to it was the diagrams I'd given him. He'd done a good job. Ancient bronze has up to 15 percent tin, the rest copper. Nowadays we put zinc and lead in. The ancients finished off their bronzes with the meticulous minuteness of a watchmaker, but we haven't the love in us any more. Bren must have slogged like a dog. It was nigh perfect.

I took it to my old garage amidst the garden's undergrowth. Under the anglepoise lamp, the little leopard ran at a low crouch, forepaw extended and tail taut, a beautiful hunter's lithe line. I held it up admiringly.

Bronze corrodes. Leave it in air and it goes green or blue—that's the patina housemaids used to clean off with vinegar. But fakers don't want to remove that antique-looking patina. We want to put one on.

Fakers use household salt and copper nitrate, then a bath in a little ammonium chloride and oxalic acid in weak vinegar. But that can take weeks, even. The method I'd chosen was gentle heating, and brushing with powdered graphite.

Silver was my trouble.

The Roman leopard's "spots" were to be silver vines. The Romans loved vine-leaf design. The easiest thing is to heat the whole leopard over a coke brazier and rub it all over with a soft pencil. Do it a few times and your bronze looks ancient as civilization itself. Then you can inlay what you like.

Eleven hours with a Flexidrill later, my bronze leopard's skin was full of vine-leaf-shaped pocks. Another five hours, and sixty-eight leaves were cut from silver sheeting. A quick nosh and rest for two hours. Then an epoxy-resin job, sticking the vine leaves into the hollows. Of course I'd underscored the hollows with a planishing punch that the Japanese silversmiths call sobayase, but that's only common sense. The big danger's using too much epoxy—it forms a thick wodge so the silver stands up proud. You only need to do one sloppy and you've blown it.

After that it was an endless slog with a gas blowpipe and a million pencils, rubbing and heating and rubbing the exposed bronze to produce a lovely rich patina, fraction by fraction. Then, with considerable heartbreak, a dot of strong acid to corrode little patches, and in those pits a scattering of cuprite powder, then bronze fillings to make a thick green-colored patina made by the chemicals I've mentioned. Forgery's got to be more reasonable than truth, you see. A little bit of the right sort of damage carries conviction.

I stuck it upright in a box of sawdust while the patina developed, and left to get on with the rest of my life, where things still hung fire. A few more applications and the Roman leopard's own mother would be proud of it. So would I.

24

Sometimes I think that time is always its own best ally. One theory of art claims that all creativity is the reuse of time, the actual refashioning the stuff as if it were wood. That might be so, but there's a grim side: Time does things off its own bat. It just doesn't hang about waiting. Sometimes it steps out of line, goes its own way, springs surprises. Age isn't all laughter lines.

This week's surprise was time's tardiness. God, it went slow. Now everything was ready I just couldn't settle. I went with old Robie and okayed a patch of eleven acres in New Black Field next to Pittsbury Wood, for him to grow bionic or whatever it's called. He asked if Councillor Ryan knew.

"No," I answered. "It's a secret, see?"

"Farms can't keep secrets, Lovejoy."

Me, with feeling: "I'm realizing that, Robie."

Ledger interviewed me about the fire at Harold Ayliffe's, how come I'd been so handy to rescue that lass and all that. I told him I'd just been strolling past, and heard Enid's screams. . . .

He said, "Oh, aye," and left. Where's trust gone these days? The newspaper reports were subdued. I'd awarded Lize scoop four, and promised her a further stupendous run, five to eight, in a package deal sealed hazardously between design sessions with Suzanne York and analyzing Manor Farm's performance with Mrs. Ryan.

Then I called Clive to do me the hanger job we'd discussed in tomorrow's exhibition at the museum. I'd give him the item the next morning at 8 o'clock. Fixer Pete would be my link man. He said okay, pleased.

After that time did its stuff, footdragged to Wednesday midnight. I can't say I like time passing, but I do like it to do one damned thing or the other, stay still or get on with it.

Eons later, it crept to four o'clock in the morning. I worked on my leopard, finishing touches. Time oozed to five o'clock. I brewed up, fed the birds, considered washing up, didn't. Days later the trannie awoke to its usual hysteria. Six o'clock. I had a bath, fried some bread for my breakfast. Read. Waited. Read. Walked about. And . . .

Six-thirty A.M., same day.

Time grinned, having me on, dozed. I listened to the radio, checked that the brass carriage clock was ticking (Mrs. Ryan's elegant gift; rubbish). All electronic indicators seemed to show that time was cracking on, hard at it. The trannie played a million more records.

Six-thirty-eight, same day.

Epochs later, six-forty. I thought, do you believe it? But there's no mileage in patience when time's being stupid so I thought sod it, rang Fixer, and said let's go. He tried telling me everything was on schedule but I'd had enough and hit the road.

Ten o'clock that morning I happened to be in the Castle Museum, nearly accidentally, when the new exhibition of local antiques opened. And, surprise, there was my leopard looking dug up yesterday, but authentic. The legend gave it: "Recent Find, Anon; Romano-Brit/Celtic." Good old Clive.

There was a lot of attention. Winstanley was at the bookstall, smiling hello. Sir John looked fit to kill, and demanded in a funny voice if I knew anything about the newly discovered bronze. I said, "No. Nice, though, eh?" He went off steaming.

Dealers came, including Joe Quilp and his gorgeous Varlene. She hugged us all—whether collectively or individually I can't remember—and cooed that Joe "could make so much *money* from all these *lovely* things, dwelling . . ." before sweeping off to adorn the main gallery. Joe tottered after, calling that these lovely things weren't his, dwelling.

And by eleven the antiques mob were there in force. I drifted, nodding, saying coming to Big Frank's wedding and all that, being pleasant. I had to cope with three dealers who'd not received invitations, so blamed Fixer and promised it'd be all right on the night.

My big chance came when the place was packed. Den Hutchinson found me and said sorry about sending regrets for Saturday. He knew Big Frank'd understand. "Besides, Lovejoy," he added, "I've been to six of his others."

"Okay, Den." He was into the exhibits before I called, "Oh, Den. You'll miss the antiques."

Den screeched to a stop. "Antiques?"

"Yes, the antiques . . . whoops!" I gave a false laugh as if I'd almost betrayed a prime secret. "Er, nothing, Den." Forty antique dealers were fixing me with their beady eyes.

Den said, "Antiques? At Big Frank's wedding?"

I laughed a hearty laugh. "Don't talk daft. I didn't even mention antiques."

"You did." Helen was close by, curious. "I heard you."

"Look, Helen." I pretended anger. "I was joking."

"Lovejoy. You did a raffle at some restaurant." Good old Jessica, gliding up. "Are you doing another at dear Big Frank's ninth nuptials?"

"Eighth," I said. "Slip of the tongue, for heaven's sake . . ."

By the time I left there were desperate shouts going up for Fixer Pete. By teatime there'd be a thriving black market in our wedding invitations. Ledger passed me at the park gates. I smiled a beatific greeting. He frowned. He really hates optimism, especially mine. Well, I hate his.

At the farm all was go. I rehired Sid Taft, as an offering to the gods. Veronica Gold had rung seven excited times on the answer phone. I called back. She was full of how she'd expect me at a rehearsal. I ask you. Telly'd make parrots of us all, given half a chance.

Lize had left a carbon copy, really quaint, of her article in tomorrow's *Advertiser*. Pretty dramatic stuff. "Antiques Ferret to Flush Felon" ran her headline. That worried me less than her incorrect punctuation of a conditional clause, but she'd laser me if I criticized. I only hoped Ledger could read.

Sir John was in a sour mood. He kept me waiting for five minutes. I said nothing, just read about Turner's use of ochres. Miss Minter wasn't speaking.

Buzzed in, I fumble-felt the vestibule curtain for lurking butlers, blank. I went in, declined to sit when his eyelids lowered to point me where.

"I discovered you own that Roman bronze, Lovejoy." The hatred was white-hot but the compliment made me pink with pleasure. "You defaulted on our contract."

He'd found out, as planned. "Wrong, Sir John."

"*Wrong?*" He wafted round the desk, practically foaming at the mouth. "You undertook to discover who was deflecting all the locally discovered antiques. Now you have joined the enemy."

"Wrong twice."

He screamed, "That genuine Roman leopard is proof, Lovejoy!" His yell was a decibel above a whine.

"Want real proof?" I swiveled, taking in the antiques everywhere about us. "You can have the leopard Saturday. For a price."

The silence of bafflement. "Price?" He understood that.

"Your dud, Sir John. The one here. You give it away publicly."

"Give?" He couldn't understand that at all.

"Don't worry. I'll not tell. People will admire your generosity."

His eyes roamed the room. "To whom?"

"To absent friends," I said sadly.

He tortoised into himself, thinking. Finally he nodded a curt agreement, to my astonishment. But there'd be a bill.

"Thank you," I said. "Tell your secretary to stay on duty all Saturday, all night if necessary. When I phone she's to enter this office, and instantly fetch me the antique that I tell her to, unquestioned."

"Very well. Which is it?"

"Tell you Saturday," I told him. "Halloween."

The day speeded up, now I'd started it off.

I went to Lize's office and told her to include a photocopy of my signed statement when she blew the news in tomorrow's *Advertiser*. Blankly she asked what signed statement, so I had to type out one and sign it there and then.

"It says I've sold my story to you," I explained. "Or other reporters will be outscooping you."

She was appalled. "But this says I've paid you a fortune . . ."

"Nobody ever pays me, love," I said irritably. "People only say they do."

"Darling," she said, quite brokenly. "A national scoop, murders, police, an illicit ring. How can I ever repay you?"

I cleared my throat. "Well, actually . . ."

I'd need a quiet haven tomorrow night. It would be doing Lize a kindness to let her put me up.

Three more jobs to set up. First, I showed Tinker the bronze leopard in the museum. They charged me another quid admission, swine, just for one measly look at my own thing. I gave him a letter, typed and signed.

"Tomorrow morning, Tinker. Eight o'clock, before the museum opens, you come here with Clive and reclaim this bronze. Then bring it to my cottage."

"Eight o'bleedin' clock?" he said, paling.

"Do it. Then you have the Ruby, until church on Saturday at Big Frank's wedding." Tinker, driving my motor, would then be an exposed risk, not me, which for once was the right way round.

He eyed the leopard balefully. "This little dog really ours, Lovejoy, or are we nicking it?"

"It's all legit, Tinker." I gave him some notes. He brightened. "Now tell me where's Joe Quilp."

"Arcade." Exit muttering.

Joe Quilp proved the accuracy of Tinker's mental radar hadn't failed. He was in Eve Harris's at the Arcade trying to dissuade Varlene from ordering a beautiful Victorian ostrich-feather fan, silver-mounted.

"But, Joesy-Woesy," Varlene was cooing as I hurried up. "It'll go with my new evening dress."

"It won't," he was saying in agony, wringing his hands.

"Joe," I thundered, grabbing him. "You swine, blabbing rumors!"

"Eh?" He was bewildered. I shook him angrily. Varlene adored herself in the mirror.

"Don't try getting out of it, Joe!" I bawled. Antique dealers' heads popped out all down the Arcade.

"Out of what, Lovejoy? Honest to God—"

"You revealed it's my Roman bronze in the castle, and you've let on I'm raffling an item from Sir John's collection at Big Frank's reception. I'll frigging murder you, Joe."

"Lovejoy . . ." He was starting to gurgle so I relaxed a bit. He'd need his voice to complain about my mistreatment.

Varlene wasn't taking a blind bit of notice. "I'll need new shoes, dwalling."

"Well I'm not, see?" I yelled loud as I could. "I'm not. It's only rumor." I dropped him and marched off. It'd be all over town in an hour, confirming the rumor I'd begun earlier. There'd be a right scamper for cars, mid-afternoon on Saturday, as dealers everywhere changed their plans. I shed my angry sulk as soon as I was round the corner. Good smiles are rare. I deserved to enjoy this one while it lasted.

That night I persuaded Mrs. Ryan to my cottage. Her estate manager's house was too much a part of Manor Farm to be cosy. I said it would be more romantic. She said oh darling how sweet.

And we loved and stayed.

I did a thing in a casserole. I'm no cook; the last meal I did was in Latin. This smelled all right but got a bit runny, chicken and carrots and a bay leaf. Margaret Dainty had started it for me earlier, got it through the raw stage. I can do spuds, though they never mash right and make you gag. Then peas; though I'm always a bit sorry for the little blighters when I split the pod and surprise them all lying there. The pudding I bought, a blancmangey thing, with five spares in case Mrs. Ryan got night hunger. Candles. Coffee. Wine from Ollie's supermarket, price label scraped off. Two paper napkins, and I was Ivor Novello, suave, elegant. I'd even talcumed my feet.

Mrs. Ryan was bowled over, in a manner of speaking.

"This is all very splendid, Lovejoy," she said, smiling. A compliment, from the landed gentry!

"I thought you deserved it, love."

"As long as it's not farewell." She spoke lightly, but her eyes were in the wine.

"Please don't joke about things like that, love."

"I'm sorry, sweetheart." She came beside me, effusive and apologetic, which always leads to the inevitable. "Forgive me."

"Of course, doowerlink." I forgave her repeatedly until she left for the farm on her chestnut nag at six next morning.

By eight I'd had my fried bread, fed the birds, and had Toffee reluctantly swathed in her trug. Tinker blearily arrived at half eight, with the leopard bronze. "He made me sign for it," he groused. He hates Popplewell, the curator.

"Drive," I said. "Lize's, down the estuary."

He cackled, his beer fetor making me hold my breath to avoid retching. "I'll take her off your hands for a pint, Lovejoy." He chuckled and coughed all the way at that quip.

Suzanne York's car was parked by the river bridge, as I'd arranged. I halted Tinker and walked across. She wound the window down, looking frightened.

"Morning, Lovejoy. Isn't it cold?"

"Perishing," I agreed, though it was quite mild.

She looked so worried. "Lovejoy. What if it's another failure?"

"The restaurant? It can't fail."

"Sandy's gone insane. He's on about TV, Victorian underclothes, weddings."

"Just go with it, Suzanne. I'll be there. It's called the day of reckoning."

"Lovejoy. I heard you saw that Dorothy Moran. You're not . . . meddling in things we shouldn't, are you?"

"That from a woman?" The joke fell flat.

"Whatever happens, Lovejoy, I know you've really tried. Thank you." She watched me cross to the Ruby, and called, "Lovejoy? God bless."

The old parting. I didn't reply.

Three big television vans were parked in the High Street. As we trundled past somebody shouted my name, a woman's voice full of authority. I told Tinker to keep going. We'd all see plenty of each other before long.

25

To me, rest's disturbing, though everybody's different. Like, Renoir hated winter. He thought cold was nature's sickness. He lived for sunshine and warmth. Me, I love autumn but Lize is a Renoir type. Her flat's torrid temperature steams the sap from your bones. In the first hour I blotted my copybook by opening a window for air. She crashed it shut with an angry squeal.

Not only that, but there wasn't far to stroll. Bedroom, kitchen, living room, tiny hallway, and that was it. No place to kick your heels. She saw to my breakfast, then zoomed off to war, pale but game as they come. Tinker had wended his merry way in the Ruby, leaving me with a suspicious budgerigar and a dozing Toffee. "Good job we don't leave civilization to cats," I told Toffee. Not a stir.

The window showed St. Leonard's old church, vehicles distantly drifting toward the wharfside. Beyond the roofs, a ship's funnel and a few masts. The back window showed a street of old cottages and wall paint of scandalous colors. I felt encased.

Toffee woke, dined, licked her paws, the dirty devil, decided on kip.

Desultorily I speculated on exactly how Richard II had invented the hankie—I mean, was he out pillaging one day and suddenly shazam, like St. Paul's retinal detachment near Damascus? Or was it the product of a chaps-we've-got-a-problem think tank?

I brewed up. Instant coffee. Grue.

On the other hand, some inventions are the product of compelling need. The Earl of Sandwich invented the sandwich so he could continue gambling without getting marmalade and grease on a running flush. . . .

Should I wash the dishes? Postpone, postpone.

Then again, some world shatterers happen quite by accident, like the recipe for bakewell tart—though you've got to call it pudding, not tart, in prim old medieval Bakewell.

Toffee snored. More coffee.

By a fluke I happened to have some stuff on witchcraft. I read it from boredom, and not from any kind of apprehension. I mean, with Enid the Loopy as its local harbinger it could hardly be Macbeth time.

Toffee rose, yawned colossally, tramped round her cushion, collapsed. I played with the budgie, which finally said, "It's my round, Liza," in a voice oddly Lize's. I put it back in its cage. The windows showed the same roofs, church, ship's funnel.

Ten-thirty. The *Advertiser*'d be out now.

Ten to eleven the phone started ringing. I let it. Eleven o'clock police appeared below, pounded on the door, talked into their squawk box, drove off. The phone rang and rang. Good old Lize would now be doing battle with Ledger. He'd be demanding the meaning of the story she'd published. She'd be stonewalling, private sources are sacrosanct and suchlike lies.

Finally I switched the telly on. A hard time lay ahead, and Mrs. Ryan'd kept me on my metaphorical toes all night. Toffee sensed potential warmth and swarmed on me. Luckily it was an afternoon sociology program, so I slept.

The nastiest moment came sixish, with me having fried some cheese. Lize came tearing in with a yelp, switched the lights off, and leaned disheveled against the door, panting. In the telly's flicker-light she looked bleached. Toffee slept on, unconcerned; her tea wasn't due for an hour, so the universe's tribulations could get stuffed. That's cats for you. Somebody hammered on the door, shouting.

"You okay, love?" I divided the fried cheese.

She took a restoring breath, yelled furiously at the door, "Go away!"

"Do a deal, Liza," some bloke bawled. "*The Times.* The *Guardian.*"

Lize screamed, "You bastards turned down my articles on fowl pest two years ago. The boot's on the other foot now!"

She came and flung herself all over me. "Oh, Lovejoy, you hero!" She was triumphant, giggling like a little girl who'd got away. "What a day! I'm thrilled! You know who's out there?" She was on my lap. I was trying to eat a forkful. "There's that wino cretin from the *Guardian*. That groper stringer for the London *Times*—"

She gave me a wet rapacious kiss, her tongue everywhere, but I'd already put her cheese on a separate plate for God's sake, so pulled away. We parted like rubber bungs, pop.

The riot continued, with more cars squealing outside and people calling up at the window. Lize ran angrily and drew the curtains. I put a small table lamp on. She looked radiant, rocketing on a high.

"This, Lovejoy," she cried, "is ultimate reporting!"

"How the hell'm I going to get out tonight, Lize?" I had the little leopard to bury, at spot X in New Black Field. I didn't want the paparazzi spoiling my least favorite murderer's surprise.

"All arranged, Lovejoy." She spread her hair. "When you've finished that revolting concoction, prepare for your reward. You've put me at the pinnacle of my profession. It's rape for you, my lad."

"Can I have your cheese first?" I said. I'd a lot to get through in the next forty-eight hours.

At eight-thirty a plum-voiced Hooray Henry knocked, announced he'd prepared the documents, and pushed a couple of envelopes under Lize's door. She and he held an intent whispered conversation through the letterbox. The envelopes contained blank paper. Lize waited a second, then called loudly that he should meet Lovejoy as arranged.

"Decoy," she whispered to me.

The cars outside roared, doors slamming and blokes shouting. Like a car-chase serial. Two minutes and they'd all gone.

"Clever girl," I told her.

"See?" She showed her watch. "Nine o'clock. You're free as air. Want me to come?"

"Yes," I said. "But no."

By eleven I was back, muddy but unbowed, and laughing in the bath about today's success. I even let her show me her *Advertiser* pen drawing of me, wild and threatening. Midnight on Saturday, Antique Dealer Lovejoy would "replace" a priceless bronze antique at the very spot where George Prentiss had met his savage death. "It's what my pal would have wished," A.D.L. told Your Reporter today. "I have every faith our wonderful police will soon solve the tragedies that have so lately beset our fair countryside."

Lize smirked. I said, awed, "You wrote *this*? Strewth, Lize."

"Great, eh?" She was Toffee, purring with delight. "It's called heightening the dramatic tension." She lodged her chin on my shoulder, her arms round me so she could read on. "It's even better further down. I've got Ledger's Sterling Values."

The report was full of naught shall avails. I felt ill. "You deserve a good spanking for this gunge, Lize."

She hugged, thrilled. "Thought you'd never ask, Lovejoy."

I made her feed Toffee first, then awoke early as a daisy into Saturday. Eve of All Hallows, aka Halloween.

Today, Big Frank's wedding day with Ro. Today Suzanne York's final cast of the dice in Sandy and Mel's epoch-making restaurant at Dogpits Farm. Today the confrontation with Veronica Gold, star of stage, screen and telephone. Plus the showdown with killer swine Ryan. Plus the exposure of his nefarious scheme with the mad major and Candice. Plus the revelation, to let Sir John recover his poise. Then the neutralization of Sykie, Uncle Tom Cobley and all.

Loving calms you. It's the only true antitoxin. I smiled about everything, did my teeth, and got ready. I was tranquillity itself. Lize spruced me up like a fourpenny rabbit, with a new shirt and tie.

At two o'clock I phoned Veronica Gold. She was ready, her camera crew merrily clinking bottles in the background. At two-ten I rang the White Hart and told Tinker to drop by and collect me and Lize for the wedding.

Lize screamed, "Wedding? Am I coming?"

"Eh? Course."

She was there aghast in her dressing gown, mopstick in one hand and a sudsy pan in the other. Her hair was everywhere. "You're taking me to a wedding *and didn't tell me?*"

I'd always thought women liked weddings. "You look great, love. Anyway, you've twenty minutes—"

She went berserk. I had to grab Toffee and scarper. I honestly think she'd have killed me. See what I mean? You try to please them and never a bit of gratitude do you get. I think that's real thoughtlessness.

From the Welcome Sailor I called Sir John's secretary. She barked a breathless "Hello?" on the first bell.

"Good girl." At least one woman wide awake and eager. First taste of sin. Or her umpteenth, seeing she was Winstanley's longtime partner? "Lovejoy. Ready?"

"Which is the forgery?" she said.

I drew breath to say the fake ivory tankard, then paused. Telling her the truth would unleash that high-quality fake onto the market. Instead, I could spring a genuine antique to glorious freedom, and leave Sir John gloating over a dud.

Well, which? I admit I'd promised him honesty, but why change the habit of a lifetime? In my visits I'd noticed a lovely night clock by Edward East, complete with oil reservoir and two wick burners, genuine, rare, and clever. I coughed a bit, and said, "The fake's the East night clock by the left cornish, love. Fetch it to Dogpits at five o'clock." She started asking all sorts, so I rang off and watched the street.

26

What's more boring than a wedding? Answers on a postcard. Yet boredom, unlike beauty, really is in the eye of the beholder. I mean, each of us was taking this jaunt differently. As we breezed through town at nigh twenty that afternoon, even my little Ruby was feeling a sense of occasion, what with a white satin rosette on the bonnet and streamers.

"Like me gaudies?" Tinker too. The old devil had shaved, nearly, and had a white carnation in his filthy beret. "Fixer's lads did that at nine this mornin', silly get."

"Fixer's been helping to arrange it," I explained to Lize, as always trying to be nice. "But I've had all the worry."

Lize was still thin-lipped in the back seat. "You could have told me weeks ago, Lovejoy. Ten minutes' notice!"

She was really pretty in her best suit, gloves, a hat, all peach, with matching shoes and handbag. I'd never seen her dressed nice before. Usually she strives for the roadmender look, and achieves it. I tried, "You don't look too bad." She shot me one of her specials so I gave up. Sigh.

As we hit the village road I reflected on Mrs. Ryan. Not comparing her and Lize, honestly, but just wondering as Manor Farm's outermost acres crept into view. How does a husband condone his wife's nefarious activities? I mean, does he say casually over breakfast, "Oh, darling. A spot of spying for you today. Just give Lovejoy the old how's-your-father, a rape or two. Find out what the blighter's doing. Give him the estate manager's job, if it'll help." And what about the bird herself? Is sex loyalty negotiable? There are some beautiful examples to prove it's so. The exquisite Louise de Querouaille's my favorite. Louis XIV of France sent her to spy on his cousin Charles II after our Restoration. Mind you, the odds were on her side, her being gorgeous. She was so successful that she conceived one of Charles Two's illegitimate offspring in a lull between horse-races at Newbury. She became Duchess of Portsmouth ". . . starting at the bottom," her commentators say with brilliant malice—

"God," I muttered.

The old church is at the end of a lane. A couple of cart tracks, a pond, the squire's hall, and fields. That's it, normally. Today though the place was heaving. Cars were everywhere. People milled about. The women were really pretty, colors and flowers. I grinned, delighted. Everybody had showed.

Suited blokes were flagging us along. Two charabancs were already there, their drivers having a smoke. Bells were ringing—*bells*? Our church's bells were stolen in 1408. Yet there in the grassy churchyard was an entire set of cage bells, four stalwart ringers. I'd thought only East Bergholt had a genuine set. . . . I swallowed and hoisted a firm grin. What the eye doesn't see you can't get nicked for.

We went clattering among people like royalty, the mob parting and giving us gladness. We had difficulty nearing the lychgate, but Tinker's cry of "Best man 'ere, y'idle sods," got us through. A couple of dealers mouthed questions. I gave them a meaningful wink, mostly because their guess was as good as mine.

Fixer Pete was there, more like Errol Flynn than ever, when I gallantly handed Lize down into the throng. She was smiling herself now, infected by the general gaiety and slyly checking the other birds to make sure her clobber wasn't being bettered—or, worse, copied—by some enemy. Fixer really comes into his own on these occasions. He wore a morning suit, pinstriped trousers, gray topper, and self-delight.

"Good day to you, Lovejoy. Miss."

"How do, Fixer."

"No changes from now, Lovejoy," Fixer pleaded in an undertone. "Incidentally, the vicar's Reverend Larkin—genuine," he said hurriedly as I gave him a sharp glance. "Honest to God."

"Our church big enough for this lot?" All round people were walking with what they considered becoming gravity up the grass path to the church porch. A couple of girls trailed two cameramen on wires among the gravestones.

"No," Fixer said happily. "It's sixty too small. The service will be relayed—"

"Great." I took Lize's arm firmly to walk us on. Once Fixer starts on plans you're stuck for the generation. He passed me a little box. "I can't do valuations today, Fixer—"

"It's the ring, Lovejoy," he whispered, annoyed.

"Are they exchanging rings?" Lize was getting into it now, earlier fights forgotten.

"Not likely." Big Frank's fifth wife had had a segmental platinum-gold ring specially crafted for him. He'd instantly traded it to a London dealer, part-exchange for a Queen Anne locket, thus sowing the seeds for wife number six *et seq*.

Fixer said, more tactfully, "No, miss. Big Frank's a traditionalist in affairs of the heart."

We walked through the porch, one of Fixer's lads pinning us to carnations and introducing me to Reverend Larkin, a jubilant spherical cleric hugging himself by the door. The church was already half full, some young stranger giving out Purcell on the pump-organ. Lize signaled me to the front right pew. She and Tinker sat behind. I felt daft on my own, but Hepsibah Smith, our choir mistress, was in so I wasn't stuck for something to gawp at. The choir wore black cassocks. They used to wear red locally until the Queen blitzed some archbishop with the terse reminder that red cassocks were by royal permission only. The flowers were in great decorative sprays—Sandy's hand here. The hassocks were silk and white wool: Mel.

In fact I'd quite a lump in my throat. The ancient church looked glamorous, regal, with sun shining through its fourteenth-century stained glass. You could feel the waves of lust from the antique dealers busily pricing the reredos, our ancient font, our alabaster knights sleeping with pious somnolence and absent toes (villagers still pinch holy alabaster to cure sick sheep). Leaving all that aside, the dealers had come to support Big Frank. That counts a lot with me, because friends are friends. Me and Rowena in her cottage came to mind so I changed the subject.

The church filled with a rush as Fixer's whippers-in were tipped off that Ro was on her way. And, creaking new shoes, here was Big Frank, eyes on the silver crucifix above the tabernacle. Heartbeat time.

"Unusual, Canterbury cross, in silver," he whispered. "Don't suppose any parish has the matching ciborium, Lovejoy? I've an American buyer—"

"Stop that this instant!" Lize leaned whispering between us. "Remember where you are!"

"It wasn't me," I whispered, narked. Big Frank sighed. We sat like lemons while the church quietened so that Tinker's rasping cough could test its raftered accoustics unhindered. People looked round, shuffled. Tension grew. Somebody dropped something. The organ played on. Old Peter was pumping away round the side, the long ash handles shoving his elbows into view. Tension. More tension. In fact so much that I nodded off and was only fetched conscious by Lize's nudge from behind. Bloody nerve; she was the reason I was knackered in the first place.

The organ drew breath, and parped into the Bridal March. The congregation rose with thunderous quiet, and there was Reverend Larkin beaming from the altar steps. Rustle rustle of approaching satins, and we were off.

Ro came alongside, on Harry Bateman's arm. I caught my breath. She was radiant in white silk with lace, though sadly modern, and freesias for her bouquet. She didn't glance my way. I felt really rather peeved, after all my friendliness at 2 Sebastopol Cottages and the way I'd slaved over these arrangements.

"Dearly beloved," Reverend Larkin intoned, rapturous. "We are gathered here . . ."

I smiled soulfully at Hepsibah Smith. She looked away, coloring. Honor among choristers.

The service was great, marred only by the choir's late entry during the anthem—I knew they'd never manage it without me—and an entirely forgivable hiatus when Reverend said, "The ring, please," and stood with his hand out. It honestly wasn't my fault that Hepsibah Smith's cassock never does conceal her shape; anyway I didn't know I'd have to produce the ring just like that.

Tinker's croak saved me. "In your bleedin' right-hand pocket, Lovejoy." Sweatily I hauled out Fixer's little box and got the lid off after a struggle. I owed Tinker a pint for that—I could feel the animosity vibing from Lize and Margaret and Helen toward the old soak for his language.

Mr. and Mrs. Big Frank led us in procession after signing the book, the organ belling away, and I was collared by a pretty lass with two tiny bridesmaids as fighter escorts. "I'm Jenny," my new partner whispered, "and I've heard about you."

Where do you look when you walk down an aisle? I tried the

floor, the rafters, the west window's stained glass. I tried saying hello, going red as I caught the grins of the dealers and the fond smiles of the women, until Jenny Knowall squeezed my arm to shut up. I settled for Ro's nape in front of me until we were mercifully out into the sunshine and Reverend was handshaking and smiling, "Never mind, Lovejoy. Everybody's hopeless about the ring." A pint to the right bowler next cricket season and I'll have his head knocked off, making cracks like that.

Fixer Pete was at the waiting cars, grinning like a Cheshire cat and talking into a million-way wrist radio, ten-four and whatnot.

"Gone well, Lovejoy," he said, pleased. "So far."

"Wasn't it a lovely ceremony!" Jenny exclaimed.

"Such a relief," I agreed, smiling. Fixer said hurry into the limousine. Twenty to four. Dead on time, as the saying goes.

27

The limo put us down outside the Minories. Already there was a crowd assembling. I didn't want Sandy turning out to welcome me. In fact I'd rather pretend I didn't even know him. A coach-and-four waited, the horses plumed with white cockades and a coachman in bright green livery.

"Right," I told Jenny and the two littles. "Be sharp."

We scampered in. A nice thrombus of buses and charabancs was forming up. Several motors waited, engines running; these were the latecomer dealers who'd sensed something was in the wind.

Beryl had help today, her sisters and a team of women whose job was rushing about with mouthfuls of pins while Sandy screamed abuse at them. He was resplendent—I think that's the word for a Richard III scarlet velvet doublet with yellow-diamond sequined hose and enormous bishop sleeves. His Faust slippers, in orange lamé, blinded me. His worst feature was a giant striped hat.

"Yoohoo, Lovejoy!" he trilled. "Like my accessory?"

"Er, great." I was thinking we've got fifteen minutes and here is this goon wanting me to praise his handbag. "Where's Ro, and Big Frank?"

"Upstairs being *welded* into that dress." He twirled admiringly before a mirror. "It's nearly as old as she is. Lovejoy, my special effects!"

He flipped open the pink shoulder bag, tasseled velvet. It blared out "Light Cavalry." He tittered, rounded on Jenny. "You. Upstairs, side gallery." Jenny and her pair scuttled off with half-a-dozen matrons, as he called sweetly after, "Jenny dear. In our next incarnation shall we give *shape* a try, all rightee?"

Jenny's laughter floated back. It narks me. Birds like Sandy, despite his cruel invective. I was directed to the Georgian nursery gallery ("On the positively clear understanding you don't play with the dollies, Lovejoy," from Sandy, setting the entire place laughing). They changed me into an austere frock-coated doctor, cape and all. I felt a twerp.

Reverend Larkin arrived in all this caper, three minutes late from traffic. The daft nerk looked full of enjoyment. Gloomily I sat in the hallway listening to the females hurtling about. This masquerade was all very well, but the lovely brass-faced clock by Joseph Knibb was chiming four o'clock, nearly time for a magnificent wedding reception and sundry jollity. For me it was one step nearer night, when I would meet the murderous Ryan in Pittsbury Wood and risk getting myself executed. I honestly felt abused. Why always me? Then I thought of Ben and George, poor sods. Of course it hasn't always been me.

Ro descended the stairs. I caught my breath. She was exquisite in those Honiton lace flounces, sleeve frills, and that lace bertha. Sandy spoiled it all by coming ahead of her shedding tears of self-love, holding a freesia spray, handbag playing "Sentimental Journey" enough to pop your eardrums. Jenny and the titchies were pretty in bridal cottons, white satin slippers. Beryl followed, her team flutteringly seeing the veils didn't tangle. We had an ugly delay when little Millicent, one of our tiny bridesmaids, suddenly wanted the loo, and a further one when Babs, her deputy assistant, wanted a turn.

We were a full ten minutes late when finally Beryl stood by the outside door and anxiously asked Sandy if we could go.

We looked a sight, but the women thought it beautiful. Sandy was really moved: "Think of the lacework if dear Jane'd worked for me!" Dear Jane was little Miss Bidney, lace-maker of Devonshire, who, suddenly summoned to London for a royal commission—Victoria's wedding dress no less—promptly fainted.

There must have been over two hundred people thronging the pavement when Ro and Big Frank stepped out to applause and excitement at our historic pageant. All traffic was stuck. People were standing out of cars to see. A TV crew darted and swooped, poles held aloft. Why do half of them walk backward?

While me and Jenny waited as the bridal couple departed, Beryl came up behind and whispered a thanks to me for putting her museum on the map. "And for inviting us to the reception, Lovejoy. So sweet."

"Fair exchange, love. I insisted that you got invited." I'd have to pat Fixer on the head for thinking of that.

We were twenty minutes late getting away. Mel still blames me.

The High Street, full of Saturday shoppers, became a crowd-lined thoroughfare with folk oohing and aahing at Ro's queenly progress. We overtook it as it clattered past the George, and arrived at Dogpits first. And I almost lost my nerve. Dogpits Farm seemed suddenly the center of the known world.

Suzanne's restaurant was gone. In its place stood a lovely Gothic facade in Accrington brick, only vaguely familiar as the former exterior of the rehabilitation unit. The ornamental shaping, the reticulated windows, were all there, with the great sculpted arches. It was terrific. I was dying to see the hall's interior but Veronica Gold advanced, talking into a black drumstick. More backward-walking blokes in jeans.

Inside, the hubbub was at least that of a football crowd, with sudden laughs and the clink of glasses. Pierre the head waiter and sundry serfs shepherded us through a lounge of subdued wall panels cleverly lit from gas mantles. It was like waiting to go on stage, in a small room with an altar, would you believe, with a series of three stained-glass windows set in the wall above it. Only repro, of St. Botolph's magic *Descent from the Cross*, but it couldn't be faulted.

Mel pranced through in a tantrum about the flowers, and Suzanne flowed out to admire the dresses. She was lovely with little Millicent and Babs, taking them see the altar close to. And she said I didn't look stupid at all, which was news. She gave Jenny the coldest of nods.

"Why's the altar set up here, love?" I asked her. "Is this where the film. . . ?"

The signal came then, with flunkies sprinting. They took my sherry off me before I'd had a swig, which was unfair because, when the curtains were peeled back and me and Big Frank stepped down, the place was crammed with tables groaning under brimming glasses. Everybody turned to look, presenting a sea of faces.

And the altar was where the bandstand had been—so I realized the small anteroom had rotated, church windows and all, complete with Reverend Larkin beaming in his 1830 getup. The cameras were rolling, if that's the phrase, by the alcove windows with one high on a ladder.

Me and Big Frank made it to our places, the women dealers sniffing and the blokes enviously playing mind games pricing our borrowed raiment. During the pause before Ro and her entourage entered I had a quick scan, and approved. Sandy had somehow got a score of cast-iron chandeliers, which shed a fine light from gentle gas mantles. His adaptation of the windows to the low alcoves was achieved by old sash-raisers—God knows where he'd got those. The brass oil lanterns were reproduction, but in this day and age (customers will nick anything antique) precautions are only natural. The walls were an unbelievable Cumberland slate. The effect was of distances so elastic that you could achieve any impression you wanted by judging the light. The ceiling was a patterned Adam, another winner. That, the oak woodwork, the hint of balustrades, and that original clerk's Davenport desk for Pierre to run things . . . I bent my head, moved. It was splendid, as splendid as anything new I'd ever seen. Most of the furnishings were old, and back among people where they belonged. Everybody must have slaved. My vision blurred a bit.

I'd have been even more moved if I hadn't noticed Councillor and Mrs. Ryan seated nearby. And the major and Candice being showily snob. And of all people Ledger, with a homely lady in pearls, toasting me silently. And Tinker, lost but game.

An organ sounded, I think one of the old positive-pressure manuals—I couldn't see for the crowd—and the place rose to greet the bride. I was getting more than a little narked at the proprietorial grin on Big Frank's silly face as he stepped out to stand beside Ro's ephemeral form.

Sandy wept uncontrollably, this time into a papal flag hankie—his joke—rimmed by tiny cowbells. He sounded like the Swiss Alps throughout, but smiled glitteringly toward the cameras.

It was a lovely ceremony. This time I remembered the ring, but thought all the time of a small bronze leopard lying alone cold in the ground of New Black field, out in the dwindling day.

"Ladies and gentlemen," Suzanne announced from an arched alcove that mysteriously appeared to one side of the stage. "This evening we take pleasure in welcoming the lovely and famous Veronica Gold, who not only came to film our Victorian wedding, but to broadcast her award-winning show "Old Is Gold" from here."

She continued over the cheers, explaining the show would start at nine after the break, and meanwhile for everybody to enjoy themselves. Sandy and Mel were fetched out of phony self-effacement to be presented with bouquets as cameras whirred.

Sandy started his account of the wedding dress well before time: "*Very* few of us, *dear* Queen Vicky excepted, can wear simplicity with grace," he bgan, spinning Ro on the dias. "The eight-piece bodice emphasizes the *terribly* low wide neckline. Risky? But of course! Actually, one has to be, well, slim as *me* to carry it off. Note the point-waist, sitting above the true waistline?" Doubtfully he prodded Ro with a long finger. "It's here somewhere . . ."

Added attractions were the antiques in the assembly room. All guests were invited to inspect. . . . The stampede, thinly disguised as a casual sprint, overwhelmed part of the proceedings, but Sandy already had his audience and was in his element.

Weddings are a thrash now, between church and the late-night swigging. There's teatime after the reception. Then dance and booze, then the evening disco, and you stagger to your pit at cock shout. For once I was pleased because—chatting to Goldie, praising Suzanne, introducing Beryl, seeing that Lize met the newsworthies—I could keep a weather eye on my major suspect.

"Ten hooks and worked bars," Sandy was cooing, spinning Ro, "were quite enough for Queen Vicky's back fastening. It's *nearly* enough for *dear* Rowena."

Ryan accosted me boldly enough, saying he admired the brickwork, and being charming to Lize. The swine could really turn it on. Well, let's see how much charm he'd muster when he came sneaking after me in that dark forest waiting out there. . . .

"No wonder you weren't at work today, Lovejoy," Mrs. Ryan murmured to me, circling conversationally. She looked good enough to eat in a light calf-length clinger with the central split hem she knows I go for. "Busy."

"It was hell," I concurred. "Mostly night work, though."

"Was it indeed." She eyed Lize, and asked what now.

"Now?" I said, puzzled. "You mean the telly show?"

"With you, Lovejoy. And me." Her head tilted, checking we were safe to talk. "Has my estate outlived its usefulness?"

Her stare makes honesty difficult. "I have greater need of your estate than ever." How true, I thought. Luckily she misunderstood.

"Shhh." She smiled and pressed my fingers.

Ledger spoke, too. Mrs. Ledger, all pearly homeliness, was surprisingly a musician, cello and keyboard. She argued quite well how reputations were chancy—like, Bach was more famed as a player than a composer in his own day, and better known for being a jailbird than for fathering twenty children. I countered by asking if she had any antique musical instruments. She hadn't, but her husband Ledger played the Boehm flute, another shaker. You never really know people, do you.

At nine the place was rearranged for the telly show under Sandy's direction, with Goldie's assistants arguing and Suzanne going anxious. They did it with models, attired from Beryl's museum, for each alleged period. I was made referee, and sworn to good behavior. Ro captained the bride's team and Big Frank the bridegroom's. Helen, Liz Sandwell, and Margaret—lovely in a limp-concealing long dress—opposed Harry Bateman, who can only recognize antiques by their lack of a digital clock, Brad, and Mannie (who'd conformed by displaying a carnation on his caftan). Sandy paraded each antique on, which was galling to the cameras, but on the whole it went well.

Goldie really seemed to come alive during the filming. Of course she was all excited from having done a full commentary on an antique real-life Victorian wedding ("The very priest is genuine, viewers!") but even so I was astonished. She had a battery of signals to direct the cameras, for example to focus on Mannie's bare feet; I saw it come on the monitor. And she was witty enough when folk applauded in the wrong places or dropped a glass, making jokes to gain a covering laugh.

She introduced me at halftime, and I bumbled about a Norwich school painting, giving tips to the unwary purchaser, like at least measure the damned thing and all that.

By the second half most of the antique dealers were tipsy and laying heavy bets, and every bad guess was greeted with a storm of clapping or boos. They had extra blokes to flag everybody quiet so Goldie could speak. What with the cheering I began to think, Oh, hell, another rollicking for Lovejoy, but oddly enough the day kept giving out surprises, for when Ro's team won and Goldie finally closed the transmission, calling "Goodbye, viewers!" over a storm of yelling and stamping, she came running over to me and hugged me. I pulled away because she looked rotten in that makeup but no, she dangled on me patting my face.

"Lovejoy! Superb! We've never had . . . oh, God! It was real real *real*!" As bad as Lize.

And the T-shirt brigade were all round saying Oh darling, things had nearly gone wrong. I'd assumed Veronica would be wild because some of the panel were still attired in the early nineteenth century and some not, but even that was somehow a plus. They're a loony lot.

It was some time before I could get away and sit out on the balcony in the cool. The day had long since burned out. Ledger came by after a second, as I knew he would. Once a peeler, always a peeler.

"Something out of Sherlock Holmes, Lovejoy." He chuckled, gesturing. Him in his dinner jacket, me like a caped Dracula, music, light, and chatter from the tall windows.

"What're you doing with an antique flute, Ledger?"

He laughed, wagging. "I knew that would irritate you, Lovejoy. But question is, what're you going to do with a valuable Roman bronze in Long Tom Field, isn't it?" I snickered a mental snicker. Only me and the killer knew it was in the New Black.

"Lize's speculative reporting? Give over, Ledger."

"Oh, aye. She gave me a written statement. No grammatical errors, Lovejoy, but a pack of lies all the same." He glanced over the balcony. "See that glowing cigarette? That's a constable." He gave his a sardonic grin, half lit from the ballroom. "Truth is, Lovejoy, a worm couldn't get into the field where George was killed. Let alone you. Or your opponent."

"Opponent? Don't talk daft." The silly old coot left then. I wrapped myself in my cloak and sat on a balcony seat for a doze.

28

It was ten before I missed Ryan in the crush. My heart gave a nasty lurch. Naturally I'd checked every so often through the blue haze to see nobody had slipped off to wait in the woods— that was my ploy, not anybody else's. Quickly I reentered the mob and mingled cheerily, watching. Candice was missing, too. Grinning and calling greetings, I made my way to the men's loos. No sign. I talked a bit with Ro and Big Frank— enthroned in state before their going away—and managed to escape after Veronica Gold laughingly demanded my autograph. Sandy was holding court, waspish jokes about practically everybody. Pierre advised me about a private room to have a lie-down for my sudden headache, off the corridor lounge.

Minutes later I was through the double doors and prowling Suzanne's house. I'm too clumsy to be a really good prowler, but with common sense you stand half a chance. My mind reasoned: Ryan's a friend of the major; is he also close to Candice?

The house was quite small, nothing like I'd expected. Lights had been left on. A television was going somewhere. I made the upstairs without a tremor. Only one room had voices, Candice going on at Ryan with the occasional riposte from him. I was so relieved he was still here I hardly bothered to listen at first.

". . . not a question of getting the stuff out of the ground, Candie," he was giving back. "It's doing it so we keep the takings."

She: "You're like dearest Christopher." The name was an expletive. "Caution's for old men."

"It's for successful men, silly cow."

"Oh. Forceful, is it?" She went little-girl voluptuous. "Want to pick a page, sailor? A drawing? One of the figurines. . . ?"

"I've a lot on tonight." Same words I'd used.

"Switch the bed on? Start the mirrors? Or are you getting like groveling George?"

Ryan's voice sounded suddenly uneasy. "George was none of my doing. You know that." Oh, aye, I thought sardonically. Keep up the innocence, lad. See how much good it does you.

"Do I?" Candice's voice had thickened.

She gasped, laughed. There was a sudden stirring inside, so I eeled away. It looked like I'd found where George was taking the book; Candice was the collector of erotica. It only dawned on me as I scurried along the corridor that if I'd had half the sense I was born with I could have asked Big Frank when meeting him on the London train that day. He'd been collecting erotica for a "local lady," wouldn't say who. He'd even asked me to find him a fertility pendant. I'm thick.

George had probably been caught—by Clipper's men, hard at their electronic wizardry? He must have been trying to approach this house unseen, hoping, poor fool, to contact his former wife and please her by a gift right up her own street. No mistake there, from what she'd so enticingly revealed. Candice and her bedroom gadgetry would occupy Ryan long enough to give me a head start.

For the sake of appearances I nipped back into the restroom, from which I planned to emerge, whistling noisily. Bentham looked up drunkenly from the couch.

"Lovejoy. You've been with Candice."

"Not me." I kept cool. A rumpus now would spoil things.

"Don't lie, you bastard." He tried to rise, fell back. "She fancied you from the outset. A tramp." His head wagged in drunken mystification. "I can't handle her, Lovejoy. She frightens me."

"Take what you can get and scarper. A bird like her."

"You're an animal. I'm an officer and a gentleman."

Aye, he looked like one, with puke stains down his red mess jacket, and drunk paralytic.

Ledger too had gone from the reception throng. About time.

Pittsbury Wood was silent. I'm sure there are different sorts of silence. This particular night's silence was heavy, oppressive, though usually all that means is that the weather's turning sultry. Tonight was cold. No breeze. No rain. A moon was having a hard time of it, lifting its chin over cloud rims, then down again. That highwayman poem came to me from school as I stood waiting: "The moon was a ghostly galleon tossed upon cloudy seas . . ." Romantic twaddle. Anyway, Boothie was around, with Decibel. I'd saved his life that day, so he'd not let me down. The old poacher's invisible presence warmed the chill from my spine.

From where I stood near the edge of the wood I knew that beautiful New Black Field lay on my left. Six furlongs distant, round Charleston's Long Tom Field, Ledger's police would be waiting for me and for the murderer—in the wrong place, happily, thinking poor George had been killed there. Only the true boss murderer, Ryan, would come to the New Black here on the edge of the wood, for only he'd given orders that had done George in. And where. And he'd dig the leopard up to prove it. Of course I didn't know what to expect, but there were some certainties. One was that Ryan would come. He had to, to protect the knowledge of where George Prentiss had died that night. And since I'd announced to the whole wide world of the *Advertiser*'s readership that I shared that knowledge, he had to come for me. There'd be no witnesses. He'd arrange a mock-up road accident, something elsewhere. I watched the big field glow in sudden moonlight, fade as swiftly into blackness.

A good idea of mine, I approved inwardly, to choose Halloween. Local people don't wander abroad, especially in the last hour. They're not superstitious, of course—all that spooky rubbish is for kids' toffee papers and Hollywood matinees.

These witching hours are a godsend to a poacher. And he'd got Decibel, loyal and silent hunter. Can you honestly think of two better allies? I mean, anywhere? The police surrounding Long Tom Field would be chilled to the marrow. Serve them right.

Nothing out there yet. Another quick moon rinse, then blackness settled. I tried to think my way through the tenor part of Rincke's Mass, the Introibo, but found myself dangerously near to humming aloud and shut up.

Ledger's police were getting paid overtime for squatting in a ditch doing nowt. I was out in the same cold, cold night free of charge. I smiled. Ledger's lads probably had their ears out for the sewing-machine chatter of my old Ruby. Tough luck. Here in the forest sounds carried oddly. They become distorted, every susurrus a threat.

Leaving the party at Dogpits and cutting up through the northeast pasture had been easy. So easy, in fact, that I'd wondered if Ledger had deliberately made it so. Unprofitable line of thought, that. No. I'd simply been Hereward the Nightwalker, silently slow round the winter wheat field. I'll bet even Boothie would have had a hard time finding me, if I hadn't told him my exact waiting spot. "Don't move," he'd cautioned, "once you're in position."

Well, I wasn't moving. Movement makes noise. It makes stealthy crackles.

I wasn't moving. So why had I just heard a crackle? I listened to nothing. I relistened, very closely, to nothing. To utterly *absolutely* nothing?

To a cra-ckle . . . *then* nothing.

Relax, Lovejoy. Tom Booth and good old fang-toting Decibel were around. Allies. I'd already proved that, hadn't I? Relax, because no noise is nothing is absolute zero.

Leaf rasp. And cra . . . ckle. Now, noise is noise, no?

No snuffle of night creatures, no comforting hoots, no badgers shuffling. *Why not?* I'd been standing still for yonks, so long that the fauna had begun to disregard me. But now they'd gone silent. But don't they only do that when somebody is moving in a wood?

Not *a* wood. *This* wood.

Going crackle? A pace a minute? Slower? My throat dried. Sweat dampened my hands. I didn't move. I felt like praying, swearing I hadn't moved, honestly God I haven't, as if that proved I'd not misbehaved.

"I can hear you, Ryan." I spoke before I could think.

The crackling stopped. Silence. A terrible wave of hate wafted at me from the dark.

"Ryan?" I gulped. "The wood's surrounded." Something clicked, to my right.

"Now, Councillor." A pathetic whimper. "Don't . . ."

It wasn't Ryan. He'd never carry a gun. His wife had told me only last week he even turned westerns off television. And he only rented out the land for duck shoots, never went himself.

"Boothie?" I said, sweating down my back. My legs began trembling. But you'd never hear Tom Booth click a gun hammer, not unless he wanted you to. "Decibel?" A croak. "Here, boy."

Crackle. Oh God. Moving around. Crackle.

"Clipper?" I said louder. "Clipper?" But Clipper and his men wouldn't come, not with the police skulking within earshot.

"Major?" Too drunk to stand. "Ollie?" I croaked, "Candice? Harold Ayliffe? Enid? Sir John? Winstanley?"

Another click, close and deliberate. The second hammer. And a rustle, as in arms raised when somebody—

I screeched and ran nightblind, arms ahead, the killer plunging after. No doubts now. I was whimpering, rushing hunched, my eyes screwed up against malicious whipping undergrowth. Direction didn't matter. Distance was everything.

But I swear that bloody foliage had it in for me. It snatched my top hat off. It had a high old time lashing my face, scratching my hands, neck, head. My thatch of hair was drag-combed over my face, thorns stabbing my skin.

The killer's breath was stertorous. *I could hear him.* I fled through a sharp groove where water suddenly sucked my feet under. Then the forest floor slammed up, jarring me so my teeth rattled. The ridge? A thinning, suddenly easier passage. I thrashed on in a straight line. I must be on the Celtic ridge, higher than the rest of the wood.

And I saw the fire, only a glimpse, but a definite bonfire among the trees. A bole thumped my chest as I changed direction, ploughing along the arc of raised ground. Thinner meant faster. My chest was searing so I hadn't strength to bawl for help. Wavering, I battered yelping along the ridge until I was about opposite the fire, then slithered down among brambles and shoved through a small brook making a hell of a noise, no silent Trapper Jim.

But stupidly I'd made an angle for him to cut across. He too'd seen the fire. His crashing pursuit was to my right, encroaching, trying to cut me off from the fire and nearly succeeding. I flopped wetly into water, some small pond, floundered through and ran low, blindly, arms out and careering into everything in my panic. Twenty steps, just enough to make him change direction, then a ducking spring right, directly toward the flickering.

Chanting. Scouts? Guides? Anyway, a trillion witnesses.

"Boothie," I gasped, shaky from exertion. God, I wished I'd kept up circuit training, but I'd only done it once, half an hour to please Magdelene.

I forced through, smashing foliage. A bonfire was there in a small clearing, but no people. Jesus. I moaned, ran as the man butted through the tangle behind me, his breath an audible fast sough.

Fastest way across. I ran at the fire, leapt through with my lunatic cloak flying out behind me—and tumbled on Enid.

They are there in my mind yet: Enid, eyes opening as I hurtled onto her, three other kneeling women, mouths opening to scream. I fetched them all down in mid-chant, their white gowns flashing legs and arms as we rolled over in sparks, smoke, and their frightened screeches. With my yowling plea, gibberish, it must have seemed like Doomsday.

They scrabbled up and ran, screaming. All except poor batty Enid, who, with the silent calm of madness, got herself together and knelt, eyes on me. I was spent, utterly done for.

"Lovejoy."

Billiam was there, stepping sideways round the fire. He looked in as bad a state as me, gasping, matted, disheveled. He held a double-barreled shotgun. It went up and down with his rasping respiration.

"No," I pleaded. I tried to crawl, put my hands together in supplication. I'm pathetic.

He tilted his head for me to move away from Enid. I hauled myself up beside her. She rose, solemn and docile. I stepped behind her, almost retching. Billiam moved, aimed.

"Protect me, Enid," I panted, keeping her between me and the gun.

"Magister?" She looked at me, eyes blank.

"The gun won't harm you," I bleated. "Honest."

Billiam sidestepped, looked along the barrels at me. And Enid, bless her, said, "Yes, Magister." She walked one pace between me and mad frigging Billiam. Her arms were outstretched protectively. I swear she was smiling. I cringed and hunched over, whimpering, arms wrapped round my head, eyes closed. The explosion made me whine one long loud whine.

Silence. The only rasping breathing left was mine. A footfall, soft. I was untouched. What. . . ?

A dog's cold snout touched my hand. I screeched, leapt away on my bum, and saw Decibel standing over me, coming to lick my face. Then he went to Enid and nuzzled industriously at her cheek, sneezing when a hair strayed.

Boothie was standing over Billiam's darkstained prostrate form in the firelight. He held his shotgun the way countrymen do, lock across his left wrist and the gun pointing down.

"Enid," I said. She was so still. Decibel had lost interest and was wanting more night games, the psychopath.

"She's not hurt, Lovejoy." Boothie's remark was so full of criticism I'd have clouted him if I'd had the strength. "It was my gun, not Billiam's."

"You've killed him?" I got up, trembling.

Tom's leathery old face was carefully void of expression. "He was chasing you, with intent to kill, when he stuck his foot in an ancient mantrap. His gun went off accidentally and he blew his own face open."

"Mantrap? There's no mantrap." And Billiam hadn't shot—

Boothie jerked his chin in exasperation. "There'll be one in a minute, Lovejoy. Gawd, but you'm slow, booy."

"And the girl?"

"She's like to remember only what you tell her." He looked so blinking calm, ready for a fag and a pint. Decibel, bored now his night-stalking was over, had flopped down near the fire's warmth. "Brave lass, eh, Lovejoy?"

"He was chasing me," I blazed up. "Where were you, you idle bugger? I told you—"

"And I'm telling you, Lovejoy. Rouse her before the peelers come, and give her the tale." He stared reflectively down at

Billiam's corpse. "I knowed it was him. He tried to kill me at my cottage."

"You could have warned me, you burke!"

"Shush, lad. Them three women'll be by presently, bringing the whole village like as not. Anyway, where was the evidence, my word against his? This way, he'll not be back to do any more killing." He fetched something clanking from the undergrowth, grunting with the effort. Chains rattled. A sickening clang and crunch of iron teeth on bone as the mantrap closed. I retched. Boothie's breath shrilled gently as he worked.

Enid was stirring. Decibel snored. A police whistle sounded somewhere. In the distance undergrowth rattled.

"Here they come, Lovejoy."

"What about the gun, Boothie?"

"Why, it's the one he stole from my cottage, simpleton." He was chuckling. "That's what I'll say. My fingerprints is on it, seeing it was that I shot him with." He made a gentle tongue noise. Decibel rose and was gone, hardly parting the firelight. "I'll borrow his, see it gets back to his place. It's not been fired."

Enid was another minute coming round. I cradled her as she murmured in alarm.

"Am I hurt, Magister?" she said. "The gun . . ."

I cleared my throat and intoned, "Have you no faith?" I wanted the peelers to admire the tableau. "Did I not promise you unharm? The gun turned back upon itself, and destroyed the evil one."

"I conjured you from the flames, Magister," she explained.

"Eh?" I only live round the corner.

"And you protected me, Magister."

"Didn't I just," I said gravely. "My duty, Enid."

And it was thus they found us, Enid resting in my arms and gazing in awe from me to the huddled mass that had been Billiam. I'd told her to tell her story to the police once, then say nothing to anyone about it forevermore. We magisters have to make these decisions.

29

The statement was taken on tape in a police car. I'd refused to accompany them to the station, but graciously let them drop me back at the party about one o'clock.

"Doing my night rounds," I told Ledger. "I was a bit concerned when I saw the fire. Councillor Ryan's so keen on conservation."

"Billiam's dead, Lovejoy."

I gave a realistic shudder, easy. "Poor, poor, Billiam." Who'd told me that Candice liked his books, if nobody else did. Who was jealous of George's continued obsession with his ex-wife, and accordingly clobbered him in the New Black Field, then carried poor George—dead or dazed, either would do—to be gored by Charleston, to cast the blame on the bull, the moonspenders, anyone. Who had killed his old confidant Ben Cox, for fear he realized the truth about George's death. Billiam had found it easy to encourage me to go calling on Ben, and make me suspect. He'd also tried to do for Boothie, in fear that Tom's suspicions were accurate. I'm thick. "Quite deranged, Ledger,"

I said sadly. "Came at us with that gun. I tried to protect the girl, of course. My one thought. The others ran screaming." I paused a second. "Do you think it might be drugs?" He snorted, baffled, angry, and suspicious. "I'd better make a full report to Councillor and Mrs. Ryan."

Sandy was exhibiting the Queen Victoria size four-and-a-half shoes, having a whale of a time. Veronica smiled when I signaled that we meet on the balcony. She came smiling, glass in hand.

"Reward time, Lovejoy. Kiss for your penny." She swayed against me, murmuring, "You've given me quad ratings, darling. An authentic Victorian wedding. And my show'll go galactic—"

I disengaged. "Your crew still around?"

She sensed news, sobered in a flash. "Why?"

"Not far from here's a wood. In it you'll find the corpse of one Billiam Cutting, the famous romance novelist. The witches' fire still burns. It happened dead on midnight, at Halloween."

She drew away, staring. "Lovejoy. . . ?"

"Deadly serious, love. The wood's already roped off, police everywhere."

"I don't *believe* . . ." She dropped her glass, literally just opened her hand so it smashed. It could have cut me, silly cow. "Lovejoy, if this is true . . ."

"They've collared one witch at the cop shop," I said. "Name of Enid. You can ask for Inspector Ledger—"

And she'd gone, shouting for a phone, her crew, Boysie, Arnie, Jim. . . . So much for romance. The balcony doors wafted shut on the party din. I waited there until Councillor Ryan emerged.

He tried to be hearty. "Your Bela Lugosi outfit's all grubby, Lovejoy. Been rolling in the mud?"

"Shut it, Councillor." I said nothing more, just sipped at a lemonade, an awful thirst on me. He froze, relaxed, nodded for me to go ahead.

"You've guessed, eh, Lovejoy? Thought so."

"Only from Munting." A figure had slipped onto the balcony behind me. I saw the movement reflected in Ryan's eyes. You can't hide a flash of light in the dark, however small. "Billiam's shot dead, Councillor. The peelers are all over the forest." I paused, said conversationally, "Like a drink, Winstanley?"

A pause. Confidently I sat with my back to the trellis. I'd more friends in the adjacent party than they, that was for sure.

"No, thank you, sir." Winstanley came round to stand by his partner.

"Both of you were in on it, eh? You, Ryan, did the deal with Clipper and his treasure-hunters—making it easy for them to lift all the archeology from the New Black Field, square after square. And you Winstanley, you brokered them."

"Why would I do that, sir?"

"Money." I saw Ryan sag in defeat. "And Miss Minter, Sir John's secretary, was your lover. You funneled the finds into the mitts of London dealers—who gave you first offer of their own stock for Sir John's collection, on legit purchase. That way you also gained sly commission."

"All this is regrettably true, sir."

"It was only when Ben Cox came doddering up to ask Sir John if he'd bought any Roman bronzes that Sir John realized he was somehow being bypassed. Right?"

"Indeed, sir."

"We had nothing to do with the deaths, Lovejoy," Ryan said brokenly. "You must believe that."

"I do. You're money crooks, not people crooks."

"Thank you, sir," from Winstanley. Time to divide the cake. Snag: it was their cake, but I held the knife. "Might I ask what will happen, sir?"

We were all half-lit from the balcony windows. I smiled. The moment felt great. "Generosity, Winstanley," I said.

Ryan groaned. "Generosity? Lovejoy, let's deal."

"No, ta. Dealing time is over."

"It might be very remunerative, sir," Winstanley murmured.

I went pious. "From now on, lads, our reward's in heaven." I meant theirs, not mine.

The news that Councillor Ryan had signed over the archeology rights of his entire estate to Cox's trust was played up in the *Advertiser* for all Lize was worth. More, Ryan even made a speech about it to the Rotarians, playing down his generosity— to which he endlessly referred. He also funded the Victorian wedding costs at Dogpits Farm restaurant and antiques center. His humble eloquence brought tears to everybody's eyes, especially his own. Sincerity's really moving, isn't it? I'd gone along, not because I like that kind of occasion, but to jog Ryan's memory should he falter. Wise really, because momentarily he forgot to offer his entire estate's amenity rights in perpetuity to the local borough. I cleared my throat, and he quickly remembered. Ergo, no building forever. A trust, headed by local archeologists, was formed on the spot to keep the pledge. Access would be allowed for all religious purposes, which in good old East Anglia includes Enid's merry coven. They were still nervous at actually having had a spell work, when they conjured me from the flames. I'd already arranged with Enid to give them weekly guidance on the magic arts, for a small fee.

I was especially glad when Ryan's speech closed, somewhat shakily, with an offer to waive the cost of reconstructing the rehabilitation unit.

Ledger made me attend the coroner's court on Billiam's death. Boothie and his dog were also there, he having strolled into the police station one day and asked what was all this about his being reported dead, as he'd only been on holiday. Billiam's verdict was accidental death. I didn't really listen to the proceedings, because I'd had a disturbing message from Sykie earlier. Today was the last of the month Sykie'd given me, and would be calling on me at five "to square up, Lovejoy." This always means paying Sykie whatever he simply guesses you owe. I'd had some of his squaring up before. It's painful stuff.

That same day I drove Jo over to the rehab unit.

"W-w-what am I d-d-doing here, L-L-Lovejoy?" Jo asked.

I'd let her carry Toffee. She'd dressed posh, looked really nice but ectopic.

"Dr. Pryor's a bloke who can cure some stutters."

"C-c-cure?" She was looking doubtfully at the horrible new brick facade. "Me?"

"Well, worth a try, love, eh? And it's free." I'd sent him the money I'd got from selling the fake bronze leopard to Sir John, who'd be mad at the treachery, but I was used to that.

She went in, hesitant, then with sudden resolution. I drove back to my cottage, using the track past Charleston's field. "You're in the clear, Charleston," I yelled, chugging past. It glared balefully. That's what thanks you get for risking your neck for people. But I was quite chirpy still as I pulled in to my gravel drive. First time I'd been free for years, it seemed. All over. Free, at peace.

Enid was in the porch.

"Hello, love. Anything up?" I hauled Toffee down.

"Magister, I have come to serve."

"Oh. Good." Serve who? With what? I unlocked the door and entered, her following. Maybe it was time for her tablet. She gazed around, pleased.

"Is this where you enact, Magister?"

"Er, usually. My, er, mantra and that." I lowered Toffee, who strolled about, stretching. "Look, love. This magister thing. Call me Lovejoy."

"Lovejoy," she repeated solemnly. "A symbolic?"

"Eh? Oh, aye." Five more minutes and I'd be as barmy as

her. The phone rang. "Put the kettle on, love." The receiver said it was Vanessa.

"Vanessa?" Did I know a Vanessa?

"Are all aerial photographers Vanessa?" She cut through my bluster. "I guess from the *Advertiser* you liked my sky shots."

"Great, great."

"There's the little matter of—"

"How about you call round, love?" We fixed on six-thirty.

The phone summoned me back before I'd even sat down. "Lovejoy? Suzanne."

"Hello, Suzanne." There were three letters in the vestibule, two bills and one that needed opening. "How's your rotten old restaurant?"

She laughed. "Don't be silly. I wanted to thank you. The supplies of naturally-grown produce for my restaurant will be a winner." She meant Robie and his nondaft farming. "About money."

"Still some out there in the world, is there?"

"For you, yes. I'm appointing you adviser on our antique displays." We both waited for her to plan phrases sufficiently bent for her purpose. The envelope held a brief executive command from the George. Veronica was in Room 209, it seemed. What is the matter with people? Have they no homes to go to? "I've set aside a room here for you, Lovejoy."

I said how kind and she said not at all, come soon because the check was ready. I promised. Narked, I quickly rang the George, and got Veronica in a babble of voices.

"Veronica? What the hell's this?"

"Lovejoy?" She was dangerous, honeysweet. "Glad you rang. Seven sharp. First of thirteen shows, lover."

"No, ta," I said. "Promise I'll watch, though."

"You won't. You've signed the contract. Remember giving me your autograph at the reception?" The treacherous bitch. She was still laughing as I slammed the receiver down, in time to catch another ring. Free? At peace? That what I said?

"Lovejoy? Lize." She sounded so breezy.

"What?" On guard, Lovejoy. She'd never accepted Lize before.

"Just wondering what time you'll be home, sweetheart."

Home? I was already home. "Eh? Oh, sevenish."

"Right. If you get home before me, switch the oven on. It's a casserole."

"Right," I said, heartily as I could with a headache. Casserole? Oven? What *is* this?

Enid was kneeling on the peg rug, silently pouring the tea. With every passing second she looked better and better. The doorbell. There stood Candice, majorless.

"Sorry, Candice," I said. "I'm just off out."

"I don't intend to stay, Lovejoy." Flounce skirt today, a sling jacket, which were all right. But she wore an antique plaited glass headband, yellow and white. I'd not seen one since the Sudbury auction three years gone.

"No? Pity," I said to the headband.

"The major's . . . left." Her tone told me he'd got the sailor's elbow. "About your arrangement with my aged aunt, Lovejoy." She heard Enid's quiet movements indoors, merely smiled. "I could be very troublesome, disrupt her wonderful restaurant, spoil those new displays of Sir John's collections those two queers are putting on, ruin your sexpot's telly broadcasts. Or."

Long pause. "Or?"

"Or you and I can enlarge our mutual perceptions, Lovejoy."

"Any particular time?" I asked that beautiful headband.

"Eight-thirty sharp?" she said into my eyes.

I saw her car off, with enthusiasm, and went indoors. Enid sat-knelt waiting. She'd even found a saucer among the shambles, clever girl.

"Enid," I said. "I need a quiet house. Just for a few days. To restore the, er, spirit energies."

She rose. "Yes, Magist . . . Lovejoy." She hadn't got the tea right, but you can't have everything. I listened as she phoned.

"Evadne? Magister is to confer the blessing of his presence on us." Pause. "Where will you leave the key?"

God, but her tea was the pits. I rearranged my expression to spirituality in time for Enid's news. "Evadne's home will be honored, Lovejoy. Her husband is at sea, currently off Durban."

A clipclopping sounded in the side lane. I thought, it *can't* be. "Evadne? One of your, er. . . ?"

"You spared her in the wood, Magister."

"So I did." The horse-hooves clopped closer. Mrs. Ryan. There's no stopping some folk.

"Will we leave now, Lovejoy?"

I closed my eyes an instant, made a mysterious magic pass, quite convincing considering the circumstances. Maybe Evadne was the curvy blond one.

"Yes, love," I decided. "Bad karma here."

I slammed a bewildered Toffee into her trug, grabbed Enid, and ran for it.

FOR THE BEST IN PAPERBACKS, LOOK FOR THE 🐧

In every corner of the world, on every subject under the sun, Penguin represents quality and variety—the very best in publishing today.

For complete information about books available from Penguin—including Pelicans, Puffins, Peregrines, and Penguin Classics—and how to order them, write to us at the appropriate address below. Please note that for copyright reasons the selection of books varies from country to country.

In the United Kingdom: For a complete list of books available from Penguin in the U.K., please write to *Dept E.P., Penguin Books Ltd, Harmondsworth, Middlesex, UB7 0DA.*

In the United States: For a complete list of books available from Penguin in the U.S., please write to *Dept BA, Penguin,* Box 120, Bergenfield, New Jersey 07621-0120.

In Canada: For a complete list of books available from Penguin in Canada, please write to *Penguin Books Ltd, 2801 John Street, Markham, Ontario L3R 1B4.*

In Australia: For a complete list of books available from Penguin in Australia, please write to the *Marketing Department, Penguin Books Ltd, P.O. Box 257, Ringwood, Victoria 3134.*

In New Zealand: For a complete list of books available from Penguin in New Zealand, please write to the *Marketing Department, Penguin Books (NZ) Ltd, Private Bag, Takapuna, Auckland 9.*

In India: For a complete list of books available from Penguin, please write to *Penguin Overseas Ltd, 706 Eros Apartments, 56 Nehru Place, New Delhi, 110019.*

In Holland: For a complete list of books available from Penguin in Holland, please write to *Penguin Books Nederland B.V., Postbus 195, NL-1380AD Weesp, Netherlands.*

In Germany: For a complete list of books available from Penguin, please write to *Penguin Books Ltd, Friedrichstrasse 10-12, D-6000 Frankfurt Main I, Federal Republic of Germany.*

In Spain: For a complete list of books available from Penguin in Spain, please write to *Longman, Penguin España, Calle San Nicolas 15, E-28013 Madrid, Spain.*

In Japan: For a complete list of books available from Penguin in Japan, please write to *Longman Penguin Japan Co Ltd, Yamaguchi Building, 2-12-9 Kanda Jimbocho, Chiyoda-Ku, Tokyo 101, Japan.*

FOR THE BEST IN MYSTERY, LOOK FOR THE Ⓟ

FOR THE BEST IN MYSTERY, LOOK FOR THE Ⓟ